# Sins of
# A Wicked
# Duke

# SINS of A WICKED DUKE

## Sophie Jordan

**AVON**

*An Imprint of HarperCollinsPublishers*

This is a work of fiction. Names, characters, places, and incidents are drawn from the author's imagination or are used fictitiously and are not to be construed as real. Any resemblance to actual events, locales, organizations, or persons, living or dead, is entirely coincidental.

AVON BOOKS
*An Imprint of* HarperCollins*Publishers*
10 East 53rd Street
New York, New York 10022-5299

Copyright © 2009 by Sharie Kohler
ISBN-13: 978-1-60751-939-3

Printed in the U.S.A.

*For Jared*
*Because you're the kind of man who gives*
*his wife a card on Father's Day.*

# Acknowledgments

There are several who read this book in its various parts and forms, and even more who listened to me talk it to death and always offered sage advice—ahhhing, nodding, laughing, and eye rolling when necessary. Thanks to each of you: Tera, Robyn, Ane, Christy, and Lindsay. And, as always, I could never do it without the wonderful May Chen. Thanks for helping me bring another one the final mile home. Long-overdue thanks goes to Tom Egner for all my amazing covers. And Maura Kye-Casella, my agent-extraordinaire, my friend, my sounding board—thank you doesn't cover it.

# SINS of A WICKED DUKE

# Prologue

**T**ears ran cold paths down Fallon O'Rourke's cheeks, but not a sound passed her chilled lips. Not a sob. Not a whimper. In the past fortnight, she'd bled all noise from her tears. Tucked into bed on the second floor of the Penwich School for Virtuous Girls, she held herself still as death and managed not to shatter into sobs.

Her breath fanned before her in frothy clouds of white, one after another. Shivering, she huddled beneath the threadbare blanket and wondered if she would ever feel warm again. If a night would ever descend when her feet did not ache from chill. *Oh, Da.*

"Pssst."

Fallon lifted her head. Two girls crouched at the foot of her bed, blankets draped over their thin shoulders. She recognized them. Not because they looked so very different from the other whey-faced girls in starched pinafores to march the halls every day, but because they had watched her since her arrival with a curious intensity. Their wide, solemn eyes followed her everywhere, unlike the other girls who minded their affairs, busy about their own misery.

And it was misery. A constant battle against the hunger, the cold . . . *each other.*

She sat up, tense and instantly wary. A pair of older girls had jumped a smaller girl only yesterday, stealing her meager ration. Yet she possessed nothing these girls could want. And at thirteen, she was bigger and heavier than most here. The dark-haired one looked as if the wind howling on the moors outside could knock her over. No doubt her rations were stolen with some frequency.

Fallon shifted, rising up on her elbows. Almost in reminder, her back stung from the strap Master Brocklehurst had administered to her only today, punishment for daring to remove her cap from her head. Any more such beatings and she would soon be as pitiable as the forty-odd girls battling for survival at Penwich.

Wetting parched lips, she spoke. "Yes?"

The oldest-looking of the pair—possibly older than Fallon even—blinked bright blue eyes, the only color in her otherwise wan face.

"We mean you no harm." She rounded the bed. "Come with us."

Perhaps it was the kindness of her voice . . . or simply that she spoke at all in a place where none seemed inclined—or permitted—to speak. Whatever the reason, Fallon swung her legs over the side of the bed. Slipping on her well-worn boots, she laced them up and followed the girls past cots of sleeping girls and downstairs.

They crept through the kitchen where Cook slept, snoring loudly near a hearth of dying embers. Fallon focused on the back of the smaller girl, watching the rhythmic sway of her dark plait, thick as a man's wrist, bouncing against her back.

A blast of frigid wind met Fallon when she stepped outside, slashing her cheeks. The older girl took her companion's hand and held out another for Fallon. She looked down at that hand, hesitating to take it in her own.

The girl smiled, as though understanding. "My name is Evelyn." She shrugged. "Evie." She dipped her head toward the smaller girl. "This is Marguerite."

Marguerite lifted her gaze, revealing witchlike eyes that glowed gold in the murky night. She gave a shy nod.

"Come along," Evie directed before plunging into the winter's very teeth. She and Marguerite moved over the frozen ground with the speed of hares, the frayed hems of their nightgowns flashing beneath their blankets.

Biting her lip, Fallon glanced behind her, almost as though she suspected the specter of Master Brocklehurst to rise up on the night. He had enjoyed her beating. She heard it in the pant of his breath as he brought the strap against her back and saw it in the gleam of his eyes when it had been over. He would relish doing it again. She swallowed against the tightness in her throat. She did not wish to give him an excuse. Evie and Marguerite grew smaller, their gray blanketed figures dirtlike smudges on the white horizon.

Muttering, she dove into the slicing wind, her legs working fiercely through the drifts to catch up with the other two as they rounded the back of the sprawling school.

Moments later, she arrived at a ramshackle stable crouched in Penwich's shadow, a stitch pinching her side, cold snow slithering down the inside of her boot. The girls held the door open for her, and Fallon helped them fight the wind to close it. With the thick wood door shut, the wind sounded far away, a dull howl in the distance. Evie and Marguerite clambered up a ladder to the loft. Fallon followed, clearing the top as Evie dragged a bucket from behind a pile of hay and Marguerite crouched in a corner, unraveling a bit of cloth.

Chafing her hands together, she watched Evie crack a thin sheet of ice from a bucket of milk. Evie grinned. "Goat's milk."

"Where did you get it?"

"Jean-Luc from the village leaves it up here for us once a week when he delivers coal."

Fallon glanced up from the bucket. "Why?"

"Marguerite speaks French. He fancies her a countrywoman."

Fallon glanced at the dark-haired girl, gasping as she revealed a large hunk of cheese from the cloth. "He leaves that, too?"

Marguerite offered a portion to her. Fallon barely stopped herself from falling upon it in a ravenous fit.

They ate in silence, taking turns at the bucket of rich milk. Falling back on the soft hay, Fallon sighed, replete. Evie rose and opened a shutter in the loft. Dropping in the hay beside Fallon, she tucked an arm behind her head and stared out at the wintry night.

Fallon felt a moment's peace. Perhaps the first since Da's death. She frowned. It would not last. Best she not become too at ease. "Why did you bring me here? With you?"

Evie replied, "You look like you needed a friend."

Fallon nodded, her throat tight at the unexpected kindness. Friends were lost to her. And family. She scarcely recalled her mother, lost to fever before she could truly know her. Da had been everything. And now he was gone. She could use a friend or two.

Marguerite spoke, her voice a feather's stroke on the air. "Girls at Penwich come and go—"

"They most often *go* in a coffin," Evie muttered savagely, her blue eyes glinting.

Marguerite continued, "You're not like the other girls. We saw that when you shared your bread with Helen."

Fallon shook her head. "Helen?"

"Little Helen. About five years old."

"Oh." Fallon nodded, remembering. Some older girls had filched the child's food, and pinched her arm viciously when she started to protest.

Marguerite drew her knees to her chest. "You reminded us of . . . well, *us*."

Fallon digested this, unable to respond for the

thick lump in her throat, simply pleased to have found affinity with two other souls. To no longer feel so terribly alone.

"There!" Evie shot up off the hay, pointing to the ink-dark sky as a single flash of light arced across the night. "Did you see that? A shooting star! See it?"

Fallon nodded, staring.

"Quickly, make a wish." Evie jammed her eyes tightly shut, her lips moving in a rush as she proclaimed, "I wish for adventure! To visit places far, far from this vile place." Opening her eyes, she fixed her gaze on Marguerite, nudging the smaller girl. "Come, what do you wish for?"

Wetting full lips, Marguerite stared thoughtfully out at the night. "I wish . . . I wish to *matter.*"

Evie nodded slowly, then turned her attention to Fallon, who had been holding her breath, knowing her turn would come. Her heart was greedy. She wished for so much. For the impossible. *For Da.*

She settled on the important, and, hopefully, attainable. "I wish for a home."

The streak of light left from the falling star vanished after the words left her lips, but Fallon could still see it in her mind against the night sky.

Their hastily formed requests lingered on the air, the words floating as reverently as prayers uttered aloud in a chapel.

*I wish for adventure.*
*I wish to matter.*
*I wish for a home.*

# Chapter 1

**F**allon's steps slowed along the cobbled walk as she approached the modest brick town-house, home to Widow Jamison. Her toes pinched inside her boots and she longed for her other pair—the men's boots tucked under her bed that Mrs. Jamison deemed unacceptable. *A female on my staff shall look as a female ought to and not wear articles intended for men.* Fallon sighed and shook her head. Her vanity had long ago accepted she would never be feminine or dainty. Why could not the rest of the world?

The hour was late. She had lost track of time during her visit with Evie and Marguerite. They had a great deal to catch up on—more than their correspondence had ever been able to convey in the two years since they parted ways.

Her gently swishing skirts cut through the night's low-rising fog. Burrowing deep into her cloak, she stopped and gazed ahead at the looming townhouse, lingering in its shadow for a reason she could not pinpoint. Wariness skittered through her as she studied the shadows dancing along the pale brick facade. Dark sensation zinged through her, prickling her nape. An awareness she could not easily dismiss . . . an instinct that had been bred into her ever since her father's murderer dropped her on Penwich's steps.

Her fingers curled around the cold steel gate surrounding the residence. Shivering in the frigid night, she commanded herself to move out of the chill and into the warmth of the house. And yet she could not move.

Then it came to her with the suddenness of a hare bolting from the brush. Lights blazed from the front parlor window. A low hum of conversation floated on the air, gentle as wind.

Usually, the house sat silent this time of night, Widow Jamison and her three pugs long since tucked into bed following her evening "tonic." What marked the situation as even more unusual was the fact that the widow had departed yesterday to visit relations in Cornwall. Most of the staff had made free with the night to follow their own leisure pursuits, but certainly none had decided to make merry in their mistress's absence. In the parlor, no less. The stern housekeeper would never permit such an occurrence. So the question remained: Who was in the parlor?

Deciding it none of her affair, she eased the gate leading to the back of the house open, shutting it carefully, making certain it did not clang.

Fallon paused as she slipped inside through the servants' back entrance. Loud, indistinct voices overlapped. A female's shrill laughter carried from the front of the house. Then a second female laughed, the sound just as coarse. Fallon winced and resumed her pace down the narrow corridor, her swift steps falling dead on the well-worn runner.

Who could possibly be in the house? Mrs. Jamison possessed no female relations who would make free of her home in her absence. Only a . . .

Fallon stopped, cold dread and absolute certainty sweeping through her simultaneously. She closed her eyes in a long blink and shook her head. *Reginald.* Of course. Or Reggie as his doting mama called him.

The rare times Mrs. Jamison's thin lips curved in smile were during her son's visits home from school—only twice since Fallon hired on, but twice too many. She had grown well acquainted with the face of *darling* Reggie on those visits—a face like so many gentleman and noblemen scattered throughout her life. Not gentle. And not noble.

The lad was near her age. Even without the spots on his face and gangly awkward limbs so disproportionate to the rest of his body, he struck her as far younger than her own twenty years. But his youth hadn't fooled her. Nor his mother's blind, absolute affection for him. It hadn't taken her long to learn why all the maids steered clear of him.

She had very nearly flung a book at the cad's head when he corned her in the library. His mother's sudden appearance had stopped Fallon before she did anything so dire. Instead of reprimanding her son, the widow had sent Fallon off with a swift warning. *I'll have no tarts working beneath my roof. Take better care to cover that outrageous hair of yours and get yourself to the kitchens.*

Her face still burned at the memory even as the insult echoed with dreaded familiarity. Master Brocklehurst's charge of vanity frequently rang out through the halls of Penwich for any girl whose hair showed beneath their caps. With her

fiery tresses, Fallon had always attracted his particular ire.

Lifting her wool skirt, she increased her pace,
eyeing the long length of hall. The small room
she shared with another maid was at the far end,
near the set of stairs that led up to the family's
quarters.

Suddenly another sound rose on the air, min-
gling with the distant laughter. Her pulse skittered at the dull thud of approaching footsteps.
She didn't know whether to quicken her steps or
freeze in her tracks. The heavy tread grew. Air
froze in her lungs.

A shadow descended, casting a pall over the
corridor's floor. Her heart seized in her chest.
Clutching the edge of her cloak near her throat,
she prayed merely another servant approached,
retiring for the night.

She lurched sideways, hoping—absurdly—to
blend with the wall. She watched as black Hes-
sians became visible, then buff trousers, then an
opened waistcoat and rumpled lawn shirt. Her
gaze drifted up and dread clawed through her.

*Reggie.* And well into his cups, if his rumpled
appearance and the slight sway to his stance were
any indication. His bleary eyes had no trouble
spotting her where she hugged the wall.

"There you are, love." *Hiccup.* "Fancy that. Thought I would have to search every room to find you." *Hiccup.*

Inhaling deeply, she shoved off the wall and strode forward, chin high, intent on reaching her door. And bolting it solidly behind her.

"Good evening, sir."

"Good evening, sir," he quipped, his smile mocking as he waved an arm, his loose sleeve billowing like a dove on the air. "You speak well." *Hiccup.* "Like a lady." He smirked as if he told an amusing remark.

She resisted snapping that she was as educated and polished as any lady of his acquaintance— that he needn't act so bloody surprised over the fact that she could string her words together in an intelligent fashion. Despite her poor beginnings, she was not an uneducated guttersnipe. Penwich had seen to that, wiping practically all hint of an Irish brogue from her voice. The school might half starve its pupils and beat them for the slightest infraction, but they had not scrimped on providing a topnotch education. Indeed, Fallon was well suited for life as a governess. Unfortunately her lot was that of a maid assigned kitchen duty.

A familiar anger burned through her blood. *Gentlemen* like Reggie had seen fit to rob her of any other opportunity . . . dismissing her on the grounds of impertinence when she had not been more *accommodating* to their wishes. With so many dismissals and too few references, a position more suited to her qualifications eluded her. Her fist curled at her side. Da's voice whispered across her mind. Almost as if he stood beside her. *Careful, Fallon girl. Don't let 'im get your goat.*

Sighing, she uncurled her fingers and stowed away her frustrations. Such emotions would only get her sacked. Yet again. Far better that she diffuse the situation.

"If you would pardon me, Mr. Jamison." She attempted to step past him.

He blocked her, moving faster than she expected for one so deep in his cups. "I thought you might like to join me and my friends in the parlor for some sherry." Leaning forward, he brushed the back of his hand against her cheek. "See how the other half lives."

He pressed a finger against his wobbly-mouthed smile. "I won't tell Mother. Come." He clasped her arm. As if he had every right to do so. Her teeth ground so hard her jaw ached. But didn't they *all* behave that way? As if they possessed *every* right?

The top of his head did not even reach her chin. It would be a relatively simple matter to plant her fist in his pug-nosed face and knock him down. As much as her father had lectured her on controlling her temper and abiding the ill treatment of her betters, he had also taught her it was acceptable to draw a line when risk to her person loomed imminent.

Drawing a steadying breath, she cautioned herself that it had not come to that. *Yet*. And she must prevent such a situation from arising. Otherwise she would be at the mercy of the agency again. Specifically Mrs. Harrison. The image of that proprietress rose in her mind, her sour face and buglike, unblinking eyes not the least bit merciful. She would not refer Fallon if she were sacked again. No matter the excuse.

*Dignity and forbearance. Dignity and forbearance.*

Like all those years at Penwich when she had bit her tongue and born Master Brocklehurst's switch to her back. For whatever imagined infraction. She would bear more. She *could*. With as much charm and humility as she could manage, she pasted a smile on her face. "Lovely as that sounds, sir, I must decline."

"Ah, you must not." *Hiccup*. "As your employer, I insist." His slight chest swelled with importance.

"I command it. I told all my friends about you—my fiery-haired Boadicea." His fingers flexed on her arm, his grip softening into a caress.

"Boadicea?" She winced.

"Yes. She was a Celtic queen who fought off the Romans—"

"I know who she is," she inserted pertly, then bit her tongue. *Dignity and forbearance.*

"Indeed." *Hiccup.* "Then you recall she was a giant of a woman with flaming hair. It is said she rode bare-breasted into battle." His gaze dropped to her chest almost on level with his eyes.

Her cheeks smoldered. That particular bit had been left out of her history lessons.

He trailed his hand down her arm, his fingers reaching her tightly fisted hand. "If I don't return to the parlor with you, they will think I've invented you." *Hiccup.* "We can't have that. Now. Do as you're bade and come along with Reggie." He winked. "I promise you shall have a *grand* time." From the way he licked his fleshy lips, Fallon guessed he expected he would have a grand time, too—with *her.*

Da had warned her of men's lascivious natures—especially when it came to women they considered beneath them. *Easy pickings.* Aside of her own father, the years since had concreted her feelings on that score. The Penwich School for Virtuous Girls had boasted a few girls who were less than virtuous. And yet Fallon had never faulted them. They bartered what they possessed for what the school failed to provide—food, clothes . . . affection.

Post or no post, she had no intention of stepping into a parlor full of inebriated men scarcely out of leading strings.

"I work for your mother. Not you, Mr. Jamison."

Something tightened in his face, reminding her of a spoiled boy denied a treat. He flicked a hand in the air. "And who do you think shall inherit? Once I reach majority, all this shall belong to me." His gaze roved over her. "That includes you and every other servant in this house. If you wish to keep your post, you would do well to remember that."

Her fingers tightened around the strings of her reticule. It took every ounce of willpower to not swing it at the insolent pup. If she remained one moment longer, she would strike him where he stood.

"Forgive me, sir, but I forgot I have something I must do."

With that rather inane comment, she gave a fierce tug and freed herself from his grasp. Lips tight, she spun on her heel, perversely satisfied at her final glimpse of his startled face. Likely a servant had never denied him anything before.

"Where are you going?" he sputtered behind her.

She didn't reply. Hopefully she could disappear into the night and tomorrow this whole encounter would be but a dim memory for the sot. A few times around the square and she would return, well after he had returned to his friends in the parlor.

She hurried out the servants' door into the frigid night, her heels clicking over the cobbled path that circled the house. Passing through the gate, she forged ahead, heedless that it clanked loudly behind her. Her breath puffed before her in frothy clouds.

The sudden echo of the gate clanging open and shut again scraped the air. She froze and shot a look over her shoulder into the murky night. *It couldn't be. He couldn't be.* She quickened her pace.

"You there! Girl! Wait."

Heat licked her cheeks. *Girl!* Really! She possessed a name. And she happened to be older than he, the little toad.

"Stop, I say!" He was tenacious. A bulldog with a bone. She pretended not to hear him and turned down a street leading from the square, onto sidewalks lined with darkened shops. Feet pounded behind her. For a brief moment, she contemplated breaking into a full run but decided against it. A tad dramatic, and she was a pragmatist at heart. A pragmatist who needed her post come morning.

Sighing, she stopped and turned to face him, legs braced a bit apart. "Mr. Jamison," she began as he came to a halt breathlessly before her, his face red from exertion . . . and something else. Something that sent a trickle of unease down her spine. "Go home, sir. Return to your friends. I remembered I have an errand to—"

"At this hour?" he panted. "Nonsense. You're trying to escape me. Most impertinent."

"Please, sir. Just go home."

Panting, he clutched his side, all evidence of hiccups gone. "You dare to command me? Hold your tongue, girl."

"Please, Mr. Jamison," she said tiredly. "I have no wish to offend—"

He raised his hand from his side and snatched

her wrist, his eyes glowing with a sobriety absent moments ago, before his jog through fogged streets. "Then you best be a biddable creature and follow me back inside the house."

She glanced down at her arm. At the pale hand, smaller than her own, gripping her. Anger churned in her stomach. Extending the spot-faced lad any courtesy at this point took every ounce of will she possessed. Da had long ingrained in her the importance of showing proper humility to her betters. But he had also instilled in her a healthy respect for herself—for the safety of her person.

"Do you hear me?" Reggie tightened his grip.

She inhaled thinly through her nostrils. *Sorry, Da. But even you would agree this is one of those circumstances.*

Her stomach churned. Not so much at what she was about to do, but at the consequences that were certain to result.

She nodded, an eerie calm sweeping over her. "I hear you, sir. Now hear me." She locked gazes with him. "Unhand me or . . ." her voice faded.

"Or what?" Amusement brimmed in his voice.

"Or I shall make you."

"Make me?" He laughed, tossing back his head. "Are you daft, girl?"

"Laugh all you like." Her voice lowered a degree. "You've been duly warned."

"Warned?" He shook her arm again. Hard enough to give her discomfort. She winced. "You have cheek, girl, I'll give you that."

She had more than cheek. Breath gusted from her lips. He was going to learn that the hard way. She wrenched free of his grasp. Grabbing him by both shoulders, she lifted her knee. Using all her force, she kneed him in the groin.

His startled gaze collided with hers the instant she made contact. The choked gurgle to follow brought a grim smile to her face. She released his shoulders and stood back, watching as he collapsed, a twisted pile of man. Low, pitiable moans tripped from his lips, reverberating through the chill evening air.

"You're fortunate my skirts hampered me." Propping her hands on her hips, she added, "It could have been much worse."

"Worse!" he wheezed, sprawled on the ground and clutching himself in the most undignified fashion as he rolled side to side.

"Indeed."

His face burned varying shades of red and purple beneath the muted glow of gaslight. Spittle flew from his lips as he spoke the words she had dreaded. And yet if the truth be known, she had grown so accustomed to hearing them, they did not distress her as they should.

"Your services are no longer needed."

Fallon sighed. Sacked again. Of course.

# Chapter 2

**D**ominic Hale, Duke of Damon, parted the curtains of his carriage as he idly fondled the female beside him. Her plump breast over-filled his palm, precisely the way he preferred a woman's breast to fit in his hand.

Her name escaped him, but their names always did. And, after a day or two, so did their faces.

Inhaling the cold night, he stared out at the gas-lit street, searching, it seemed . . . for something, anything. But then he had been doing a great deal of that lately. Restlessness plagued him. As it had halfway around the world, following him home. He had hoped his return would restore him to his proper self.

He grimaced, deciding the word *proper* a far from apt description for him. The cheap perfume that rose to sting the inside of his nose mingled with the stink of opiates that had floated about the gaming den where he spent the evening.

He exhaled, dreading his next breath. While he might appreciate the feel of the woman in his arms, her overpowering perfume was another matter. He inched closer to the window, trying not to breathe too deeply.

The second woman in the carriage mewled for his attention. She dropped off the seat to curl at his feet in a mass of ruffled silk. Her hands slid up his boot, fingers working into his thigh like a kitten flexing her claws.

He brushed a hand over her hair as she worked at the front of his breeches, eager for the tide of sensation to flood him. In a matter of moments, her soft hand closed around the length of him and she lowered her head into his lap.

Dropping his head back against the squabs, he let the clatter of hooves fill his head, enjoying her expert mouth bringing him to life. An evening of carnal pleasure yawned before him. Two women should keep him fairly occupied. Distracted. His body could burn in a way his heart could not. The nights, the drink, the gaming, the cards, the women . . . for a brief time they brought him warmth. *Feeling.* They broke through the numbness. Temporarily at least.

He gazed at the shining puddles of rainwater outside the carriage and waited. Then, after a few moments, frowned.

The usual sensations eluded him. The harsh pleasure he knew so well, the wild, searing sensations that reminded him he was alive . . . none emerged. Even as his body responded, the awful emptiness clung to him with a tenacious fist.

Through heavy-lidded eyes, he stared out at the night, catching the hazy reflection of the carriage in the glass of the darkened storefronts they passed. Suddenly his view was broken, the string of shops interrupted by a pair of tussling figures.

He straightened against the squabs at the glimpse of a female, her dark cloak whipping in the night as she fought a man. He caught sight of a pale face with impossibly wide eyes. Dominic shoved the woman's head from his lap, turning on his seat for a better look. Unfortunately he could see no more. The carriage had passed the pair.

Hastily rearranging his clothing, he rapped on the carriage roof. "Halt!"

The women squealed in dismay as they jerked to a stop. The one on the floor rolled onto her back in a flurry of fuchsia skirts, her tiny slippers kicking in the air in a desperate attempt to gain leverage.

Dominic had never aspired to be a gentleman. Quite the opposite. Still, he found himself seized with an impulse to act, to do something that could only be deemed *gentlemanly*. Amid his travels, he had saved others—all urchins. Helpless souls, innocent victims. As he once had been. Before he grew to manhood. Before Mrs. Pearce broke him. Before a life of depravity became second nature.

Lurching from the carriage, he hastened down the sidewalk, jerking to an abrupt stop at the sight before him.

Hands propped on her hips, the female—a towering Amazon—stood over her attacker. Or perhaps more appropriately, her victim. In the brief time the carriage had passed the pair, she had turned the tables on her attacker. Scratching his jaw, he eyed the hapless young man writhing at her feet, clutching himself between the legs. His flushed face contorted, and Dominic winced.

"Do you need any assistance?" he asked rather lamely. Clearly she did not *require* help.

Her head snapped up, bright eyes focusing on

him. Beneath the gaslights, he couldn't be certain their color, only that they glittered boldly, her gaze direct in a way he had not seen before. On a woman, at any rate.

She looked him up and down as if he were little better than the wretch sprawled at her feet. Her nostrils flared as though she did not like what she smelled. Likely the cheap perfume of his companions. "I have the situation well in hand, thank you, sir."

He nodded, eyeing the mass of her hair, gilded fire beneath the gaslamps. He hungrily drank the sight, memorizing the color, envisioning it on canvas, trying to imagine what mix of his oils might best recapture it. "I see that."

Her gaze fixed distrustfully on him. Granting him wide berth, she stepped around her erstwhile attacker and continued down the sidewalk, her steps bold, confidant. *Extraordinary.* Nothing like the dainty steps of most women.

Tossing one last glance at the groaning young man, he moved to catch up with her. "Perhaps I can offer a lift?" He motioned to his carriage.

She paused beneath a street lamp and he was allowed a moment to fully appreciate the glory of hair. He could scarcely take note of her face for all that hair, beckoning his eyes. The mélange of red, gold, and brown tumbled past her shoulders, the pins sticking out oddly. He imagined with all the pins removed it would reach her waist. A sudden image of her astride him, his hands sliding over her long legs as she rode him, her head tilted back so that the incredible mass of her hair tickled his thighs, speared him in a blinding flash of heat.

Her eyes narrowed beneath brows several shades darker than the rest of her hair. "You stopped for me?"

"You appeared in need of help." He cocked his head. "I trust you are unharmed."

She sent a glare over her shoulder. "It would take more than that boy to gain the upper hand with me."

"Ah." He nodded gravely while he marveled at her mettle. "Then he is the one in need. Should I tend to him?"

Her lips twitched, but she did not smile at his jest. Indeed, he wondered if she ever smiled. There was something hard about her. Something unyielding, as if she never allowed herself to relax.

He spoke again into the hovering silence. "I fear you've made me feel quite useless. You must allow me to convey you to your destination safely."

Her gaze drifted to his carriage, and he could tell she was debating the matter. He found himself staring at her shadowed profile, the high brow, the strong line of her nose, the full, wide mouth. She was no beauty, to be sure. But there was something about her. Something untamed and earthy. No doubt many a man yearned to part those long legs of hers and sample such an uncommon woman.

His cock stirred, straining against his breeches. Excitement zinged through him. The excitement eluding him earlier. He dragged his gaze away from her, his mind quickly working . . . determining how best to seduce her into his bed for the night. That's what he did best, after all. When he wasn't bedding a woman whose morals were as equally flawed as his own, he corrupted innocent and well-heeled ladies. That was his life's vocation. And painting. When he lost himself in a canvas, he felt alive. Plowing a woman's thighs and creating a new world on canvas . . . it was all he knew. All he did. All that ever penetrated the numbness dwelling inside him.

"The hour's late." He glanced up and down the street. A hack passed the silent store fronts, its dark curtains drawn. The driver's eyes narrowed on Fallon with insolent speculation. Hardly a safe setting for a lone woman. "The next man you come across may not be so easy to dissuade as that boy." He motioned to the lad who now staggered away at the far end of the street.

Eyes as cagey as a cornered animal, she assessed him. No doubt wondering whether he was one such *next* man.

He'd nearly forgotten his companions, but remembering, and hoping their presence might reassure her, he murmured, "I'm not alone. I have companions. Ladies." Of a sort.

Some rigidity seemed to lessen from her stance then. She studied the carriage a long moment. "Very well. A lift would be appreciated. I'm venturing to the Hotel Daventry."

Dominic took her elbow and led her to the carriage, pausing to call up the destination to his driver. Only a short time to change her mind. The Hotel Daventry was but five minutes away.

He could not help noticing as he assisted her within his coach that she smelled spicy—a peppery blend of sweet and savory. As a boy, he spent a good deal of time in the kitchen, avoiding Mrs. Pearce in preference of the cook's kind attentions.

This woman evoked those long-ago memories, smelling of baking bread, savory stew, and chocolate tart all at once.

Once inside, she nodded a greeting to the other two women. He took the seat across from her and found himself quickly sandwiched on either side by feminine bodies soaked with familiar cheap perfume. His appreciation for the woman across from him only grew.

"Picking up strays, Damon?" the female to his right purred. "Two of us aren't enough?"

He sent her a quelling look. Even in the dim coach, he detected the flood of color in the girl's face. She held his gaze though, square chin set at a proud angle, watching him and his companions closely, and he was fired again with the need to have her, to possess her, to find his release in her body.

The other female snickered as her hand slid up his thigh. "I'd heard you had an enormous appetite."

Angling his head, he watched his Amazon intently, rubbing a finger lightly over the top of his lip. "What's your name?"

She did not reply for some moments, her gaze dropping to the woman's hand inching up his thigh, higher and higher until she palmed his cock through his trousers. That wide, luscious mouth parted with a soft gasp of outrage, and her eyes snapped to his face. "Fallon," she bit out. "Fallon O'Rourke."

Wine, he decided suddenly, his mind racing over color pallets. He would paint those lips a deep ruby wine. After he tasted them, of course.

"Fallon," he repeated, leaning back and smiling. He liked it. As different as the woman herself. A woman he vowed to have. In his bed and on his canvas.

He stretched his legs out before him, letting a booted foot slide between her feet. Lips set in a mutinous line, she tried to arrange her feet so that they did not touch. She shot a pointed look to the woman's hand on his crotch. He merely stared at her, arching a brow.

She blinked and forced her gaze away from his lap, staring at the carriage wall as if a fresco of vast interest were painted there.

He scowled. *A prig.* He had hoped that an un-accompanied woman who felt free to prowl the streets alone at this hour of night might be a little more receptive. Unfortunate. He had little use for *good* women.

The hand on his cock grew bolder. Insistent. Annoying, as she sought to free him from his trousers. He seized her wrist, in no mood. At least for her. "Enough."

Fury glittered in Fallon's gaze. "Let me out. Stop the coach," she quietly commanded.

He laughed. The sound curled through the air, dark and low. "We're almost there. Sit back. Relax."

Just *looking* at her sent his blood smoldering through his veins. Woke him, revitalized him as he craved.

Filled with a sudden desire to see those eyes widen even more, to see just how far he could scandalize her, he brought one of the tarts over his lap. Watching Fallon, he tugged down her gown. Plump breasts spilled over the top of her corset. Bending his head, he touched one large nipple with his tongue, tickling it until the dark tip was moist and engorged. The woman on his lap squirmed and panted out her pleasure.

Fallon made a small sound, part distress, part something else. She looked away, but only for a moment before her gaze dragged back again, watching the scene he played out in horrified interest.

The woman on his lap threaded her hand through his hair and gave a violent tug. "Harder."

His Amazon's eyes flared wider.

His blood pumped faster.

Fallon's slender hand drifted to her neck. She stroked the side of her throat with deceptive idleness.

He bit down, catching the nipple between his teeth. The female shuddered in his arms, her body in spasms against his mouth.

Fallon inhaled, the ragged sound a sharp rip in the close confines of the coach—almost as though the act had been done to her. Her hand slid down her neck, stopping at her cloak's ties. Her fingers played with the frayed ribbons at her neck for a moment before her hand dropped, falling to her lap.

Satisfaction curled deep in his gut at the sight of that trembling hand. She was not unaffected. He watched her as her hand curled into a fist. Oh, she was angry. Outraged. Like any good woman ought to be. But she felt something, too. And it was that very thing he wished to explore. Both with his body and his painter's brush.

Eyes feasting on her, he enjoyed the rise of color staining her cheeks as he bit down and sucked the beaded tip. The woman on his lap writhed. Fallon's mouth parted. The coach jerked to an abrupt stop. Before he could move, Fallon was off her seat and flying from the coach. He dumped the woman from his lap to the seat across from him and flew after her. She made it only a few feet from the carriage before he caught her arm.

Swinging around, her eyes flashed fire. "Release me."

The hotel loomed beyond her. A pair of footmen near the door watched them curiously.

He opened his mouth to apologize, then stopped himself. He wasn't sorry. He had enjoyed every moment of her discomfort. To say otherwise would be a lie. Of all his faults, dishonesty did not rank among them.

He stepped close enough to murmur against her ear. "What I did to her—I would greatly enjoy doing to you."

The sound of her sharply indrawn breath tickled his cheek. "You're a libertine."

"Indeed." He released her. Fishing out his card, he offered it to her. "But I can bring you pleasure. You're . . . curious. I see it in your eyes. Let me show you how it can be."

"You see nothing."

"I see a woman." His finger descended to her bottom lip. She froze. He tested the fullness, stepping closer until their bodies brushed each other.

He traced that plump bottom lip, pulling her mouth open a bit, stroking the moist inside just a fraction. Her breath rushed free and he grew hard, imagining that sweet breath wafting over him a moment before she took him into her mouth.

Gritting past his arousal, he stepped back and placed his card in her palm, folding her fingers closed over it. "In case you ever have need of a friend."

She glanced down at her hand with a befuddled expression.

"My address," he explained.

"Oh!" Comprehension settled on her shadowed features. "I don't think so." She began to crumple the card. "I don't need a *friend* like you." Her glittering eyes shot a scathing glare toward his carriage where his companions waited.

He smiled. "One can never have too many friends."

She snorted.

He brushed back a thick strand of fiery hair curling over her shoulder—soft as silk on his fingers. She flinched. His smile slipped. "Perhaps if I had you, I wouldn't require other such friends."

The words were absurd. *Untrue.* He did not know what motivated him to utter them. He closed his hand over her hand. She gawked at him. He nodded to their clutched hands. His skin burned where he held her. Her eyes widened at the contact, proving she felt it, too. Unfortunate she would not act upon it.

"Keep the card." Smiling grimly, he pivoted on his heel and returned to his coach . . . and to a night of carnal abandonment. Even if it was not *her*, his body would find the release it needed. He always saw to that.

Fallon glared at the elaborate coat of arms on the carriage door as it closed with a decided click. Chest tight and prickly with outrage—and other emotions she could not identify—she debated searching for a large rock to throw at the departing vehicle.

The image of the dark-haired devil with smoky blue eyes lingered in her head. Heat swept up her throat, scalding her cheeks as she recalled the things he had done. The things she had watched him do. Insufferable rogue. She glanced down at the card clutched in her trembling hands and read the first line of the fine elegant script.

*Dominic Hale, the Duke of Damon.*

She snorted. A duke. Of course. Bitterness flooded her mouth, thick enough to make her nearly gag. A bloody lord of the realm . . . and the most licentious man to ever cross her path. Of course. She shook her head, her gaze scanning the Mayfair address. 15 Pottingham Place.

*In case you ever have need of a friend.*

Friend indeed! Did the cad think she would one day appear on his doorstep seeking his special brand of *friendship*? Did he think his blue-gray eyes so mesmerizing that she could not resist? His tall lithe physique—so rare among men—impossible to deny?

*The Duke of Damon.* She tilted her head and stared thoughtfully at the departing carriage. It rang a familiar chord. Likely his reputation preceded him.

The image of his tongue circling that woman's nipple flashed through her mind and she closed her eyes in one long blink, denying that her stomach dipped and twisted at the memory. Very well, he had been . . . *intriguing*. In a dangerous and totally uncouth manner.

Opening her eyes, she scanned the card again. *15 Pottingham Place.* With a savage mutter, she crumpled the card in her hand and tossed it into a puddle. Strides swift and sure, she ascended the steps into the Hotel Daventry.

The world would stop turning before she *ever* crossed the threshold of 15 Pottingham Place.

# Chapter 3

"**F**allon? What are you doing here?" Evelyn knotted the sash of her wrapper over her slim figure. Reaching into the corridor, she pulled Fallon inside the room, sparing a quick glance up and down the hall's length.

Fallon stumbled into the elegant bedchamber where she, Evie, and Marguerite had taken tea earlier. "I hope you don't mind my coming."

Evie's forehead creased with concern as she turned from the door. "Of course not."

"I won't get you in trouble?" Fallon demanded, careful to keep her voice low, knowing one of the rooms on either side of Evie's belonged to her young charge.

Evie fluttered a hand in dismissal. "What are you doing here? Did you forget something this evening?" she asked, glancing about the room.

"Not quite," she hedged. "I met with some trouble upon returning home." *Home.* She twisted her fingers, wincing. The word sadly rang wrong. Had she ever possessed a true *home*? A place of her very own that no one could take away?

"Oh, no." Evie sighed, shaking her head.

Fallon nodded. "I've been sacked."

Evie's hand flew to her mouth.

"I'll return tomorrow to collect all my things. As things stand, I don't think it wise to return tonight."

Evie wrapped an arm around her shoulders and led her to a striped chintz sofa. "Of course not. But what happened? You said the new post was going well."

Biting her lip, Fallon sank down beside Evie and reluctantly confessed the night's deeds. Well . . . all save the last bit. No need to describe her encounter with the wretched Duke of Damon.

"I'm sorry to prevail upon you like this. I've no wish to jeopardize your new position." She lifted one shoulder in a weak shrug. "I have nowhere else to go."

Evie cut her off with a swift shake of her head. "You will stay here for the night. And after that . . ." Her voice faded. Uncertainty flickered in her soft blue eyes. She squeezed Fallon's hand. Fallon nodded, understanding. In the morning,

Evie sailed for Barbados to deposit Miss Pratt into the hands of her waiting groom.

Untying the strings at her throat, she removed her cloak. "I'll find something tomorrow. A new post. A better one." She gave a small, brittle laugh. "I always do." Well, perhaps not *better*. But she did not want Evie to fret.

"Perhaps you can explain what happened to Mrs. Jamison. Surely she cannot fault you for her son's—"

"She can," Fallon interrupted again. "She will." She shrugged with a lightness she did not feel. "Family tends to stick together, I've learned. Mrs. Jamison won't take the word of a maid over her precious son."

"Oh, Fallon, you've the worst luck."

Luck. Fallon supposed she could believe that. Believe that luck alone—or lack thereof—was responsible for all the events of her life. But to believe that, she must accept that she bore no responsibility, no control over her own life. And that, she refused to accept.

"Oh, Fallon." Evie glanced around her well-appointed room, biting her lip when her gaze landed on her large trunk. Fallon imagined she was contemplating a way to smuggle her into her luggage and stow her aboard ship.

Fallon's gaze drifted, appreciating the fine rose-wood furniture, the four-poster bed, the counterpane that looked plump and inviting, definitely down-stuffed. A marked improvement from the cots they slept on at Penwich.

As though reading Fallon's mind, Evie muttered, "You deserve all this, too. You're just as qualified as I to hold such a position."

Would she have had this? If she had stuck it out and taught a few years at Penwich as Evie had done—earning the experience and letters of reference needed to land such a coveted post?

*And seen Brocklehurst's face one day more than necessary?* Fallon shivered. He never had it in for Evie and Marguerite as with her.

"I land on my feet." She would not have Evie depart for Barbados worrying for her. Not when she was about to embark on her long-waited adventure. "I'll find a new situation tomorrow."

"You're welcome to stay here until we depart in the afternoon. Hettie never ventures into my room." Her smooth brow creased. "Are you certain you will be able to find another post in so short a time?"

"Of course." And if not, Fallon vowed it would not be Evie's cross to bear.

Evie shook her head, her plait of honey brown

hair tossing on her shoulder. "I don't know," she began, but stopped at the sharp screech erupting one room over.

Fallon jumped where she sat, her hand flying to her heart. "What on earth—"

"Eve! Eve! I need you! Get in here at once!"

"Good Lord. Is that your charge?"

Evie closed her eyes in a weary blink.

The screech came again. "Eve!"

Fallon arched a brow. *"Eve?"*

"She insists on calling me Eve."

Master Brocklehurst had called her that, and Fallon knew how much her friend hated the designation. "Sounds like a lovely girl." She gave a shaky smile.

*"I haven't all night, Eve!"*

"Weeks aboard a ship's cabin together." Evie shuddered. "I'm starting to wonder . . . this might not be the adventure I planned." Rising to her feet, she strode to the adjoining door, rolling her eyes. "You'll have to excuse me. The royal highness beckons. It's only the fifth time she's called upon me tonight."

Facing the door, Evie squared her shoulders. "She probably needs me to stoke the coals in the grate. Again." She motioned to the wardrobe against the far wall. "Feel free to make yourself comfortable. I have a night rail that should fit well enough." She gave a quick apologetic smile. "If a bit short, though."

Lifting the latch to the adjoining room, she quickly entered and closed the door behind her.

Taking advantage of Evie's offer, Fallon rummaged through her things until she located a spare nightgown. Closing the wardrobe, she passed the grate, the warmth from the coals a comforting stroke on her bare calves. For a moment, she allowed herself to forget tonight . . . to forget the duke with the mesmerizing blue-gray eyes and wicked smile and all the sinful things he had done within the shadows of that coach. And without.

Face burning, she fell back on the luxurious counterpane. At least she had a night of comfort. With Evie, no less. Stretching her arms over her head, her thoughts drifted to the duke again. *Bloody man—men!* They could be as depraved as they liked. They could do whatever they wanted. Even if they lacked coin, they could venture out and find respectable work without suffering all the nonsense she endured.

After tonight's debacle, Mrs. Harrison at the agency would never consider referring her again. And the only work she could find would be of the variety no respectable woman would contemplate.

*Oh, Da, you never thought I'd sink this low, did you? Too bad I wasn't born a man. Surviving would be a spot easier.*

As a man, she would be someone who could go about their day and perform their duties without being forced to defend their person. Someone whose presence would not make the women of the household uncomfortable simply by breathing and occupying the same space. Someone who Mrs. Harrison would not turn away.

With a sharp breath, she shot up straight on the bed. Suddenly, the world righted itself. Everything became clear. The impossible so . . . *possible.* If she only possessed the temerity to see it through.

Scooting to the edge of the bed, she stared at her reflection in the vanity mirror. Her eyes stared back, wider than usual, glowing with alarm and . . . excitement. The amber brown glowed with a hope she had not felt in some years. Not since the first time she was unjustly sacked.

Her father's voice whispered through her mind again.

*Ah, Fallon, lass. You've your father's mettle.*

"Yes, Da. I do," she whispered, sliding her legs to the floor and moving to the vanity, so accustomed to talking to her father, even all these years after his death, it did not strike her as odd.

Sinking onto the stool, she spread her hair out over her shoulders. So like her mother's, Da always said. And part of the reason, she suspected, that she attracted such unsolicited attention. Master Brocklehurst had certainly found fault with it, calling it wanton and sinful. As if she could help the unusual color of her hair— neither red, blond, or brown, but a mélange of all three.

Seized with impulse, she fumbled through the drawers, searching, a grim smile curving her lips. Her fingers landed on a pair of scissors.

She clutched them in her hand for a while, simply staring at them, the cold steel injecting a sharp bite of reality to the moment. *Do you really want to do this? Yes.* Her hair had caused her enough grief over the years. She lifted her gaze back to her reflection. But perhaps she could help with that.

Inhaling, she lifted a heavy lock of her hair off her shoulder and began to cut.

\* \* \*

"Heavens, what have you *done*?"

Fallon ran a hand through her short-cropped hair and rotated on the stool to face Evie. Her bare toes brushed the silken tendrils scattered about the floor. Her once waist-length hair now stopped at the back of her neck, just above her shoulders. She shook her head, unaccustomed to the lightness.

"Your beautiful hair," Evie moaned, touching her own honey brown hair as if it were in similar jeopardy.

"I cut it," she unnecessarily explained, placing both hands on her knees and hoping that would still their shaking. She still could not quite believe what she had done . . . or what she yet intended to do.

Evie shook her head and pressed a palm to her temples, her long, elegant fingers jutting from her head. "How did this happen? I only just stepped from the room."

"You know me. When I make up my mind . . ." Her voice faded and she shrugged.

Evie motioned to the hair strewn about the floor. "But . . . why?"

Fallon moistened her lips. "It occurred to me that I wouldn't have half so many problems keeping a position if I were a man."

Evie's brows winged high. Silence hung between them for some moments. Her lips, almost too full for her thin face, worked. "You cannot mean . . ."

"Why not? Men are paid a better wage. I could save toward a nest egg. It wouldn't be permanent."

"You cannot possibly expect anybody to confuse you for a man."

"I'm tall enough."

Evie stared pointedly at her chest. "And what about those?"

She glanced down at herself. "The rest of me may be big, but these are not." One small thing for which to be thankful. "I suppose I can bind them to be safe."

"You're still a woman. The way you walk, gesture—"

"People see what they want to see. And when it comes to servants, nobs don't look too closely. No one gives footmen or grooms special notice. The problem before was that I could never blend in." She ran a hand through her shorn hair. "Now I can."

Evie squinted at her hair. "It looks . . . brown."

Reaching behind her, Fallon held up a small vial of skin cream. "I used this. It makes my hair look darker. It will do for now. Until I purchase pomade."

Evie sank down on the end of the bed, her slim hand circling one of the posts, knuckles white. "You really mean to do this." There was admiration in her eyes as she uttered this, but also alarm . . . fear. The latter drove home just how mad this scheme actually was—it could be Fallon's salvation or ruin. But what choice remained? Bleak alternatives rose up in her mind, and she shoved them all away. *Never.* She could never resort to that.

Chin high, she pasted the most encouraging smile she could manage on her face. "Tomorrow morning I shall present myself to Mrs. Harrison at the agency. All will be well. You may depart for your adventure with no concern for me."

With a sigh, Evie stood. "If you're to do this, let's see it done right."

The rest of the night passed in a blur. Evie first tidied up Fallon's efforts with her hair and then left, returning shortly with garments bought from the hotel porter. After minor adjustments with needle and thread, Fallon was appropriately attired.

Outfitted in her new clothing, she stared hard at her reflection, gooseflesh breaking out over her skin. "I don't know whether to be appalled or pleased."

Evie nodded behind her, face slack with astonishment. "If I had not assisted you with the transformation, I would never believe it.

"I actually *look* like a man," she breathed.

"Well, you can *pass* for one at any rate," Evie offered. "Or rather a boy."

"A young man," Fallon amended, smoothing a hand over her slicked-back hair, pleased that the red-gold hue was scarcely visible. It simply looked an average brown.

"Yes. Perhaps seventeen or eighteen. Thank goodness for your height."

Fortunately, the narrow shape of her face stopped her features from appearing too soft or delicate. She had never been an apple-cheeked maid. Her features had been too strong, her jaw a bit too square.

Evelyn cocked her head to the left side, her expression thoughtful. "Still, you are a *pretty* man."

"I've seen pretty men before." Fallon nodded, whether to convince herself or Evie, she couldn't say. Half the men about town aspired to look as she did—a veritable dandy. The ones who gave her grief over the past two years had certainly been prettier than herself.

For some reason, the Duke of Damon's face floated before her. Definitely *not* a dandy. The angles of his face looked carved from stone. Nothing soft or *pretty* about him. And he had been taller than her. Not like any gentlemen she had known before. Men of his ilk were not the sort found sipping tea in drawing rooms. Her lips twisted. He likely haunted bordellos and other unsavory establishments. Banishing the wicked man from her thoughts, she surveyed her new self.

Propping a hand on her hip, she strove for a manly pose. "And what name shall I give myself?"

# Chapter 4

Sick dread curled dark fingers around her heart as she stared down at the slip of paper shaking in her hand, then back to the house before her. On the other side of an ornate, Spanish iron gate stood a three-storied townhouse of white Caen stone. Another quick glance at Mrs. Harrison's quickly scrawled words and the bronze address plate confirmed there was no mistake. The world had stopped turning. Flown off its axis. She stood at the threshold of *15 Pottingham Place*. The Duke of Damon's home. The very residence she vowed never to enter.

She hovered there for some moments, recalling the dreadful man. The wicked gleam in his eyes as his tongue laved another female's nipple. *Wretch.* Did she really wish to place herself in his sphere?

*Only you're not you. He'll never look twice at you now.*

With a decided nod, she pushed open the gate and circled around to the back and knocked on the servants' entrance. She required a roof over her head tonight. She couldn't afford to be choosey.

Moments later she sat in the spacious kitchen, a plate of biscuits before her and the oddest-looking butler she'd ever clapped eyes on interviewing her for the position of footman.

Fallon had worked in enough households to form certain expectations. One of which included butlers looking . . . well, butlerish. But should she feel any surprise? His master hardly seemed concerned with propriety. Like many an aristocrat who believed himself above reproach for no other reason than the position granted him at birth. Bitterness churned inside her, tightening her chest as she thought of her father, dead on a distant island. All because of Lord Hunt's selfish whim. Blasted blue bloods always did whatever they pleased. Rot the lot of them.

The butler looked her over critically with one good eye—a discerning blue eye as stark as the black eye patch covering the other eye.

She forced herself not to fidget, not to show the least sign of anxiety even as that single blue eye seemed to strip away her garments and see her—

the real her. Or at least she imagined he did. This was the moment. If anyone sniffed out her deception it would be here, now, with this man. Ironically, the discerning one-eyed butler.

"Mrs. Harrison referred me." Unnecessary to volunteer—as he held the letter from her in his hands—but she did so anyway, feeling the need to fill the silence. She held her breath, waiting.

After a long moment, Mr. Adams leaned forward in his chair and selected a biscuit from the plate. "Excellent biscuits," he called over his shoulder to the cook, a thin woman who stood at the stove stirring a pot with a sinewy arm. Great stains of sweat marked the armpits of her dress. The woman grunted in response.

Mr. Adams fixed his eye on Fallon again, his expression sober, considering. "What do you think of young Francis here, Martha?"

Evie had decided on the name, thinking the closer to her own the better. Yet hearing him speak the name, she had the impulse to look behind her.

The cook gave a second grunt in response.

"My thoughts exactly," he answered vaguely. Lifting a napkin, he dabbed at his mouth with a fastidiousness she would not credit a dangerous-looking one-eyed man. Butler or not.

Fallon looked helplessly between the butler and the cook. It had been a relatively simple matter to impress Mrs. Harrison. The woman had not questioned her too closely regarding her references—all fabricated, of course. The older lady had gushed in response to Fallon's flirtations, happy to send her on an interview this very day, proving what Fallon had suspected all along. Men had it better.

Mr. Adams broke out in an easy grin. "Well, lad, I think you might be just the thing we're looking for. You even appear the size of our last footman. His livery should fit you well enough." The butler puffed out his chest. "Might be a bit antiquated to some, but this is a ducal household. All the footmen wear full livery."

Fallon nodded, smiling, but strangely, she felt no relief. A properly enthusiastic response failed to slip past her lips. She had achieved precisely what she sought. Why did she suddenly feel as though a noose had settled about her neck? A flash of the duke's dark head bent over the woman's bare breast flashed through her mind, and she knew why. If she reflected long enough . . . she could almost imagine his hot mouth closing over her breast. Her belly clenched.

She swallowed back an unladylike snort of disgust—or rather, an ungentlemanly-like snort. She gave a small tug at the hair brushing the back of her neck. A little late for second thoughts now.

"Come, Francis, I'll show you to your room and summarize your duties.

Mr. Adams shoved one more biscuit into his mouth and shoved to his feet. "Splendid biscuits, Martha. Send some up on his lordship's tray when he wakes."

Fallon glanced at the sunlight pouring through the kitchen window. Typical slothfull blue blood. Well past noon, and still asleep.

"Our lord has an incorrigible sweet tooth." Mr. Adams's lips twitched and he angled his graying head, giving Fallon a nudge in the ribs as they departed the kitchen. "In fact, incorrigible might be the best word to describe him." He winked his one good eye. "A bit of the ladies' man. And he enjoys his drink. And the card tables."

*Incorrigible.* Fallon sniffed and thought back to the man in the carriage, a woman on either side of him. Incorrigible seemed to adequately sum him up—or better yet, insatiable. Of course, the butler failed to mention his master's penchant for orgies among his list of vices.

Mr. Adams paused on the steps, his single eye narrowing. Too late, Fallon realized she perhaps sniffed too loud.

"A good servant holds his tongue and looks the other way, if you gather my meaning."

Ah. That was the formula for a *good* servant, then? She fought down a wry smile. No wonder she kept getting sacked.

He continued. "His lordship is one with a taste for . . . indulgences. You've likely heard his moniker bandied about Town. Since his recent return, tongues have been wagging."

At Fallon's blank look, he elaborated, "The demon duke?"

*The demon duke?* She nodded. Apt.

The butler's gaze grew shrewd. "I hope you won't find any objection to working for such a man, lad."

The question was posed. A test. She thought for a moment. Did she object to working for such an incorrigible toff? She stopped short of rolling her eyes. Had she known any other sort? Working in the guise of a man—no longer a female deemed easy pickings—it should not matter one whit to her how incorrigibly her employer lived his life. A footman, she would fall beneath notice. Safe in obscurity. As she preferred.

"Who am I to object?" Fallon waved a hand. "I'm but a humble servant.

"Indeed," Mr. Adams murmured. Hesitation

lurked in his eye. "We are all loyal to His Grace. It is our privilege to serve him."

*Privilege?*

"I hope you will come to feel the same way."

*Loyal? To that libertine?* She stared hard at Mr. Adams, failing to understand how such a wretch could inspire loyalty among his staff. Fallon knew firsthand that servants did not have to *like* their employer to perform their duties. In her experience, that was rarely the case.

Perhaps his behavior had been truly singular. An uncommon incident that she had the misfortune to witness. Even as she thought this, she dismissed it. She knew his type. Her father had worked for such a man. A wicked, amoral man who got away with anything . . . even murder.

Mr. Adams halted on the stairs and faced Fallon, his one eye unblinking. "We're both men here, Francis, so I'll be blunt."

Fallon squared her shoulders, nodding, trying to look manly and grim at the butler's sobering tone.

"We look the other way over the master's escapades and clean up after him in the morning. And we don't prattle about it outside these walls." Mr. Adams motioned a gnarled finger at the narrow walls of the stairwell. "Or to the women of the house. No use offending their delicate sensibilities."

*Delicate? Ha.*

"His Grace's reputation is sullied enough without us bandying about what goes on under this roof? Understand?"

Where had she landed herself? Sodom and Gomorrah?

Fallon gave a brisk nod. "Of course, Mr. Adams."

As long as she had a warm meal and bed and funds enough to save for a place of her own—a genuine home—she could do near well anything. Mr. Adams turned and resumed his ascent. Fallon followed.

# Chapter 5

Fallon smiled and stretched herself beneath crisp sheets. For a long moment, she listened, enjoying the sound of her hard-won silence.

Her gaze skimmed the four walls surrounding her. A table, dresser, wardrobe. All superior pieces of furniture for a servant's room. And hers. All hers. For however long she resided here at any rate. A room of her own. Solitude. Not since Da died did she have a room of her own . . . or the blessed peace and silence that came with it. She would not fool herself into believing this was home. Home was permanent. Lasting. Something no one could take away. Something she vowed to one day claim for herself. Still . . . it was a marked improvement.

A far-off screech shattered the early morning. Voices reached inside her room, pulling her upright.

"She's mad! Get her away from me! Help! Help!"

Morning light scarcely bled through the curtains of her room. Sliding out of bed, she hastily dressed in her livery, stopping long enough in front of the dresser mirror to apply pomade to her hair and tie it at the back of her neck before securing the scratchy wig in place. Wig secured, her femininity was even less discernible.

Outside her room, the din grew. With one hand on the door's latch, she bit her lip, contemplating whether she should remain in her room. Hide. She had settled in so late yesterday, she had yet to make the acquaintance of all the staff and could not stop her shiver of nervousness. Someone might uncover her deception . . . perhaps the master himself, if he was about. Another shiver coursed through her. Unlikely. At this early hour, he would still be abed.

She would have to face her new world sooner or late. Sucking in a deep breath, Fallon pushed open the door and stepped into the corridor, immediately discovering that she was not the only one roused from bed.

A horde of servants scurried down the corridor. She was scarcely spared a glance as she filed into step with them, clambering up the servants' stairs. Excited murmurs filled the air, the steady drone of voices a backdrop to the loud shouts carrying from the second floor.

"What's he done now?" a maid giggled behind her hand, bright eyes dancing.

"Might have something to do with the tart he brought home last night." Another maid cheerfully volunteered, blushing when she caught Fallon's stare.

At that blush Fallon recalled herself—she was not Fallon anymore but Francis. *Francis.* The name tripped through her head in a silent mantra. She squared her shoulders and joined the rest of the servants hanging their heads over the railing to watch the spectacle below.

Mrs. Davies, the housekeeper Mr. Adams had introduced her to yesterday, waved a broom overhead and chased a woman attired in a scarlet evening gown down the stairs. Large melonlike breasts jiggled, nearly spilling free of the indecently low-cut bodice.

"Out! Out with you, you thieving trollop!"

Several of the servants tossed down encouragement to the housekeeper, and jeered insults to the disheveled female.

Fallon turned her head slowly, eyeing the stretch of servants on each side of her before looking back down. Despite their neat and tidy appearances in starched livery, she felt as though she rubbed elbows with a bloodthirsty mob that stood witness to an unsavory execution.

Cheers went up when the housekeeper bounced the broom off the woman's head. The hapless creature shrieked and grasped her head, fingers desperately trying to disentangle the broom's straw from the snarled mess of her hair.

"Teach you to steal his lordship's silver!"

"Mrs. Davies! What are you doing?" Mr. Adams's voice boomed from the marble-floored foyer far below. Hands on his narrow hips, he watched the display with less humor than the rest of the staff.

"Call the watch, Mr. Adams! We have a thief in our midst."

"Mrs. Davies. That is His Grace's . . . guest." Even as he spoke, his single eye traveled over the woman with disfavor.

"Guest, umph! He didn't invite her to rob him blind, did he?"

Suddenly, a deep chuckle rolled over the air.

Fallon froze, a tremble skating through her as she and the dozen other servants turned and strained to gain a better view of the man bearing that sherry-warm voice.

Caught in the web of that masculine laugh, she brushed a hand over her wig, satisfied at the feel of it atop her head. He certainly would not know her. She hardly knew herself when she looked in the mirror. Still, she felt her shoulders sink in an attempt to melt into the throng of servants.

"I'm scarcely blind, Mrs. Davies," the familiar voice said, the velvet sound knotting Fallon's insides.

The brassy-haired female on the stairs looked up. With one hand pressed to her heaving bosom and the other still clutched to her head, she pleaded, "Damon, darling! Help me! Tell this witch to cease beating me." She cut a vicious stare to the housekeeper. "Surely she has a cauldron to stir."

The servants hissed and booed at the remark.

Mrs. Davies's face burned an unbecoming red. "Your Grace! Surely you did not give leave for this . . . person to rob you."

Fallon followed Mrs. Davies's gaze—and that of everyone else—to the renowned Duke of Damon.

And her breath caught.

Attired in nothing more than buff-colored trousers, he stood at the top of the landing. Broad-muscled chest bare for all to see. A wicked serpent tattoo covered the top half of his chest, winding its way onto his shoulder. Shocking. She had never seen the like. And on a duke, no less.

His dark hair, nearly as long as her own, fell in straight lines around his face, brushing the muscled curve of his shoulders. He more resembled a pirate than gentleman. Her gaze flew back to his body—his chest and that wicked multihued serpent that seemed to dance and writhe above one flat brown nipple.

Her gaze crawled over the rest of him, eying the thin dark line of hair disappearing into his trousers. The sight made her face flame and she had to remind herself that she was supposed to be a man and not someone affected by such a sight. Not like the many blushing maids surrounding her.

"Celeste," he drawled. "I wondered where you disappeared." Humor rumbled in his deep voice. He dragged a hand over his chest, the motion slow, indolent and somehow . . . sexual. "I woke up to a cold bed."

"Would you please tell this beast of a woman to stop beating me?" she snapped in exasperation, swiping a hand at Mrs. Davies's ever persistent broom and trying to grab it.

"I caught her stealing the silver, Your Grace." The housekeeper delved into her apron pocket and waved the evidence before setting each item on a step—a candlestick, creamer, and caster.

"Celeste." The duke clucked his tongue, gray eyes dancing with devilry. "And I thought my company was reward enough for you."

"Darling, dearest, I would never steal from you." Celeste implored with her eyes.

"Lying whore," one of the maids at Fallon's side snickered.

A sudden pounding tread filled the air. "Your Grace! Your Grace!"

An aggrieved-looking man joined the duke on the landing, flushed and breathless, his face reddening even further at the duke's state of undress. His gaze darted around like a wild bird, widening, she presumed, at the sight of so many people gathered to witness the sordid spectacle. With a deep breath, he lifted his chin high above his severely starched cravat and smoothed two hands down his dark plum-colored jacket, as if the single motion composed him.

"Who is that?" Fallon whispered to the maid beside her.

The pretty maid slid her gaze to Fallon, her brown eyes warm with interest as she answered,

"That popinjay is the valet, Mr. Diddlesworth."

"Please, Your Grace." The valet waved his hand in a small, elegant circle and executed a deep bow. "Let me assist you back to your chamber. I've laid out a lovely Pashmina jacket with a silk vest—"

"Good God, man," the duke broke in with a swift shake of his head, dark hair rippling. "You're not discussing clothes with me again, are you?"

Diddlesworth motioned to the duke's bare chest, sputtering, "B—but you are not dressed, Your Grace. I only thought to assist—"

"Don't be a bore, Diddles*wart*," Damon chided, eyes hard. "Nothing interests me less than one of your diatribes on wardrobe."

The valet's cheeks glowed red. "Diddles*worth*, Your Grace, *worth*."

Servants tittered. And Fallon was absolutely convinced she had entered a madhouse. Bedlam. Utter Bedlam.

"Very well." The valet's nostrils quivered. "I shall attend to your wardrobe myself, then. And rest easy, Your Grace, the Pashmina is stunning, and that genius of a tailor just sent over some checked trousers that will flatter—"

"Diddles*wart*!" the duke ground out. "*Go.*"

"Of course." The valet hastened away, muttering the proper pronunciation of his name several times beneath his breath.

"Damon, love," the woman on the stairs whined, making her way up toward him, rocking her hips side-to-side in her rumpled silk gown, full lips pulled into a pout.

"Celeste," he returned with a cheerful evenness of voice, looping an arm around the newel post. Fallon's lungs constricted at the appealing flex of bicep looped around that white marble. Even the dark hair beneath his arm looked manly and enticing. Absurd.

The duke watched Celeste's progress with a remote expression, his gray eyes flat . . . little resemblance to the pools of glowing pewter from the night in his coach. And still, his smile remained fixed. Frozen on a face of carved stone.

"Give her the silver, Mrs. Davies." His grin twisted, became a wicked, lopsided smile that would lure any woman to the dark side. "It was well worth the pleasure of last night."

The servants on each side of Fallon stirred, tittering.

Celeste straightened as if a poker prodded her backside. Color spotted her cheeks. "I'm no whore, Damon."

"Just a thief," Mrs. Davies inserted.

The duke held up a hand to silence the housekeeper. His grin remained in place, but it altered . . . became something tight, stiff and uncomfortable-looking on his face. The tiny hairs at her nape prickled. Something else lurked in the bend of those well-carved lips. Something guarded. Dangerous. In that moment, she realized he was no fool jackanapes to be taken lightly, however much of a libertine he may be.

Her stomach clenched and she wondered, again, if she should not have waited for another position to become available. *And what would you have done in the interim? Slept on the streets?*

The innocuous calm of his voice vanished, and Fallon was granted insight into just how malicious he could be as he sneered, "If we ever should do this again, let me save you some trouble. Just ask for a sum upfront."

Celeste gasped as if struck.

"For now, take the silver. You want it so badly." Shoving off the post, all levity had vanished from him. "Off with you now."

Cheeks red, Celeste grabbed at the silver in Mrs. Davie's hands.

The housekeeper clung for a moment. "But—"

"Mrs. Davies," the duke bit.

"Yes, Your Grace." With an aggrieved sigh, she released the silver.

Clutching the silver close to her sizeable bosom, Celeste thundered down the steps, tossing several quick glances over her shoulder as if she expected the duke himself to come after her.

The servants grumbled unflattering remarks beneath their breaths, clearly disapproving.

"Harpy," the little brown-eyed maid beside Fallon muttered.

"Don't know why his lordship wastes himself on tarts like that," another chimed.

"He could have himself a good, proper girl." The maid's brown eyes landed with interest on Fallon again. She curled a finger around a fat curl that escaped the confines of her cap.

"Off with you all. To your duties," Mr. Adams commanded from the foyer, clapping his hands.

The servants began to disperse. The petite maid lingered, smiling coyly at Fallon, her fingers now toying with the edge of her crisp cap.

A sudden voice—dark and rich as spiced cider—stoked the air. "And who are you?"

A ripple of shock swam through Fallon at the biting question. *He was not supposed to notice her.*

Slowly, she turned, holding her breath, praying he did not recognize her. He observed her with a stony expression. Tall as she stood, she dropped her head back to gaze into steel gray eyes, stopping herself just short of dropping into a deferential curtsey. His very scent wafted to her. He smelled of man and warm skin. The pulse at her neck hammered a jittery, uneven tempo.

With an arm across her middle, she bowed from the waist. "Your Grace."

"Ah, Your Grace," Mr. Adams called as he worked his way up the steps at a steady clip. "I intended to introduce Francis to you this morning."

The duke gave Fallon a quick look-over, then glanced to the blushing maid beside her. "Perhaps you should speak with him instead. Already he does not hasten to command."

Fallon frowned. "Your Grace?"

"Mr. Adams gave a directive and here you linger, flirting with a housemaid. Did he not command you return to your duties?"

Fallon gaped. *Flirting?*

The duke turned cool gray eyes on Mr. Adams. "See he understands he is not to harass the maids."

*Harass* the maids? Of all the absurd, *impossible* scenarios . . . She choked on hot words of denial, but before she could defend herself, he turned on his heels. Fallon watched as the duke disappeared down the corridor, the broad expanse of his bare back rippling as he moved.

Shaking off her stupor, her gaze snapped to Mr. Adams. "I assure you, sir, I was not—"

"The duke is protective of the females in his household."

The same duke that had so scandalized her in the coach? The same duke who just treated a lover so callously in front of the watchful eyes of his staff? He actually possessed a shred of decency? A laugh bubbled free from inside. Appalled, she pressed her fingers to her lips, and the sound escaped through her nose instead—a muffled snort more horrifying than any laughter.

Mr. Adams arched a gray brow.

Fallon sobered and amended her tone. "Of course he is. Allow me to assure you, I would never harass any of the women on your staff." That she even needed to assure the butler of such a thing struck her as beyond absurd. And to the butler of a man like the Duke of Damon, a consummate libertine? The demon duke? Was he implying the women beneath this roof were safe? From *that* wretch? She refused to believe it.

"Very good, then." Mr. Adams sent a quick

glance to the maid. "Off with you, Nancy. You've chores waiting and you've already stirred things up enough this morning."

With a coy look beneath her lashes for Fallon, Nancy scurried off.

Mr. Adams turned a contemplative look on Fallon. "Mrs. Davies is in the kitchen. She will start you on your day."

Fallon nodded. "Very good, sir."

With a final measuring look, Mr. Adams strode away.

Fallon released a shaky breath and leaned back against the railing. Not the most auspicious of beginnings, but at least the duke had not recognized her. On the contrary. He had thought it necessary to warn her to steer clear of the women on his staff. Ridiculous. But she was safe. Secure in her position. For now.

# Chapter 6

**D**ominic dragged a hand through his hair and dropped back into his bed. After a night with Celeste, he was due a little rest. His mouth twisted. Even if she had turned out to be a thief, her company had been . . . delectable.

Sighing, he idly rubbed his forehead. Delectable. And yet, he still felt . . . unsatisfied. The same restlessness that had plagued him while abroad, following him from city to city, country to country, woman to woman, still prowled inside him. Returning home had not changed that.

He had chalked up his urge to return as homesickness. Homesickness for England. Not, by any means, *home*. Home did not exist for him. He had not stepped foot in Wayfield Park since his majority. And he never would again.

True, Wayfield Park *belonged* to him. Even if the old bastard resided under its roof. Dominic could eject him, send him back to the village vicarage where he could tend his flock with unflagging zeal. But what did Dominic care if he remained in that hulking pile of bricks and rocks? His grandfather could rot and die under the frescoed ceilings that had stood silent witness to all the days of his wretched youth.

Still, there was no accounting this ennui. After a night with the voracious Celeste, he should be satisfied. Even his canvas and paints in the next room did not beckon, ever ready to block the pain . . . to fill him with inspiration. Bloody troublesome. His life consisted of two passions: shagging and painting. Nothing else could make him feel, could chase free the numbness he had learned at the knee of his grandfather. Or rather, at the skirts of Mrs. Pearce.

He stretched, his nape tingling as the memory of wild, untamed hair, glorious as a red-tinged sunset, washed over him. Her face was a bit hazy—the carriage had been dim, the streets dimmer yet—but that hair he would never forget. The viper-tongued wench he'd dropped off at the Hotel Daventry lingered in his thoughts still. His fingers itched for a brush, and he knew before the day ended he would paint what he could remember of her—all fire and wild wind. Fallon O'Rourke. Irish, he presumed. He wouldn't have her beneath him, but he would still snare her for his canvas. At least what he remembered of her.

Dragging a hand over his face, he contemplated locating her. She hadn't exactly responded to his proposition . . . but there had been something in her gaze, a spark. With the right amount of persuasion, she could come around. He had been charming women out of their skirts since his fourteenth year. He did it well. His wealth, lofty title, and wicked reputation all conspired to break down the most resistant lady. Sin had become his life's purpose.

Dominic closed his eyes and pressed his fingers against his eyelids, attempting to assuage the dull ache growing there.

"Ah, you're awake. Shall I bring your clothes to you, Your Grace?"

He dropped his hand from his eyes and peered up at Diddleworth's ingratiating smile. A flush glowed beneath the light coating of powder on his hollow cheeks.

Dominic grimaced. "Later."

"Oh." The valet's expression fell. His gaze shifted to the salver he held, scattered with correspondence. "Then perhaps we could use this time to run through your social calendar and decide which invitations to accept?"

"You mean I'm still being invited into Society?" He snorted, then grinned, recalling the incident four years ago that marked his decision to depart British Society.

He thought the *ton* had banned him after his dip in Lady Waverly's garden pond during a soiree honoring the engagement of her daughter. Especially since he had convinced Lady Waverly's daughter to join him. *Nude.* A small chuckle escaped him. The young lady had been none too thrilled about her upcoming nuptials and quite eager for a little diversion.

"Of course." Diddlesworth sniffed indignantly. "You're a duke. A coveted guest to any fête. People fall over themselves for you and rightly so."

Dominic made an inarticulate sound in his throat, even as he supposed there was some truth to what his valet claimed. The season's hostesses likely deemed his presence an enlivening element to any event.

"Let them fall over themselves then. I have no desire to go out. Not to any *ton* event, at any rate." It was no longer necessary to scandalize Society. He'd proven he was irredeemable. Precisely the demon his grandfather charged him to be.

Frustration flashed in Diddlesworth's eyes. "Your Grace, you cannot hole yourself away—"

"I've no intention of holing myself away. I intend to go out this very night." Though, why he bothered to defend himself to his vexing valet, he hadn't a clue.

Diddlesworth's face brightened. "Indeed, Your Grace?"

"To Madame Fleur's. I understand she is having one of her masques."

"Madame Fleur?" His features scrunched in a scowl. "Is she not a . . . courtesan? You're going to a brothel?"

Dominic crossed his ankles and folded his hands behind his head. "A brothel," he snorted. "Madame Fleur is legend. She would be most offended to hear you designate her venerable establishment to a scurrilous brothel."

"I can think to describe it only thusly, Your Grace. You do yourself no service crossing its threshold." Diddlesworth frowned in a manner too reminiscent of Dominic's stuffy old grandfather. The realization went down like a bitter pill, and he had to question why he allowed Adams to force a bloody valet on him in the first place. He had gone without one while abroad. He certainly did not require one now. Adams was set in his ways, though, and still believed in running a household like it was 1810, with all the pomp and ceremony of bewigged footmen and fastidious valets.

"See here, Diddle*watts*—"

"*Diddlesworth.*"

"You're not my keeper. I go where I want, when I want. If you don't care for the way I live, you're free to seek a position elsewhere. Understand?"

Diddlesworth nodded tightly, although he still wore that infernal frown.

"Good." Rolling on his side, Dominic presented the valet with his back. "That will be all, Diddle-*knot*," he tossed over his shoulder. "I'll let you know if I have need of you. Do not disturb me again."

He heard the man's exasperated breath, but this time the valet did not correct him on the proper pronunciation of his name. "Very good, sir."

Dominic smiled at the soft tread fading from the room, wondering how far he would have to go before the fop resigned. Perhaps then Adams would rest on the matter of his needing a valet. The demon duke did not require a watchdog.

"This bucket is *so* heavy."

Fallon ignored Nancy's soft exclamation and

fixed her attention on the massive arrangement of flowers she was carrying to the foyer table. Her arms strained from the effort, but she knew the average man could heft the heavy vase full of water and flowers and she best appear the average man.

"Oh!" Nancy grunted.

Fallon darted a quick glance to where the maid dropped the bucket on the marbled floor in a great display of drama, her expression one of pain as she rubbed the small of her back.

*Set the vase down and don't look back. Don't meet her gaze.* Fallon had done her best to avoid the girl—especially with the duke's warning ringing in her ears—but she had taken to shadowing Fallon.

The maid tried again. Groaning, she lifted the bucket again. "Ugh, this is so *heavy*."

Setting the vase upon the center of the marble-topped table, Fallon inwardly sighed. What choice did she have? A red-blooded man would *never* ignore an attractive woman. Especially one in need of help—however feigned. And Fallon must, foremost, appear as a man. Squaring her shoulders, she faced the maid.

Nancy smiled brightly.

Fallon cringed.

Easing the bucket down, the girl sent a reproachful glance up the looming stairs. Her lips pulled into a pretty pout. "It's all those dreadful steps." Placing both hands on her hips, she stretched, straining her breasts against the front of her dress.

Fallon stifled a snort. She had known girls like Nancy all her life—those who used their wiles to entice others to do their work. Fallon never dared. Sooner or later payment was expected. Either young Nancy was too naïve to know that or she was willing to deliver when the time came.

Swallowing down an epithet, Fallon stepped forward and took the bucket, committed to playing her part to the fullest, even if it meant breaking *her* back. "Allow me."

Nancy clapped her hands before her considerable bosom. "Oh, I couldn't let you—"

Dipping her head, Fallon rolled her eyes where Nancy could not see. "I insist. It's much too heavy for you."

"Oh, what a gentleman," Nancy gushed. Stepping forward, she squeezed Fallon's arm, her hand lingering.

"Where shall I take this?"

"The master's rooms. I'm responsible for supplying fresh coal there twice daily."

Fallon nodded, hoping that Nancy did not

expect her to carry a bucket upstairs for her twice every day.

Tossing a weak smile at the girl, Fallon headed up the steps with the bucket. She walked carefully down the corridor, mindful not to spill any coals on the rich, gold-threaded runner. At the master's door, she knocked briskly. She had worked in the kitchens, running errands for Cook most of the morning and did not know whether the duke was in residence. Rapping again, she waited several moments more. No response. Slowly, she opened the door and stepped within the shadowed chamber. The hush of the room struck her as almost reverent, almost as though she stepped inside a church's hallowed interior. Absurd considering the man who occupied the space doubtlessly conducted all manner of vice within its walls.

With the drapes drawn, it might well have been midnight. Only a bare slit of light crept from between the drapes. Red and orange embers glowed from the grate and she hastened in that direction, feeling very much an intruder.

She scanned the dark and musty chamber as she walked—the veritable lion's den. Only the lion was out, she reassured herself. A massive four-poster with a rumpled white coverlet sat against one wall. She blinked and stopped at the sight of it. *White?* Virginal and pure as a dove's breast. Somehow she expected the demon duke to sleep shrouded in scarlet sheets. Or black. She could well envision him there. The wicked handsome beast of a man at love play with one of his many paramours. A tightness grew in the center of her chest at the thought.

Thanks to him, she possessed a fairly good idea of what that entailed. At least at the beginning. In her mind, she saw that broad hand lifting a breast toward his lips, holding it, squeezing. Unfortunately, in her mind that breast resembled hers. Stinging heat crept up her neck. Her belly clenched, twisted. She pressed a hand against her stomach.

She shifted her gaze from the imposing bed . . . and shoved the image of the demon duke tangled amid those sheets—with *her*—from her head.

Strange that no one had tidied the bed yet. The chamber's furnishings, while appropriately opulent for the bedchamber of a duke, seemed at odds with the duke himself. While it was exactly the type of bedchamber she imagined a highborn lord to occupy, it wasn't *him*. He did not adorn himself richly as a duke of the realm might, but rather—when he wore clothes at all—attired himself simply. A dark jacket. A vest and cravat of abstemious black. No personal belongings littered the opulent chamber. It struck her as a mere domicile. Simply a place to sleep. Nothing more. Not even a home.

A large mahogany desk loomed like a beast before the French doors leading to the balcony. She somehow suspected he rarely sat behind its mammoth proportions. That would hint at an industrious side to the duke. Smiling ruefully, she crouched before the grate and opened its door. Likely the only thing he worked hard at was waging sin.

Resting a hand on her knee—and relishing the freedom of movement her breeches offered—she dug a shovel into the coals, adding several into the smoldering grate.

"What the devil is that racket?"

She dropped the shovel into the bucket with a clatter, her hand flying to her throat at the sudden rough voice. Whirling around, she watched in horror as the rumpled bed began to shift and move like a great beast emerging from a snowdrift. A dark head appeared, popping up amid the pile of bedding. Her mouth dried. Her throat tightened. *No.*

With one arm wrapped around a plump pillow, he rose on an elbow, blinking and scratching his head. Tousled dark hair flew in every direction before falling to his shoulders. His scaled serpent tattoo rippled with the movement of his muscled shoulder, almost as though it lived and breathed there on his flesh. Her mouth dried and watered invariably. She fought to swallow past the sudden thickness of her throat. His body more resembled a young laborer of the field than a lily-handed nobleman. And that tattoo . . . it belonged on a wicked pirate.

He blinked several more times before his gaze found her crouched before the grate. Her fingers grew numb where they clutched the bucket handle.

"What are you doing in here?" The deep throaty sound of his voice puckered her skin to gooseflesh. "I told Diddlesworth I was not to be disturbed."

She closed her mouth and rose to her feet, the glare from those hooded eyes making her stomach quiver. "Begging your pardon." She stopped herself just short of curtseying. Sketching a brief bow, she urged the butterflies in her belly to quell. "Forgive me. I was told your chamber requires coal." She motioned behind her. "And I did knock."

"Did you?" Yawning, he sat up, the white counterpane pooling around his waist, revealing his bare torso and skin far too bronzed . . . far too muscled. At least for her notions of a lazy, self-indulgent lord. The fingers of her free hand twitched in reflex, tempted to touch, to caress despite her dislike of him and all he was. Despite that she was supposed to be immune to men such as he.

"Fred, is it?" he gazed at her through bleary eyes.

Just as she thought. A footman was scarcely noticeable. Hardly memorable, it would seem, even after his earlier chastisement.

"Francis," she replied after some delay, swallowing and trying to bring moisture to her dry mouth.

"Ah, Frank."

She parted her lips to correct him and then stopped. Frank. Francis. What did it matter? As she had witnessed with his valet, he appeared fond of distorting names.

He dragged a hand through the thick fall of his hair. The dark locks fell back in place like a silken curtain, framing the strong planes of his cheeks. The ends swayed rhythmically above his shoulders, mesmerizing her. He scrubbed a hand over his eyes. "I rarely rise before noon."

Of course. Like most idle lords who spent a night carousing. Worthless, the lot of them.

Him included. "Yes, Your Grace, it won't happen again."

He dropped back down in the mound of white, rolling onto his side and dismissing her. Tearing her gaze from the broad expanse of his back, she hastened toward the door, lugging her bucket and vowing never again to visit his lordship's room. No matter how Nancy wheedled. Her feet moved quickly over the plush carpet. The sound of his sigh as he settled back into sleep carried from the big bed. It reverberated through her and she shivered, her hand trembling around the bucket's handle. Never again indeed.

# Chapter 7

**F**allon rounded the lane, panting for breath and hoping she was not too late, that Marguerite still waited at their designated bench in the park. She patted her bonnet to make certain it was still in place, covering most of her head. She had managed to pin back the short tendrils of hair, even though it took every pin in her possession to tame the shorn waves.

Fortunately, Marguerite waited at their usual bench, poised primly and looking out at the pond. Her bonnet framed her face becomingly, dark wisps of hair edging her face. Her expression came alive when she spied Fallon.

"I was afraid you weren't coming," Marguerite said as Fallon plopped down beside her. She set her bag down near her feet. Inside were the garments she would change back into before entering the duke's house.

"I had some trouble getting away." In truth, it

took longer than planned to find a water closet outside the duke's residence for her to change clothing.

"Your note said you found a new position, but nothing more. I've been beside myself with worry for days." Marguerite frowned. "What happened to your post with Mrs. Jamison?"

"The usual."

"Oh, Fallon," Marguerite muttered, her tone half pity half aggravation. Not so very different from Evie's response.

Petite and pretty as a fragile China doll Fallon once admired in a shop window, Marguerite was undoubtedly the most delicate creature to ever emerge from Penwich. Yet she never faced the difficulties Fallon had when it came to keeping a post. With her flair at the healing arts, she was a coveted commodity. As a sick nurse, she moved from household to household about the *ton*, her presence valued and respected. Employers treated her only with courtesy.

"Nothing to fret over," Fallon quickly reassured. Although Marguerite and Evie had come to her rescue all those years ago at school, Fallon loathed to think that they still felt her some pathetic creature in need of saving. "I've handled things."

"Have you now?" Marguerite arched a dark eyebrow, her whiskey brown eyes aglow.

"I've found a better position with the Duke of Damon."

Marguerite's gold-brown eyes widened. "You mean the demon duke? Surely you jest?"

Her stomach twisted at the designation. She smiled, her lips shaky. "You've heard of him, then?" It made sense. Marguerite moved in higher circles than Fallon.

"That he's recently returned to Town, yes, and that he's an utter bounder? Yes, I've heard that, too. I've also heard that his reputation rivals that of his father . . ." She leaned forward and lowered her voice, "shot dead in a duel by a jealous husband. It's said no woman was safe from him, and he preferred married ladies—the greater conquest and all that. Are you sure you're safe working for such a man?"

"You heard *that* much?"

She shrugged. "Lady Danford has me read her the gossip pages before I administer her treatments. It appears to relax her."

"I'll be safe."

Marguerite shook her head, ever the pragmatist. Always, at Penwich, she had been the careful one. The one least likely to get into trouble. "How can you be certain?"

Fallon dropped her attention to the frayed edge of her cloak, playing it between her fingers. Over the distant rise geese honked as children pelted them rather fiercely with bits of bread. Marguerite, she feared, would never understand or approve of her subterfuge.

Sucking in a breath, she confessed, "He doesn't know I'm a female."

"What?"

Fallon lifted her head. "He doesn't know I'm a woman."

Marguerite's eyes flicked over her. "I don't understand."

"He sees what I present him." She moistened her lips, bracing herself for Marguerite's censure. "And what I've shown him thus far is a man."

"A man?" Marguerite uttered the word as if she had never heard it before. For long moments she simply stared at Fallon in mute confusion.

Fallon kicked the bag near her feet. "I've become Francis."

Marguerite looked down at the bag. Gesturing to it, she asked, "What is in there?"

"Clothing." She grimaced, reluctantly confessing, "My footman's livery."

Marguerite pressed a hand to her heart as

though it threatened to gallop free of her chest. "Why?"

Fallon smoothed her hands over her wool skirts. "I think my reasons should be obvious. For two years we've met nearly every week at this park bench." She waved a hand around them. "You know all I've gone through."

"But you never even hinted that you were considering this! Isn't it a tad . . . *extreme*?"

"You remember when we were at Penwich?"

Some of the light diminished from Marguerite's eyes. She may not have gotten into trouble like Fallon and Evie, but her time at Penwich had been no less difficult. As petite as she was, she was a target among the bigger girls. Fallon and Evie could not look out for her every moment of the day. Marguerite had been bullied, her food stolen. Sick from malnourishment and susceptible to disease, she had spent a great deal of time in the infirmary—no doubt where her interest in the healing arts began. At times, Fallon feared she would perish like so many other Penwich girls.

Fallon swallowed against the lump in her throat. "We did whatever we had to in order to survive. All of us."

"I remember," she intoned, her voice soft, subdued as her mind doubtlessly traveled the dark roads of their past, of the girls they used to be, struggling for life. "And when your deception is revealed?" Her gold-brown eyes locked on Fallon. "What then? They could arrest you . . . perhaps even commit you to an asylum. They will say you are a sick woman . . . unhinged."

"I'm simply pretending to be a footman. I'm not impersonating Prince Albert. Besides." She adopted a cheeky grin. "Who says I shall be caught? I'm tall enough. I've never been the delicate, petite sort." She scanned Marguerite almost enviously. "Not like you."

"Not delicate, true, but you're all woman." Marguerite assessed her. "From everything I've heard of this duke, he's a connoisseur of womanhood. He'll sniff you out. Mark my words. You will be caught."

"He hasn't yet. In fact, he warned me against flirting with the women on his staff."

"What?" The word strangled on laughter. Marguerite shook her head, the thick sausage curl on her shoulder dancing, glinting blue-black as it caught the sunlight.

Fallon waved a hand in dismissal. "Enough of me. I want to hear about you." Anything to distract, to ease her attention from the voice whispering across her mind, insisting that Marguerite was right, that it was only a matter of time. *He'll sniff you out.*

A tremor skittered up her spine, and she couldn't be quite certain if was fear or excitement.

Fallon rose and stepped aside as a carriage pulled up in front of the townhouse, the horse's clattering hooves slowing to a stop. Setting aside the oil canister she had been using to grease the creaky iron gate, she clicked her heels together and opened the gate for the visitor, curious to see who would descend from the carriage. Another *lady*—for lack of a better word—calling on the duke?

A footman dropped down from his perch to open the carriage door, and a dignified-looking gentleman in black broadcloth stepped down. Tall and thin, he raked a haughty stare over the house, nostrils quivering as if he smelled something foul from within.

Using a brass-headed cane, he strode ahead at a firm clip, not sparing her a glance where she stood. Almost as if she did not exist. As if she were merely a statue holding the gate open for him. But then that was the rule of thumb with servants. The more unnoticeable, the better. Dipping her head, she smiled in satisfaction, watching the caller covertly as she did.

A curious feeling of unease settled in her stomach as he rapped on the front door, the line of his back ramrod straight, inflexible, reminiscent of another lord. One who had never cared if his requests were an imposition on others. *Viscount Hunt.* Unreasonable or not, the viscount expected Da to do whatever he asked. Da was simply O'Rourke. Not a person. Not a man. Not a father struggling to provide for his daughter, striving to give her a home, to be everything for his motherless child.

Shaking off bitter thoughts of the man who drove her father to an early grave, she shut the gate. The stranger rapped on the knocker. He removed his hat, revealing a head full of lush white hair. Acrimony radiated from him, and she suspected this caller bore no love for the duke. A footman opened the front door. The gentleman swept inside without a word, the door clicking shut behind him.

She stared after him for some moments, curious despite herself. Why should she care if he bore no love for the duke?

It wasn't as though she had taken Mr. Adams words to heart and adopted a sense of loyalty for her employer. It wasn't as though his naked torso flashed through her head at night. Alone in her room, when she closed her eyes, his voice did not roll through her head, filling her ears with his heated promise. *I can bring you pleasure. That,* she swore, cheeks itchy hot, simply never ever happened.

# Chapter 8

"Wake up, you forsaken sodomite!"

Dominic pulled a pillow over his head, telling himself the harsh voice that invaded his head was only a nightmare. The voice could not be real. Could not be *here*. And yet even as he told himself this, Dominic knew that the old man *could* be standing in his bedchamber—that he *would*. Rupert Collins's letters had chased him across two continents. Discovering his grandson was on English soil again, he wouldn't wait for an invitation.

The end of a cane landed on the bed, dangerously close to Dominic's side. The bed dipped and shuddered as his grandfather gave it a shake. "I said *up* with you!"

Groaning, he pulled back the pillow and leveled a glare on the one man he had never wanted to see again. And yet he had known when he returned to England that he would have to face the bastard again. Sooner or later. His grandfather would make certain of it.

The tip of his cane dug into the mattress, the cold polished wood scraping his ribs. "Up with you." At that moment, his aged eyes fell on Dominic's tattoo. He pointed a shaking finger at it. His voice quavered, "You bear Satan's symbol?"

Dominic glanced at the tattoo. "What? This?"

"It symbolizes evil."

His lips twisted. "Fitting I should wear it, then."

His grandfather's wrinkled lips disappeared into his mouth. He was a shadow of his former self. His once brawny frame no longer the intimidating figure of Dominic's youth.

Dominic knocked the cane off the bed with the back of his hand and settled against the pillows with an exaggerated sigh. "So. You're still alive."

His grandfather's gray brows winged high. "A disappointment for you, I know. You'd like nothing more than for me to be dead and rotting."

Dominic shrugged, the idle motion deceptive as his fingertips brushed the inside of his palm, tracing the puckered flesh of a scar given to him at the tender age of nine. He inhaled, almost smelling the stink of smoldering flesh. The echo of his sharp cries reverberated in his head, pleas for Mrs. Pearce, his grandfather's minion, to stop, to lift the fire-hot poker from his palm.

"I could not yet meet my Maker until I've done all I could by you."

"You mean you haven't done enough already?"

"God knows I've tried. Tried to prevent you from becoming your father, but there is yet one more thing I can do."

"I am a little too old for you to administer your usual punishments. Besides, hasn't Mrs. Pearce retired from her post as your underling?" Dominic tilted his head. The large, raw-boned woman had terrified him in his childhood. With good reason. His hand flexed at his side.

His grandfather's gaze flicked to Dominic's curled hand. "She caught you at cards. Your father nearly drove the dukedom into the ground with his gaming. Her reaction was not unfounded." His chest swelled. "The trustees charged me with your rearing—"

"Because the only living relation on my father's side was a decrepit old aunt."

"Because I was a vicar *and* the second son to a

baron. They knew you needed proper moral guidance—the very thing your father was incapable of giving."

"Yes. And Mrs. Pearce was a fine moral creature."

Emotion flickered in the old man's eyes. His voice faded. "I reprimanded her for her zealous measures that day."

"But you still kept her as my governess."

"She had your best interest at heart. As did I. You've your father's blood in your veins after all . . ."

Dominic's hands tightened upon the counterpane. He had heard the rhetoric many times before. "Why are you here?" He waved a hand wearily. "Braving the proverbial den of iniquity?"

"My last hope for your soul is to see you well and settled. I cannot embrace the comforts of Heaven until you do. If you marry a proper God-fearing woman you have a chance to not turn out like your father—"

"You mean that's the only thing keeping you alive? To get rid of you I merely need become 'well and settled'?" He asked the question with deceptive lightness even as anger churned inside him, a violent burn through his blood. He crossed his

arms behind his head, one finger tracing the mu-
tilated skin of his palm. "Marriage, hmm. Now
that is something to consider."

The worn lines of his grandfather's face
drooped, making him look like a sad-faced hound.
Amazing that his mother, beautiful as everyone
claimed—beautiful enough at the ripe age of seventeen to have snared a duke—sprang from this
man's loins.

"Indeed. I have created a list of prospective can-
didates." He patted his jacket where, presumably,
the list hid. "All goodly women. Will you consider
it?" His grandfather settled both hands on the
brass-headed cane before him, waiting, it seemed,
for Dominic's answer.

Sitting up, he punched his pillow several times.
"Not bloody likely. You scarcely look hale and
hearty. I'm wagering that you're not going to last
the winter, old man." He smiled cruelly, dark
anger swirling through him, potent and heady as
a fine claret.

"So you'll continue as you are?" His grandfather raked him with pitiless eyes—familiar in
their coldness. His gnarled hands flexed over the
top of his cane. "Oh, I've heard all about you. Tales
of your exploits abroad have carried here. You've
become as wicked as your father."

Dominic smiled, inordinately pleased at the condemnation in his grandfather's eyes. As a boy he had tried, again and again, to earn this man's approval. Never succeeding. After a time, he decided it was easier to live up or, rather, down to the old man's expectations. "Disappointing you is one of my life's greatest ambitions."

"Do you not care for an heir?"

Bitterness flooded him. "To carry on the grand tradition of this family?" Turning his neck, he forced the tension to ebb from his shoulders. "No thank you."

No doubt he would have turned out differently if his grandfather had been a different sort. Dominic wouldn't lose himself every chance he got in sin and vice, searching for an escape from the numbness. He wouldn't be all that was wicked . . . all that sent a woman like Fallon O'Rourke fleeing for cover. *A good woman. Proper.* Likely the sort his grandfather would approve of—even if she was of common stock, which he presumed she was. Rupert Collins cared more for one's moral standing than societal.

And Dominic approved of her, too. *Approved?* Hell. That seemed a poor description, but how else could he explain the constant thoughts of her that besieged him? Unfortunate that he would never see her again.

His grandfather's voice dragged his thoughts from Fallon O'Rourke. "I raised you to be God-fearing."

*Fear.* Yes, the man before him had taught him a great deal about fear. In ways he could never forget. He recalled the heavy tread of Mrs. Pearce's approaching steps in the nursery. The stinging fall of a cane on his back. The burn of a white-hot poker against the palm of his hand. Cold, endless nights spent on his knees on the hard chapel floor, stomach cramping from days of fasting. Mrs. Pearce had been larger than life itself. Dominic's world. The world his grandfather had seen fit to assign him.

And his world had been misery.

His heart was a cold stone in his chest as he stared at the only family left to him, the man that had given that woman power over him. "I would rather serve the devil than serve *your* God."

"Blasphemy!"

Dominic smiled harshly, perversely pleased to provoke him. "I suppose Mrs. Pearce didn't beat and starve the devil out of me as a lad."

His grandfather raked him with a withering

stare where he reclined on the bed. His hands flexed on the brass head of the cane.

A long moment passed before the old man turned and walked from the room, the thump of his cane gradually fading.

Falling back on the bed, Dominic felt like a pugilist having won a scrap. Why, then, did he not feel more triumphant?

# Chapter 9

**F**allon paused amid lighting the hall sconces, watching as the valet stomped down the corridor, muttering indecipherably. As he neared, she saw that his face burned an unattractive shade of red.

She didn't need to hear him to guess at his words—more recriminations against his employer. Every time he entered the kitchens, it was to express his outrage over the duke behaving in an incorrigible fashion. She recalled Mr. Adams's insistence that serving the duke was a privilege. Apparently Diddlesworth did not ascribe to the notion.

It had not taken her long to learn the older gentleman who called earlier was Rupert Collins, a former vicar and the duke's grandfather. Unbelievable as it seemed, the demon duke descended from an esteemed member of the church. Nor had it taken long to learn of the duke's descent into a bottle of Madeira immediately following the visit.

Later, the duke had stepped out, only to return hours later, bleeding and bruised from a brawl he had started at one of his clubs. At least that was the rumor circulating the household. Recalling the wicked behavior she had observed thus far, she suspected it was to be believed.

Diddlesworth's eyes alighted on her. His scowl deepened. "What are you looking at?"

Fallon turned her attention to the next sconce. Diddlesworth stopped at her side. "Here, lad. Make yourself useful." He thrust a tray at Fallon, which she fumbled to grasp. "Take this downstairs and return with some brandy."

"Brandy," she echoed, quite sure she had just heard, among his mutterings, him calling the duke a bloody sot.

"Yes, brandy." He rolled his eyes. "His Grace wants to drink himself into a stupor, so snap to it, boy."

Fallon turned, stopping when the door to the master bedchamber swung open. Frozen, she and Diddlesworth both gawked as the duke emerged, dressed in black evening attire. He held himself erect, his carriage proud. Absurd considering his swollen eye and bloodied lip. He gave no indication that he was even aware of his injury. Nor that he had spent the day overimbibing.

Diddlesworth rushed forward, grasping the duke's elbow. "Your Grace, let me assist you back to your room."

The duke shook off the other man's hand, replying in such a level voice that Fallon wondered if the prissy valet had not perhaps exaggerated his inebriated condition. "If you want to do something for me, Diddledeedee, I recommend you have a carriage brought around."

As he neared, Fallon noted a brightness to his eyes and a flush riding the swarthy planes of his cheeks.

"You intend to go out again, my lord?" Diddleworth's throat worked as his gaze darted wildly over the duke's less than tidy appearance. "In your condition?"

"Indeed, I do, Diddly. The night is still young."

Diddlesworth's face burned deep red.

A small sound escaped from the back of her throat—half chuckle, half snort.

Both men turned their attention on her. Precisely what she did not want. She might have passed the duke's scrutiny before—but she did not want him to study her further. Even with his judgment impaired by alcohol.

She swallowed, donning a bland, impersonal expression.

He took an uneven step her way, focusing those bright gray eyes on her. Or rather one good eye. The other peered out from red, swollen flesh. "Frank." He snapped his fingers and nodded as though satisfied. "I remember."

"Yes," she murmured.

"How old are you?" He staggered a step closer. She resisted the urge to retreat back and endured his nearness, the overwhelming masculinity that surrounded him like mist. A dark intoxicating mist that threatened to suck her under. She inhaled deeply through her nose.

"Twenty, Your Grace," she replied.

He shook his head. "Babe in the woods." His head dipped and he studied her closely. She struggled not to fidget beneath his assessment. "So untried. Innocent." His lips tightened and he leaned sideways, his shoulder hitting the wall with a bouncing thud. "Cling to that."

She blinked, amazed at the glimpse of vulnerability she saw in his bloodshot eyes. His lips loosened then, relaxing into a smile that did strange things to her insides. "I don't remember a time in my life where I was like that."

"Ever?" she murmured even as she was certain she should stop this conversation, no matter how intriguing. Diddlesworth seemed to concur, if his high-arching brows signified anything. She shouldn't care. Shouldn't want to know about him.

"You must have been a child once." She heard herself volunteer, trying to offer forth a smile.

Diddlesworth shifted where he stood, sending her an impatient look.

The duke angled his head, musing. "No. Can't recall a time when my soul wasn't black." He laughed then—a terrible, ruthless sound—and shoved off the wall. "My own grandfather would vouch for that. According to him, I am the devil himself."

Without further comment, he strode away.

She stared after him . . . feeling dumbstruck, and filled with absolute certainty that more existed in him than she first assumed. He no longer fit quite so neatly in the box where she lumped all gentlemen of rank.

*My own grandfather would vouch for that. According to him, I am the devil himself.*

"Ahem."

Her gaze flew back to Diddlesworth. His nostrils quivered. "No one likes ingratiating little toadies. You'd do well to remember that. Back to your duties." Lifting his nose high, he hurried after the duke.

Shaking her head, she turned and headed to the kitchens with the tray, wondering if, perhaps, a heart beat within the duke's chest after all.

"Take these to the duke's study. Lord Hunt is in there with him, so of course they'll want . . ." The rest of Adams's word faded to an insignificant buzz at the mention of Lord Hunt. Her stomach pitched.

Could it be *him*? After all these years?

The skin of her face grew cold and clammy. Sucking in a deep breath, she fought a rising tide of nausea and prayed she would not be sick. Pressing a hand to her stomach, she shook her head in fierce denial.

"What's wrong with you, lad? Are you ill?"

Fallon continued to shake her head, stopping only when she felt the curious stares of other servants on her. Moistening her lips, she accepted the lacquered cigar box with trembling hands. "No."

Duty first. No matter how she trembled at the mention of the duke's guest, her eyes burning as they had not done in years. Not since she departed Viscount Hunt's estate and began her life at Penwich.

She would perform her duty. She would venture forth. She must. And, most importantly, she would know if the past had truly collided with her—here, of all places.

Her legs moved up the steps of the servants' stairs numbly, her soft tread matching the heavy beat of her heart as she advanced toward the study. Once again, thrusting herself beneath the duke's nose. The very place she had vowed to avoid, yet where she continued to find herself. But for once, she didn't care. *She had to go. Had to know.*

The duke bade enter at her single swift rap.

"Ah, here we are. I'd begun to fear they forgot us."

Fallon's heart stilled upon hearing the voice of the duke's guest. Years had passed since the afternoon she had been called before his desk. But his voice had not changed so much. Not enough for her to forget. Always full of relentless demands. Demands Da had been unable to refuse . . . even if it meant leaving her alone in the world. Indeed, she remembered the voice. Remembered the fateful words that had so dramatically altered her life with a single declaration.

*Your father is dead, girl. Buried somewhere in the Seychelles. Take heart, though—he died righteously, performing his duties. Fret not. I'll see to your welfare.*

Bitterness twisted her heart. For once her gaze skipped over the handsome visage of the duke, instead crawling over the carpet, skimming its elaborate swirl pattern until stopping at the booted feet of Lord Hunt. Her gaze traveled up, sliding over dark trousers, to the waiting man.

Holding open the cigar box, she inhaled, readying for her first glimpse of the man responsible for her father's death. The man who sent him to the far corners of the world to retrieve . . . *flowers*, of all things. The very man who sentenced her to life at Penwich. Her gaze locked on his face, and her breath froze in her lungs.

It wasn't him.

And yet she saw him. Recognized the high brow, the deeply set eyes. The cleft in his square chin. Oh, she knew him. Saw the boy where the man now sat. As big a bastard as his father. Lord Ethan, the Viscount's son. The old man must have died if Ethan now bore the title. Strange that the thought did not gratify her. He likely died in his own bed, surrounded by family and friends. Not struck dead of disease in a faraway land with only strangers for comfort.

Her attention settled on him with unwavering intensity. The little lordling's boyish handsomeness had matured into hard-edged virility. Not so unlike the duke. They both wore a look of dissolution. From the too-long hair to the sinful curve of their lips. A perfect pair. No wonder they were friends. She should have guessed Lord Hunt's spoiled son would gravitate to someone like Damon.

And perhaps not such a coincidence, after all. She vaguely recalled that a duke lived in the vicinity of Lord Hunt's estate. On the other side of Little Saums. She had thought the name Damon familiar the first time she read it on his card. Until now it did not click.

Lord Hunt's hazel eyes, set deeply beneath thick dark brows, peered out at the world with an air of derision. As if he alone was privy to some grand jest on all of mankind.

Her stillness drew their notice. Both men fixed her with questioning stares.

"Well, are you going to gawk all day, man? I haven't been ogled so much since I was forced into Almack's for my sister's debut." Lord Hunt shuddered.

"Perhaps it's that ugly mug of yours he can't take his eyes off," Damon suggested.

Hunt shrugged, as if the notion wouldn't bother him even if it were true.

Fallon's cheeks burned. She forced herself to

approach the duke. Holding the box open for him, he made his selection. Closing the box, she moved to the door.

"Have we met?"

She stopped at Hunt's question. Good heavens. Did he recognize her? After all these years . . .

"You've a familiar face."

He couldn't remember her. Couldn't recognize her. Deepening her voice, she replied, "No, my lord."

"Hmm." He rolled his cigar between two fingers, but his expression remained fixed on her, dubious and far too intent for comfort.

She risked a quick glance at the duke, only to find him staring at her with similar intensity, all the more unnerving coming from him. The bruise around his eye was fading, yellow beginning to edge out the darker blues.

"Been with Damon long, then, have you, lad?"

She flicked her gaze back to Hunt. "Not long, my lord."

"Must you interrogate my footman?" the duke snapped. "Come. Tell me of this new thoroughbred. How does he ride?"

Hunt dragged his gaze from her face. "Not nearly as sweet as my last mistress . . . but then I had to break her in, too."

The crass reply made her face flame.

"Splendid, Hunt," Damon commented dryly. "You've made the boy blush."

The viscount swung his gaze to her again, his look speculative. "A bit green, isn't he? If he works for you, nothing I say or do should make him blush so prettily."

"That will be all, Frank," Damon intoned.

Not needing further prompting, she escaped the room . . . but not before pausing in the threshold to cast a lingering look over her shoulder. Surprisingly, her gaze did not seek out Hunt, the son of the man she had spent years loathing, blaming for her father's death, blaming for the cold, awful years she spent at Penwich's.

Her gaze sought the duke.

Her heart beat a bit faster to find him watching her, too, his look deep and assessing. Almost rueful. Apologetic. It gave her a start. Why should he look at her as though he was sorry for his friend's crass behavior? He'd practically invited her to an orgy within five minutes of meeting her. He was every bit as incorrigible as Hunt.

Lips thinning, she turned and fled, doing her best to walk in a dignified fashion, and not the mad dash she craved.

Rounding the corridor, well free of the room,

she leaned against the wall. Closing her eyes in one long blink, she sought to rid her mind of the image of the son of the man who had killed her father. More or less. Altogether not that difficult when another man crowded in, larger than life, his image pushing Hunt out.

Hunt faded, evaporating like smoke to the shadows of her mind. The handsome visage of the duke rose to take his place. Rot the scoundrel for invading her thoughts. Rot *her* for being so weak that her fascination for him grew, overriding the aversion she should feel.

Snapping her eyes open, she resumed her hasty pace down the corridor, her heart still beating a hard tempo in her chest as she fought to reclaim herself.

She stopped hard in the kitchen at the sight of two grimy-faced urchins wolfing down steaming bowls of stew. Each one of them likely bore more dirt than the soot-filled hearth. One of the lads eyed her belligerently as he stuffed a large hunk of bread into his mouth.

"Who are they?" she murmured to a passing footman.

He flicked the pair a glance. "Two street rats the duke brought home." He shook his head as if the notion bewildered him. "He does that."

"Brings home urchins?"

"Aye. Feeds them and then finds them a school. Or suitable work. All depends on their age and abilities."

*The demon duke?*

The footman moved on. She remained where she was, staring at the boys' wild, hunted eyes and thought she heard the sound of her heart crack.

# Chapter 10

"**G**ot you!" Fallon dangled the stubborn weed before her, glaring in satisfaction at the thick, gnarled root. Dropping it in the basket, she crouched back in the dirt and attacked another weed.

When Mr. Adams had requested a volunteer to help in the garden, she tried not to appear delighted over the gardener's recent fall off a ladder. Having spent most of her childhood playing beside her father whilst he worked in Lord Hunt's garden, she relished digging her fingers in moist soil. Even the slow creep of dirt beneath her nails was a missed sensation. So much so she deliberately eschewed the use of gloves. Besides, dirt beneath the nails likely advanced her image as a man.

Despite the cool afternoon, the wig felt hot and itchy atop her head. Sunlight beat down on her and a trickle of sweat ran into her brow. She wiped it free with the back of her hand and squeezed her fingertips beneath the edge of the wig and scratched furiously, inching her way higher into her sticky hairline.

"Bloody wig," she muttered.

"Take it off," a deep voice suggested from behind her.

Fallon whirled around, moving so quickly she nearly toppled into the grass and weeds.

"Your Grace," she said dumbly, hands sliding along her trouser-clad thighs, fingers burying tightly into the fabric of her trousers.

Arms crossed, he leaned in the conservatory's threshold. Garbed only in dark trousers and shirt, he was the idyllic image of an indolent lord. Only in her mind, indolent lords never looked so virile, so handsome. Their chests did not fill quite so much of their shirt. Nor did they mark their bodies with provocative tattoos. The pulse at her neck skittered wildly. Nerves. Nothing more. She inhaled thinly through her nose. *He* did not affect her. It was merely the consequence of living a deception.

"If you don't like the wig, take it off."

Her hand flew to the wig, brushing it, relieved to feel it still secure and not askew from her scratching.

"Take it off?" she echoed, heart hammering. "Mr. Adams said—"

He waved a broad hand. "You're gardening. I've never seen the gardener wear a wig while working."

"But Mr. Adams—"

"Permit me to share a secret." He leaned forward slightly, darting a quick glance over his shoulder. "Mr. Adams answers to me."

She smiled shakily, feeling foolish. "Of course."

His gray eyes glinted almost silver in the afternoon light. Silver eyes? Who ever heard of such a thing? Perhaps he was part demon in truth. "If you wish to take the bloody thing off, then *I* say you may do so."

"Thank you, Your Grace." Her fingers played along the edges of the wig, skimming over the coarse hair, panicked at the thought of removing it before him. It served as a barrier of sorts. A shield she was reluctant to relinquish. He did not recall seeing her before, but if he saw her without the wig, he might.

"Thank you," she repeated, "but I feel more comfortable wearing it."

He arched a dark brow, clearly dubious. "You do?"

"I do."

He shrugged as if to say it mattered naught to him. "Very well."

After a long moment, she bent back over her patch of grass and pulled up several more weeds, her mind racing. Clearly he appeared content to stand in the threshold and watch her. She felt his stare as she worked, tugging a stubborn weed from the earth, her pulse a skippy jump at her neck. Dear Heavens, did he *know*? Knowing, did he toy with her now? Sweat trickled down her spine.

Why was he here? Watching her? She resisted sneaking another look at him, unwilling to let him know how much his presence flustered her.

"You don't like me, do you?"

She froze, fingers locked around a rough, grimy weed. Slowly, she lifted her gaze, never releasing the weed, clinging to it as though it were a desperately needed handhold.

The duke still stood in the threshold, one booted foot crossed over the other. Unsmiling. His face carved granite.

She could scarcely form a reply, scarcely move her lips. "Your Grace?" she breathed.

"Don't feign ignorance."

"I don't know what you mean."

"Come, Frank. I can see it in your face. In the rigid way you hold yourself when I am near."

She tensed. He noticed her body? Her heart quivered, then squeezed. The very notion made her grow more rigid, more unyielding, no matter how she commanded herself to relax. Her palms began to perspire, and she released the weed to rub them firmly and quickly against her thighs.

"You're not in trouble," he continued, lips still unbending. "I'm simply curious. I don't think I've recalled anyone to take such an instant dislike to me."

The incredible claim caught her off guard. *He was the bloody demon duke.* "No one?"

He smiled a sudden grin that made her heart flip, made her want to smile back. "That shocks you, does it? By all means, speak freely."

Heat fired her cheeks. She moistened her lips. "Forgive me if I've given offense. Why should you think I don't like you, Your Grace." *And why would it matter?* She did not *believe* herself any less important than he. Merely, she knew the way the world functioned. And where she ranked within it happened to be several rungs lower than the Duke of Damon. Demon duke or not.

"I saw your face when you entered the study yesterday."

"During Lord Hunt's call?"

He nodded in confirmation, his gaze intense, and she wondered how she would fool this man if he continued to look at her in such a manner. If he deciphered her antipathy for him, how long before he uncovered her secret?

And yet she could not refrain from spilling forth with the truth. "I did not care for your friend," she confessed with the usual frankness that brought her trouble. A truth, she hoped, to distract him from the other truth. The more alarming truth. That she *did* like *him*. Far too much. The duke *intrigued* her—this man who took urchins off the streets and saw to their needs. And . . . she wanted to touch his tattoo, trace it with her fingers.

Perhaps it was Mr. Adams's words—his command for loyalty. She tried to think the duke the worst possible man. Neither good nor honorable. Certainly not the sort to inquire after a footman. And yet it didn't work. Here he was, with no ulterior motive, inquiring about her feelings. As if he *cared*.

"Hunt?" he asked. "And why is that?"

"Naturally, my opinion of your friend is not relevant, Your Grace."

"Relevant or not, I am curious. What is so offensive about the man?"

"Beyond his comments?"

Damon nodded.

She opened her mouth, prepared to offer forth some vague remark. Instead, she heard herself say, "He's unconscionable. Thoughtless, vain, vulgar." The fire in her cheeks grew to a scalding degree, and in the back of her mind whispered a question: *Am I judging Lord Hunt for the sins of his father?*

"My," he drawled. "All that?"

She averted her gaze, scanning the garden, troubled. She fidgeted with the basket handle, unable to explain without revealing the history that led to her conclusions.

"And I have somehow escaped your condemnation?" His lip curled faintly. Smile or sneer, she could not be certain. With him, she imagined little difference existed between the two.

"You're not like Lord Hunt," she was quick to reply.

"No?" He uncrossed her arms and lifted his shoulder off the threshold.

"No. You're better than that. Better than he."

"Better." His gray eyes glittered, cold as winter on the moors of Penwich. "Hardly. We are old friends. Grew up together. Hunt and I are practically the same. Trust me."

That confirmed the duke had been her neighbor, then. She released a shaky breath, glad, for some reason, that she had not known him then. She did not have memories of him to draw on that were less than flattering. Why that mattered, she could not say. Strangely enough, she needed to be *right* in liking him. She claimed he was better than Lord Hunt . . . and she needed him to be.

"No. You're not. You have a conscience. You're not"—she floundered for a moment, before finally arriving at the word she sought—"*lost.*"

In an instant, his gaze hardened, the gray icing over. The cold of that stare reached her heart and she shivered. "You could not be more wrong."

At his dark expression, her fingers stilled upon the basket. One would think she had insulted him.

"I am the very definition of *lost*. Empty. Soulless." His eyes narrowed on her, and for a moment she feared he would step toward her. She held her ground. "Ask anyone."

She shook her head. "Mr. Adams and the rest of the staff possess a great deal of loyalty—"

"Loyalty, yes," he cut in, his voice rapier sharp. "Affection? No. Faith in me? No. Never. They know what I am."

She nodded slowly, recalling the wicked man in the carriage with burning clarity, and the half-naked man standing on the landing, parleying with a woman of dubious morals before his entire household. During both outrageous episodes, he had never blinked an eye.

"If you wish to keep your position, you would do well to remember that." He turned from her and strode back inside the conservatory, the click of his boots a jarring tap on the floor. Nearly as jarring as his words.

*He would sack her if she liked him? If she thought him good and respectable?* She shook her head. Absurd. She glanced down at the weeds and began attacking them with renewed vigor, ripping them from the earth with the same hostility she had seen in the duke's gaze. A sweeping certainty swept over her. Not only did the greatest reprobate among the *ton* employ her . . . but the man was stark mad.

# Chapter 11

**A** shrill scream pierced the early morning air. Fallon froze amid her chore of
lowering an enormous framed portrait depicting
one of the duke's long-dead ancestors. The maid
dusting the bared wall behind it shot her a
startled look.

The heavy pounding of feet down a distant corridor shook the air. Arms quivering, Fallon eased
the heavy portrait back on the wall just as Mrs.
Davies's voice vibrated over the morning. "Dear
God in heaven!"

The maid cast her one more look, then, lifting her skirts, darted off, clearly intent on discovering what latest debacle plagued the duke's
household.

Fallon watched as other servants, forgetting
their duties, emerged from various rooms and followed in the maid's wake. Grunting, she returned
the portrait to the wall and fell in with the others,

locating Mrs. Davies at the top of the winding staircase.

Hands on her generous hips, the woman glared down into the foyer. "Jack! Jack, where are you?"

The brawny footman appeared below.

"Yes'm?" he called, looking up at the house-keeper.

"Fetch the watch! Before it's too late!"

"Yes'm!" Jack darted away.

Mr. Adams arrived in the foyer, calling up at Mrs. Davies for an explanation.

She looked down at him as though he were a pesky child. "He's gone and done it! Just like I always said he would."

"Woman!" Mr. Adams snapped, his gaze skimming the gawking staff with annoyance. "I would appreciate a more specific—"

Another shriek punctuated the air. Fallon glanced over her shoulder, this time convinced the cries came from the duke's bedchamber.

Mrs. Davies whirled around and flew down the hall with surprising speed for a woman of her size. The clumsy herd of servants followed, Mr. Adams pushing to the head.

"Never dull, is it?" Nancy asked from Fallon's side, nudging her in the ribs. Fallon marveled at how the girl always materialized near her. "You never know what's going to happen in this house from one day to the next."

Fallon forced a smile, unable to feel the same enthusiasm. She wanted stability. Constancy in her life. Even boring would be acceptable. Ever since arriving at 15 Pottingham Place, her life had been upheaval. And yet curiosity drove her on to the duke's bedchamber with the rest of them. Mrs. Davies was almost to the duke's bedchamber when the doors burst open.

Diddlesworth barged out, shoving past servants. "Out of my way!"

"Mr. Diddlesworth! Where are you going? You can't leave!" Mrs. Davies commanded.

"I've had enough. I'm done with this madhouse and that—that—" Diddlesworth jabbed a finger toward the bedchamber, "Caligula!"

Mrs. Davies and Mr. Adams entered the bedchamber together. Even from the corridor, Fallon heard their gasps.

Heart hammering in a way she could not explain, she stumbled ahead, pushing among the other servants, peering over their heads, her only thought of the duke, praying that he was not ill or harmed. His last female *guest* made off with the silver, after all. Perhaps the woman he selected for the previous evening's pleasure possessed even lower scruples. Perhaps she had harmed him while he slept.

Sick at the thought, she didn't even think to mind when Nancy grasped her arm, a clinging vine at her side while Fallon peered inside the room. Like the butler and housekeeper before her, Fallon gasped.

"Is that a pistol?" Nancy whispered.

Fallon nodded grimly, eyeing the squat, rotund man wearing an unfortunate checked jacket. He brandished a pistol, pointing it at the duke and his bedmate.

"Harold, darling, please. Put down the pistol!" The female's hands clutched the sheet to her ample bosom. Ashy-blond hair surrounded her in a wild cloud, reminding Fallon of the fog perpetually cloaking the city.

Propped up on a pillow, his bare chest a far too tempting sight—dark, coiling serpent tattoo and all—the duke lounged in the bed as if he didn't care one whit that a pistol waved in his general direction. "Word is you're far from a crack shot, Lord Foley. Maybe you should step closer for a more accurate aim?"

"So you can grab the pistol out of my hands?" Harold sneered. "I don't think so."

The duke shrugged as if the idea had not occurred to him.

"Must you provoke him?" The female hissed before returning her gaze to her husband. Eyes glowing with entreaty, she scooted farther from the duke, as if distance from him would save her. "Harold, darling. Please. He means nothing to me. You're my husband . . . the man I love."

Some of the tightness about Harold's lips loosened. He lowered his arm, eyes gleaming moistly as he gazed adoringly at his wife. Fallon released a pent-up breath. Thank goodness the cuckold loved his wife to the point of blindness. The duke might yet survive the morning.

"I'm so glad you found me. The wretch tricked me and was on the verge of taking horrible advantage of me."

"On the verge?" the duke queried with a drollness, shocking given the circumstances. "Two times and we were just on the *verge*? I can't wait to see what you have in store for me next, Gracie."

Fire lit Gracie's cheeks. "You're no gentleman!"

His lips curved wickedly. "And I thought that's what you liked about me."

"Bastard!"

"That's not what you were calling me earlier."

Some of the servants chuckled. Fallon simply shook her head. Was he *trying* to get himself killed?

Harold sputtered. "You've dallied the last with another man's wife, Damon."

The duke rolled his eyes and waved his hand in a small circle. "I feel as though I'm watching a Drury Lane performance. Surely if I'm to die, that clichéd remark won't be what I take with me into the hereafter?"

The irate husband's cheeks grew ruddier.

"Truly." The duke's voice changed pitch as he mimicked, *"You've dallied the last?"* He shook his head. "Not entirely original, is it?"

Harold shook with outrage. Straightening, he snapped his arm up again, pointing the pistol in the duke's direction. "I'm not overly concerned with originality."

Fallon's chest grew tight as steel-cold conviction swept over her—she was about to witness murder. And no one seemed inclined to stop it.

The duke's jaw tightened, revealing that he was not unaffected. Not as he would like everyone to think. Not as a man deserving death might duly accept his fate. Suddenly, she knew she could not stand idle. Could not watch him die . . . especially when she could stop it.

Harold's red-rimmed eyes focused with deadly intent on the duke. Fallon plunged into the room, past gaping servants who would do nothing to help the master to whom they professed such loyalty. She moved swiftly, stomping on the gentleman's toes with the heel of her boot.

Howling, his arm wobbled, and she snatched the pistol from his lax fingers.

His gaping, astonished face turned to her. "Who in bloody hell are you?"

A quick glance around revealed that everyone else watched her with expressions of equal astonishment. Mr. Adams's mouth hung open. Nancy's eyes shone with an adulation that bordered on obsession, and Mrs. Davies's head bobbed furiously in happy approval.

The offended husband took a step toward her, shaking his head as though waking from a dream. "Give that back."

She matched him step for step, moving back. "No."

The duke sat up, the sheets pooling around his lean waist, arms dangling off his bent knees.

He stared at her with hard, glittering eyes, alert, aware, his attention on her so sudden and intense she had to stop herself from squirming beneath his regard. *Grand.* So much for staying beneath notice. Finding herself the subject of such deep scrutiny—*again*—had not been part of the plan.

He cocked his dark head and merely remarked, "Frank?"

Fallon flattened a hand against her chest, her palms perspiring around the pistol. "Francis."

"Frank," he repeated with a decisiveness that rankled. Shoving back the counterpane, he rose from the bed in one fluid motion. *Naked.*

Gracie squeaked, the sound resembling laughter.

"Gracie! Cover your eyes," her husband bellowed.

Fallon would have rolled her eyes at the edict for all its absurdity had her gaze not been glued to the duke's nether parts. His *considerable* nether parts.

*That's what a man looked like?* It was a wonder any woman permitted *that* entrance into her body at all! Even as she thought this, her stomach began a slow churning twist. Her gaze roamed from that part of him to the flat belly ridged with muscle. Her belly tightened in a manner that made her want to squeeze her thighs together. Or worse, press her hand there.

"Gor!" Nancy sputtered from behind Fallon, snapping her mind from such lewd thoughts.

Striding forward, Harold wrenched his wife from the bed. Clinging to her sheet, she stumbled after him as he dragged her toward a screen in the corner.

Shocked titters emanated from the rest of the servants. Scampering feet indicated at least some of the female staff members possessed dignity enough to depart the mad spectacle. A quick glance over her shoulder, however, revealed some remained, Nancy included, riveted to the sight of the duke's nakedness.

"Out! Out with you all!" Mrs. Davies shouted.

Cheeks afire, Fallon followed the departing servants, intending to hand the pistol to Mr. Adams on her way out.

A deep, gravelly voice stopped her in her tracks.

"Not *you*."

# Chapter 12

The duke had not spoken her name, but she knew he addressed her. Slowly, she turned, her breath trapped tightly in her chest. He was looking directly at her. The gray eyes as stormy as the Yorkshire moors from which she fled two years ago. She shivered, fighting to hold his stare and not let her gaze drop. To not reveal his overwhelming effect on her.

*You're a man. Remember—a man!*

She inhaled deeply, letting air fill her lungs and fortify her, striving to cool the stinging burn in her cheeks. Men did not blush like schoolgirls.

Still gazing at her, the duke spoke. "Mr. Adams."

"Yes, Your Grace?" The one-eyed butler snapped to arrow-straight attention, his gaze trained on the duke's face, not once straying to the naked parts of him that held such fascination for her.

"Whatever we're paying young Frank here, double it."

Fallon felt her eyes grow round.

"Very good, Your Grace." Mr. Adams turned an approving smile on Fallon.

"Thank you," she murmured, sending forth a quick prayer that he saw only a footman when he looked at her. A footman he intended to give a higher wage. Nothing else need matter. Not that he stood naked before her. Not that her face burned under his scrutiny. *Not that he stood naked before her . . .*

With a nod of acknowledgment, he plucked a dressing robe off the end of the bed. Donning the black silk, he tied it at the waist and strolled toward her. Stopping before her, he removed the pistol from her hand. "I'll take that."

She nodded, breathing easier now that his body was at least hidden from view.

"Diddlesworth fled, Your Grace," Mr. Adams intoned, clearing his throat and looking over his shoulder as if he could still see the valet fleeing down the corridor, tail tucked firmly between his legs.

The duke checked the pistol, frowning when he noted the full cylinder. She guessed his thoughts. Knew he was thinking that one of those bullets had almost made its way into his chest. *Much like the fate his father had met*. Dead as a result of dallying with another man's wife.

"Er, I believe he has resigned, Your Grace."

"Did he?" he murmured.

At that moment, Lord Foley and Gracie, dressed in a wrinkled gown of ivory silk, emerged from behind the screen. *Ivory?* Rather virginal for a woman who enjoyed the attentions of men other than her husband.

Lord Foley warily eyed the pistol now held in Damon's hands. No longer in possession of the weapon himself, his ire seemed to have deflated. "Lord Damon," he said through lips that barely moved, "I trust that I will never see you speaking to my wife again."

"I don't think my *speaking* with her is your complaint, Lord Foley, but have no fear." Damon inclined his head in slight acknowledgment, hooded eyes flat and emotionless. "I have no cause to speak to her again. Might I recommend you give her the same reminder, however?"

It was the closest the duke came to implying his wife was not the unwilling participant she claimed to be. That she in fact bore some culpability.

Lord Foley swung a fulminating glare on his wife. "Come along, Gracie." His haughty tones rang out more like an aggrieved father than husband. "We best have another one of our talks."

"Again," she pouted, her lips a temptation of glistening pink. "Don't be *such* a bore, Harold. How many times must I apologize when you know I love—"

"Until it sinks in," he ground out, pulling her behind him. They drove a hard line past Fallon. Gracie sent her a coy wink. She waggled her fingers above her head as they passed through the door. "Good-bye, Damon!"

He did not respond.

Alone now with Mr. Adams, Mrs. Davies, and the half-dressed duke, Fallon moved toward the door, eager to be gone, removed from sharp eyes.

Mr. Adams's voice stopped her. "Francis, a moment please."

Fallon turned, mindful to keep her gaze only on Adams. The butler studied her carefully, thoroughly. After a moment, he turned to the duke. "Speaking of your valet, Your Grace."

"Yes. He resigned, you mentioned." He

shrugged and turned for his bed again. "For the best, I suppose."

"Perhaps you could consider Francis here for the position."

"Me?" Her voice escaped in a squeak. Swallowing, she tried again. "Me."

"Yes." Mr. Adams nodded, then frowned. "You are lettered, are you not?"

Fallon nodded. "Yes, I—"

"Very good." Mr. Adams nodded briskly. "Can't have an illiterate valet. An important part of your duties is sorting correspondence for His Grace, also dictation—"

"A splendid suggestion," Mrs. Davies seconded. "Such a fine, helpful lad."

Mr. Adams nodded. "I realize he's a bit young, but he's already proven himself far more valuable than Diddlesworth."

Damon scratched his shadowed jaw. "Not hard to do considering he ran from the room screaming like a girl at first glimpse of the pistol."

Fallon's lips twitched. Damon looked her way and she pressed her mouth into a stubborn line.

Glancing back at the butler, the duke shrugged. "Why not? As you say, Frank has proven himself helpful. Especially with irate husbands."

Bitterness coated her tongue. "And is that to be part of my duties? Disarming irate husbands?" Fallon asked before she could stop her pert tongue.

He looked at her, expression mild as he settled into the vast bed, crossing his feet at the ankles. "One never knows."

A frown tugged at her lips.

"Francis, move your things into Diddleworth's room," Mr. Adams directed.

Her chest tightened as sick dread stole over her. "Diddlesworth's room?"

Damon rose from the bed and moved toward the dressing room, apparently finished with them and having decided against sleep. She watched his back ripple against the black silk as he moved, trying not to remember what his back look liked—all muscle and tight skin—and what it might feel like beneath the stroke of her hand.

Mrs. Davies placed a hand against the small of her back and guided her from the room. "Yes. The valet sleeps in an adjoining room."

She shook her head. *Adjoining room?*

Fallon felt the color bleed from her face. Her plan of remaining inconspicuous just entered the realm of utter and complete impossibility.

"Oh. One more thing."

Her heart gave a little lurch, knowing instinctively he addressed *her* again. She gave him her attention, still trying not to appear startled as a hare caught in the sights of a predator.

"That room there—"

She followed his pointing finger to one of the doors lining the wall of his bedchamber—a dressing room, she supposed.

"—is private. No one crosses the threshold." His gaze drilled into her. "Not even you. Understand?"

"Yes, Your Grace." She nodded deferentially and . . . wondered what stood behind that door. *Torture devices of the demon duke? A harem of women swathed in translucent silks?* Clenching her jaw, she quickly told herself she did not care.

Her breath caught in her throat as the duke dropped his robe in the doorway of his dressing room, revealing a taut backside that would make even a nun's mouth water. She would be sleeping next door to that—*him*—every night? Forced to serve his every need and whim? Forced to listen as he *entertained* his women? Forced to feign that she was unaffected, that she was . . . a *he.*

How would she bear it?

# Chapter 13

"**C**ome, Frank, out with it. You've been glowering long enough now."

Fallon blinked, standing erect in her position near the railing. She had not even known the duke was aware of her presence. She had been lost, gazing out at the vast expanse of lawn and gardens, musing that Da would have reveled working with such a landscape. It was far grander than the gardens of Lord Hunt's country estate. Her fingers itched, longing for the feel of freshly tilled soil.

The duke, garbed in his black dressing robe, *The Times* spread to his left, looked up from his late-morning breakfast, fork and knife poised, waiting for her response. A glimpse of his serpent tattoo peeked out from where his robe parted, but she didn't need to see all of it to know what it looked like. The scaled serpent with its watchful eyes, ready to pounce, to devour was branded n her mind. As wicked as the man himself.

"Have I? Forgive me. I did not mean to distract you from your breakfast, Your Grace." Breakfast. If it could be called that, nearing on noon.

The debacle with the irate Lord Foley still weighed on her mind. The more she reflected, the more annoyed she became. What was wrong with the man? Did he lack all sense? Did he wish to die as his father had?

He took a bite of toast and chewed for some moments. "Are you not pleased in your new position? Quite a coup, from footman to valet."

"Indeed. I am quite appreciative." Fallon pressed her lips tight, fixing her gaze on the steaming cup of coffee on the table, looking anywhere but him . . . his hair tousled and rakish from sleep, sunlight glinting off the dark strands.

The day was beautiful. Typically, she would have enjoyed simply standing on the balcony, enjoying the outdoors. But his presence changed everything. Against her will, her gaze moved back to him.

Swallowing, he cut into a kipper. "You remind

me a bit of my grandfather with your lips pressed like that."

Immediately, she loosened her lips.

Popping half the kipper into his mouth, his intent gaze resting on her, he added, "You may have heard, I'm not overly fond of the man."

She nodded, the words tripping from her tongue with an edge that she could not seem to help. "I shall endeavor to not remind you of him, then." With a brisk nod, she attempted a smile. "How's this?" Unfortunately, it felt brittle and false on her face.

The duke snorted.

At that, her smile slipped. Fallon stared harder at his coffee, watching the steaming tendrils rise on the air, cursing her pride and sharp tongue.

The duke dropped his utensils on his plate with a clatter and lounged back in his chair with all the ease of a predator in repose. Deceptive. "Come, now. Speak, lad. What troubles you?"

Fallon's gaze swung to his. "Why should you care what I think?" She swallowed. "Your Grace," she added in a poor attempt to appear deferential.

His black robe now gaped open, revealing tempting bronze skin—the very image of wickedness. A hedonistic pasha surveying his domain . . . and all he owned within it. No doubt he would include her among his possessions. A servant to command and treat in whatever manner he wished.

"I do care." He frowned as if the realization surprised him. Unsettled him. "I am asking, am I not?"

Asking? She snorted. He wouldn't know how to form a polite request. A man like him knew only how to issue demands. Like every man she had ever known with a position of power.

"Very well." He wanted to know. She would tell him. Clearing her throat, she made certain she spoke strongly, deeply, manly. "Must you seduce every woman you meet? Have you no shame?" To be fair, she knew he did not seduce the women in his household, but she lacked the charity to grant him that much credit. Her outrage outweighed the consideration. Outrage and something else. Something dark and ugly. Tight and uncomfortable in her chest.

His mouth quirked. "Not every woman. Perhaps only half."

His flippancy grated. "With a special fondness for the married ones?"

He looked at her blandly, as if he were accustomed to servants speaking to him in such a forthright manner. "Everyone needs a hobby."

Heat washed over her face at his blasé response. "A hobby? Sin and vice are a hobby for you?" She shook her head and made a sound of disgust.

"Oh, come, Frank." He picked up his knife and fork again. "You remind me of Diddlesworth. I thought I was rid of that prig. Is your outrage going to prompt you to resign, too?"

"I shall not resign because my employer lacks morals." She stiffened her spine. *Not after going through such lengths, at any rate.*

His gaze snapped to her face and she held her breath at the savage heat in his gray eyes, wondering if she had finally gone too far. She bit the inside of her cheek, welcoming the pain. Why must she provoke him? Why could she not keep her opinions to herself?

"You wound me." He splayed a hand over his heart as if an arrow rooted there. But from the dark glitter in his eyes, Fallon could see that he mocked. The wretch was incapable of feeling. One needed a heart for that and he clearly lacked such. He was a beautiful, shallow specimen. Nothing more.

"You know what you need, Frank?"

She arched a brow.

"You need to loosen those very proper morals of yours." He stroked a finger along his upper lip, considering her intently. She followed the movement of that finger along his lip, mesmerized. "I wager a proper frigging would set you to rights."

Mouth dropping, her gaze snapped from his mouth to his eyes.

He stared at her for a long moment, his expression mildly amused. And yet beyond the amusement, something lurked in his eyes. Something dangerous. Something almost . . . angry. As though her *innocence* and virtue irritated him. Something he was not. Something at which he must scoff.

Her lips worked, but she could not speak. For once, words escaped her. Surely he was the most scandalous creature alive to make such a lewd suggestion. Or was that how men spoke to one another?

His smile faded. Understanding dawned in his gray eyes. *Awareness.*

Wariness stole over her and she shot a glance toward the lawn, ready to launch herself over the railing if he had somehow discovered her ruse.

"Bloody hell," he muttered. "You're a . . ."

She stopped breathing altogether, waiting.

"A . . . *virgin.*"

Air rushed from her lungs. She could not even muster the proper outrage, too relieved over his charge. The tension eased from her stiff shoulders.

"Christ, lad," he continued, leaning back in his chair. "The way Nancy makes moon eyes at you, I thought for certain you were . . . well . . . experienced." He shrugged one shoulder. "A matter easily corrected." Clearing his throat, he reached for his coffee and took a slow slip.

"Corrected?" As if virginity were an error one needed to rectify. The reprobate. She would show him that not all men were as amoral as he.

"I can refer you to an excellent establishment. Even put a word in with the madam. Shall I give you the evening free? It's the least I can do after your assistance with Lord Foley."

"No!" Now he would assist in expediting her—or rather, Francis's—ruin? She could have laughed had it not been so offensive. "I have no wish for a . . . liaison. I believe in waiting, sir."

"Waiting?" The duke angled his head to the side, frowning. "Waiting for what?"

"Why, for love. Marriage."

He stared at her as though she had sprouted a second head. "Come, Frank," he scolded. "You sound like a sentimental woman."

Fire licked her cheeks and she wondered if she had let her indignation get the best of her. She was pretending to be a man, after all. Perhaps it would have been wiser to act the virile, unscrupulous male, intent only on fornication. In his lordship's eyes, that would make her manlier, no doubt. More like him.

"Not all men are like you." Even as she spoke this, her gaze roamed over him, appreciating the tantalizing glimpse of his chest, muscled and firm as any field worker. She should feel disgust, scorn. Not this fascination.

"What you're saying is that *you've* no wish to be like me."

She snorted. *Like him?* If only she could be that *free*. As a peer of the realm, he could be whatever he wished. But what he chose to be was . . . wicked.

Stepping forward, she set the small half-filled coffeepot on the tray. In the pretense of fetching a fresh pot, she began to turn. "If you would excuse me, Your Grace."

A hard hand fell on her arm, burning a brand through the heavy sleeve of her jacket. "Is that not so?" he queried, one brow lifting. "I'm a bloody duke with the world bowed before me, but you've no envy of me. I'm not determined to be wicked just for the hell of it, you know."

"You're not?" Her gaze narrowed on his well-carved lips, mesmerized.

"No. It's just sinking into a woman's body . . . hell," he broke off with a rasp that made her belly quiver. Heat swirled through her, tightening and pulling in places she never knew could *feel* before.

"You wouldn't know what I'm talking about, but it feels damn sweet. It reminds me I'm alive. A definite improvement from the shit I've waded through in my life." He laughed then, a horrible, tormented sound. As abruptly as he grabbed her, he released her. "Go. Return to your duties."

At the brusque command, she fled. *Do not look back. Do not look back.* A single glimpse at her face and he might read the deep want he had ignited inside her with his words.

She slowed before crossing the threshold, gathering her composure before pushing on—a foolish female who had fallen under the demon duke's spell and thought that perhaps she could be the one to rescue him. Absurd. Especially considering the one most in need of rescue was herself.

# Chapter 14

The sound of shattering glass brought Fallon to her feet. The well-worn copy of Mary Shelley's *The Modern Prometheus* that she had borrowed from the library thudded to the floor. She had always wanted to read it, but Master Brocklehurst deemed novels trash and never permitted them at school.

Biting her lip, she stared at the door connecting her room to the duke's. The hour was late, but he usually returned home later. Sometimes not until morning. Given her reading material, her pulse hammered a bit too quickly. The noise coming from the next room only made her heart gallop and goose bumps pucker her flesh.

Deciding it appropriate to investigate—wouldn't a dutiful valet make certain all was well with his master?—she rose to her feet. Picking the book off the floor, she marked her page and set it on the small bedside table. Still wearing her trousers and cambric shirt, she gathered her wig off the dresser. Standing before the mirror, she secured it upon her head, taking care that no red-gold tendrils peeked free. With a final tug, she turned and slipped on her jacket. Satisfied, she knocked once on the adjoining door. Nothing. Silence. Pressing down on the latch, she entered the shadowed room.

Her gaze immediately flew to the movement near the window. Lord Hunt was shrugging free of his jacket as he kissed a giggling female sprawled beneath him on the chaise. Jacket discarded in a rumpled heap on the floor, he delved both hands into her hair and held her still for a deep kiss. Their tongues parried outside their mouths.

Face burning, Fallon quickly looked away, searching for Damon. Her stomach churned at the thought of him occupied in a similar manner. For heaven's sake, she was his valet! Why could she not accept that he was wicked incarnate? Why must she feel such fierce . . . disappointment at the prospect? As though she possessed some claim on him? Or hoped to?

In a flash, she realized the emotion she experienced—the deep, gnawing burn in her chest—was not disappointment but an altogether different emotion. *Jealousy.* She was jealous of any female warming the duke's bed. Any female allowed to brush her fingers, her lips, to that sinful tattoo. To trace its horrible beauty.

Her gaze landed on the duke, passed out on the bed, clearly soused, a woman curled against him. Satisfaction spiraled through her to see that he was not in a receptive mood. A frown marred his companion's face as she tried to paw him awake. Grasping his face, fingers digging into his shadowed cheeks, she tried to shake him awake. Damon groaned and rolled to his side to escape her. Dark fury spiraled through Fallon. She wanted to fly across the room and wrench the female from him. Clearing her throat, she waited for the room's occupants to take note of her.

"C'mon now," the woman on the bed purred, her hand fumbling at his breeches, dipping inside. "I came here for a bit of sport. Wake up."

"Gracious!" Unable to stay silent, Fallon clapped her hands so fiercely it made her palms sting. "It's certainly late."

Lord Hunt glanced up, scowling. "Then get yourself to bed."

The woman on the bed perked up somewhat. She crawled across the bed on her hands and knees, her breasts nearly tumbling from her loosened gown, one dark nipple dangling, exposed. "You're a lively looking one. Bet you won't quit on me."

"Look, Ethan!" The woman in his arms giggled. "Jenny wants to diddle the butler."

"Valet," Fallon automatically corrected. Surprisingly, she felt no outrage over the shocking banter. Her lips twisted with grim acceptance. No doubt a consequence of living beneath Damon's roof.

"Easy for you to laugh, Dottie. You've someone to play with." Jenny's scarlet lips pulled into a pout. Staring at Fallon, she circled her fingers around her exposed nipple. "You look like a vigorous lad."

Leveling the tart a disdainful look, Fallon pronounced in clipped tones, "His Grace needs his rest." She swept all of them her chilliest stare, the one Master Brocklehurst had used to freeze the girls of Penwich to the spot and turn their blood to ice. "Perhaps you could call on him tomorrow." She flicked a glance to Damon. Dead to the world. "When His Grace is up to visitors."

Although she heartily hoped not. She could do with an end to the parade of women traipsing through his bedchamber.

"Are you kicking us out, boy?"

Fallon met Lord Hunt's stare, determined to stand firm. "Yes." She lifted her chin. "I am."

He stared back. Likely, a valet had never shown him the door before. She held her breath, wondering what she would do if he refused. He was bigger and, of course, a man. A man of position and power. He could make her life difficult. Particularly now. His Grace was dead to the world. The viscount could trounce her for her impertinence if the whim struck him.

After a moment, he glanced to the bed, eyeing his inert friend. Sighing, he rose, gathering his jacket off the carpet. "Come along, girls. We'll divert ourselves elsewhere. I've a bed nearly as large as Damon's and appetite enough for the two of you."

Dottie stood, putting her dress to rights with several tugs. Jenny joined them. He slid an arm around both their waists. "Tell Damon I'll call on him tomorrow." Something dark glinted in his eyes, a warning she did not miss. He would take no more interference from her. "No doubt he'll be ready to play then."

She smiled tightly, knowing he was annoyed with her. She had no right to act so proprietary over the duke. She was a valet, a servant, no matter that he treated her more like an equal, more like a person than any of her previous employers . . . actually asking for her opinion and suffering her censure.

That sudden realization startled her, softening her disposition toward the wretch gently snoring atop the massive bed, explaining perhaps why he consumed so much of her thoughts.

With one woman plastered against each side of him, the viscount headed through the door, letting the women precede him. He paused and looked back over his shoulder at her. "You can relay my message, can you not, Francis? You have so many talents it seems." His lip faintly curled. Without waiting for an answer, he turned and walked away.

She looked back at the duke, relieved Hunt had left. She had never been good at disguising her feelings. And her feelings concerning the viscount were much too personal, much too spiteful given their history.

Propping her hands on her hips, she approached the bed and surveyed the sorry state of her employer. Clucking her tongue, she shook her head. A pitiful sight, indeed.

"Pitiful," she muttered. The long, lean length of him reposed in negligent oblivion.

"Wake up." She nudged his shoulder with the base of her palm, quickly snatching her hand back, the warmth radiating through the fine lawn of his shirt far too enticing. Rubbing her palm against her trousers, she studied him, the line of his jaw not quite so hard while he slept.

He moaned, turning his head to the other side, away from her. Biting her lip, she gingerly lowered one knee on the bed beside him. Releasing her lip, she cleared her throat. "Your Grace?"

No response.

Carefully, hesitantly, she placed both hands on his chest. Trying not to notice how broad, how incredibly firm and warm he felt, she shook him with both hands. "Your Grace, your . . ." she hesitated, groping for the right word, *"guests* have left."

Again, nothing. Not a sound. Not a movement. He no longer even snored. A stillness pervaded the room.

Moistening her lips, she leaned closer. "Dominic," she whispered, liking the sound of his name on her lips. Forbidden. Intimate. She had scarcely let herself *think* it before. "Dominic," she repeated.

She glanced down at his boots dangling off the side of the bed. "You need to undress—"

Hard hands closed around her arms.

She gasped, stunned at the contact, at the fire spiking through her. Her gaze flew to his shadowed face. He yanked her so close their breaths mingled. "That's what you're for, love."

*Love?* Dear God, why was he calling her that? Had he realized? Did he know who she was? In the gloom of the room, his eyes rested on her face with an intensity that fed panic to her fiercely beating heart.

"Your Grace!" She craned her neck, trying to pull her face away from his searing perusal. "Let me go!" she cried, hoping her voice did not sound as shrill to his ears as it did to hers. *Manly, Fallon. Think manly.*

His gray eyes were so close now. Too close. Only the nagging, insistent reminder that she must behave as a man stopped her from struggling in his arms. Amending her tone, she tried to sound properly dignified, a man in control and not at all alarmed—not at all like the woman inside whose heart pounded against her chest, threatening to burst free. "You've imbibed a bit too freely tonight, Your Grace. Please unhand me."

"That's not what you want, love. You came here tonight for a bit of sport. Remember?"

Relief and horror mingled through her. At least he had not recognized her. But he thought she was the tart from earlier! *Drunken sot.* Before she could correct his misapprehension, he covered the back of her head with one large hand and forced her down.

"Your Grace!" There was no stopping the shrill panic in her voice now. "Truly, I am not—"

The rest of her words were lost. A muffled exclamation as his mouth covered hers. Shock rippled through her body as his mouth moved over hers, nibbling and nipping and coaxing her lips open until the slick heat of his tongue slid inside her mouth.

She went limp, body dropping, melting over his, no longer caring that he had mistaken her for someone else. She moaned. This is what he did best, after all. What he was perhaps born to do.

Never in her life had she been kissed like this. And there had been a few kisses in the two years since she left Penwich. All chaste kisses with boys scarcely older than herself. Never a man of Damon's years and experience. Never a man she actually . . . wanted.

And there it was. The glaring, painful truth she had denied from the start. As much as he shocked her and offended her, as much as he reminded her of a past she fought to forget . . . she wanted him. A self-indulgent blue blood she wanted with an intensity that burned. Never mind that he represented all she loathed. She wanted him, wanted his kisses. Wanted to touch that serpent tattoo.

Stunned, she could not will herself to move. Could not tear her head away. Could not pull back.

And perhaps most importantly, she could not recall that she was a *man*! Or was supposed to be, at any rate.

The hand at the back of her head lowered, his palm pressing flat against the center of her back, crushing her to him. Heat sizzled through her. Her breasts ached, throbbed against their tight bindings.

"God, you're sweet," he muttered against her mouth.

His hand trailed down, fingers skimming her spine until he came to her derrière. She squeaked into his mouth as he squeezed one cheek, position-ing her against him so that his erection ground into her. Garbed in trousers, she felt the hard shape of him perfectly. To her shame, she reveled in it. Sighing into his mouth, she sank against him. Growling, he pulled her even closer.

It appeared Dominic—suddenly she could not think of him by any other name—was taking this to its obvious conclusion. Believing her the tart from earlier, she might soon find herself without her long-guarded virtue. A fact that did not send up the flag of warning it should have. Instead she only melted deeper into his hard length, a small voice whispering, *Why not?*

The pulsing ridge of his manhood prodded at the juncture of her thighs and a deep, clenching ache started there. His hand flexed on her bottom, the imprint a brand that would forever remain there. This, she knew. Long after she scrimped and saved to settle in her long-sought home—a place that was hers and hers alone—she would remember his hand, his touch. *Him.*

His kisses were drugging, deep sensuous pulls from her lips, as if he were drinking life-saving nectar and could not get enough. No wonder women dropped at his feet. A man who kissed like this—inebriated no less—was a danger to the female population. A woman could think herself special, *loved*, when a man kissed like that.

Her hand smoothed over his bristly cheek in a feverish hold as their mouths fused together. The scratch of his jaw chafed her tender palm. He dragged her higher and the broad hand on her bottom slid lower, caressing . . . dipping between her legs from behind and exerting the most sinful pressure against her core. She gasped at the sinful caress. No man had touched her so intimately before. So wickedly. Any man who tried would have suffered pain at her hands.

Through the fabric of her trousers, his fingers unerringly found her cleft, rubbing up and down in languid strokes that grew deeper with every pass. Her belly twisted. She widened her legs, seating herself against his hand. Her breaths grew faster, rushing from her lips in noisy pants as he worked his fingers over her. Slow, then fast. Hard, then gentle. She clutched a fistful of his hair, whispered pleas falling from her lips.

The tension in her belly coiled higher, tighter, a serpent ready to strike. Moisture gushed between her legs and she shuddered, crying out into his mouth.

He broke their kiss then, whispering soft words as his lips dragged a burning trail along her jaw and neck. She jerked her head to the side to give him more of her throat . . . and felt her wig tilt slightly askew.

Slapping one hand over her head to keep it in position, she cried out as his teeth scraped the hammering pulse at her neck. *This was insanity!* And yet she could not move, could not part from him, could not stop from experiencing him as a *woman.* As she never would when he had his wits about him.

He bit down where her neck and shoulder met, his tongue following, laving the tender flesh. She blinked, gasping as though emerging from a deep pool of water. In a move so sudden it left her dizzy, he flipped her on her back. For once she felt small, feminine and petite as he loomed over her and settled his large body between her parted legs.

Her gaze roved over the ceiling's flickering shadows, seeing nothing, seeing everything as his hand closed over her breast. She cried out and arched into that palm, her own hand flying to his head, her fingers delving in the silky dark strands. She could not stop no matter how many voices in her head called her a fool.

He parted her jacket and slid it off her shoulders as if every woman he caressed wore men's attire. Brandy must have addled his wits entirely. With a vicious yank, he pulled her shirt free of her trousers. His fingers grazed her soft belly, her ribs, inching ever higher.

*What are you doing? He's your employer! He doesn't*

*know it's you. He thinks he's having his way with one of his tarts.*

She moaned. Fire ignited along her flesh where he touched. When he reached the fabric she bound around her breasts, she tore her mouth from his with a frenzied hiss. Enough! She must stop him. He would certainly notice having to unwrap binding from her breasts.

Squeezing her hands between them, she shoved. "No!"

He swayed above her for a moment, and she shoved again. Harder. He fell back on the bed. Hopping to her feet, she stared down at him, trembling from head to toe.

Mumbling, he rolled onto his side, peering up at her through heavy-lidded eyes. "Where you going?" he slurred, blinking in her direction with a thankfully unfocused gaze. "Come here, you." Rising, he attempted to steady himself on an elbow and grab her hand.

She stepped sideways, easily avoiding his reach.

He fell back. With a groan, his eyes drifted shut.

With one hand pressed against her pounding heart, she watched him closely, her heart aching nearly as much as her body. He rolled his head side to side, lips moving, words a bare whisper. She inched forward a shuffling step, then another, trying to make out his words. When they came to her at last, each word punctuated with a broken breath, her heart pounded even harder beneath her palm.

*"Don't go. Don't leave me."*

Senselessly, she felt like crawling back in bed with him and folding his great big body in her arms. He sounded like such a forlorn little boy. Utterly lost. She gave her head a hard shake. Why should he sound so forlorn? He was a bloody duke, born with every advantage. He didn't know hunger. Or the sting of a strap on his back. He knew only wealth and power and how to abuse those beneath him. She ignored the fact that the latter did not ring quite true. That he in fact had treated her with more care and thought than any of her previous employers.

Stumbling, she raced from the room, fairly certain he was too inebriated to give chase . . . and too inebriated to realize he just kissed his valet. Hopefully, tomorrow he would not remember anything at all.

Shutting the door behind her, she cursed its lack of a bolt. Heart hammering, she fell against its length, taking comfort in the barrier as she waited, listening for the tread of his footsteps on the other side, sighing in relief when they never came.

She wrenched the scratchy wig off her head with a trembling hand and dragged her fingers through her short locks. Her hand slid down her cheek, coming to rest on the thundering pulse at her neck . . . where his mouth had bit, then kissed her with such heat that her knees grew weak. Her skin still felt moist there, warm beneath her fingers. A mark she would forever wear, forever *feel*. Even after she left these walls. Something, she decided in that moment, that she must do. As soon as possible. Before he learned the truth.

And before she came to forget all the reasons she couldn't care for him, and embraced the fact that she already did.

At the click of the door, Dominic jerked upright. The room spun. He inhaled, the faint odor of cinnamon filling his nostrils. And vanilla. *And . . . warm bread?* Glowing eyes flashed before him. A sense of longing seized him.

Moaning, he fell back on the bed, arms stretched wide at his sides. Emptiness, desolation swept over him. His arms moved, searching, seeking . . . finding nothing. No one.

He moaned again, the sound fading as he slipped toward sleep, his hand flexing in the bed at his side, still searching. A single, erratic thought tripped through his befuddled mind.

*Someone was supposed to be here.*

# Chapter 15

**D**ominic woke slowly, wincing at the dull throb in the center of his forehead. Perhaps he had imbibed more than customary. A consequence, no doubt, of yesterday's unsettling conversation with his valet. *Bloody hell.*

Frank's remarks had struck a nerve. Astounding as it seemed, the boy's disapproval rankled, bothering him all day until he found himself out with Hunt, joining him at Fatima's Parlor of Delights, one of the raunchiest bordellos in Town. Together they had tossed down glass after glass of brandy as they surveyed the array of women the madam paraded before them.

Inhaling through his nose, he stretched his arms out at his sides, fingers extending, reaching for the one thing he remembered from the night before. The woman.

At least he recalled beginning the night with her. *Ending* the night was a bit fuzzy. He recalled warm female skin. A wide, sweet-tasting mouth, incredibly soft beneath his. He didn't know lips could taste that soft. A slow smile curved his mouth. No matter. Headache or no, he was up for a repeat performance.

Those kisses had been spiced rum on his tongue, her response ardent and honest in its passion. Completely unexpected from any woman Hunt would recommend. And he had recommended her, known her intimately, he claimed. Perhaps Hunt did not realize what a jewel hid beneath the painted face and brazen gown—explaining why he would give her over so easily and with a pithy recommendation. He and Hunt might not have seen each other in the years he lived abroad, but he well recalled the friendly rivalry that existed between them. Years hadn't erased it.

He thought hard for a moment, trying to recall her name. No use. Whatever her name, she was unique. Enough so to be the first thing on his mind when he awoke. The last woman to linger on his mind had been Fallon O'Rourke. A canvas depicting her hung in the next room even now . . . an elusive image he had tried to perfect these last weeks. She was little more than glowing eyes and shadowed features, but the hair he almost had right. A sunset of reds, golds, and browns. He had it close. But not quite.

Determined to reacquaint himself with his night's bedmate, he turned his head, a greeting ready on his lips. Something naughty and charming, certain to entice the female to linger the day away with him and alleviate his ennui.

Yet his fantasy was dashed in an instant. White space stared back at him. Sitting up, he scanned the bed around him, seeing nothing save the rumpled sheets and counterpane. A quick survey of the room heightened his displeasure. No one.

Had she made off with the silver, too? For some reason, no cavalier remarks sprang to his mind at the notion. If this one had used him only to rob him he would care. Damn it all.

Swinging his legs over the bed's edge, he ignored the sudden lancing pain in his temples and bellowed, "Frank!"

Moments passed before the adjoining door opened. Frank stepped inside his chamber with careful steps, his expression coolly neutral. Remarkable that. Usually disapproval was writ all over the lad's bloody face . . . from the thinning of his lips, to the quivering of his nostrils.

He supposed he was fated for valets that only

ever scorned him. Dominic cursed loud enough for Frank to hear.

Face pale beneath his ridiculous gray wig, the valet set his chin at a stubborn angle. Clasping his hands behind his back, he stopped a good distance from the bed and murmured, "Yes, Your Grace?"

"Where's the girl?"

"Girl, Your Grace?"

"Yes, the girl."

Frank blinked slowly, extraordinarily reticent for him. This was not the same man who so baldly declared his disapproval of Dominic's lifestyle yesterday.

"It's not a trick question," he snapped.

Frank's lips parted, but still he said nothing. Merely looked at Dominic with his far too intelligent gaze.

"Bloody hell, don't act as if you don't know." He snorted. Servants knew everything. A valet especially would know all the activities of the gentleman he served. Frank would be no exception. From the start, Dominic had marked him a sharp lad, always a watcher, observing everything intently. Nothing escaped his detection.

"Know what, sir?" the valet asked. At this particular moment, he seemed more dense than sharp.

"Bloody hell." Cringing at the sudden pain spiking his forehead, he pressed fingers to his head, rubbing in small circles.

"Are you unwell, my lord? Can I fetch you something?" Frank moved to the door again, one hand stretching out for the latch. "Mrs. Davies's tonic perhaps?"

His lip curled at the mere suggestion. The thought of Mrs. Davies's blood-curdling tonic made his stomach heave.

"No. I don't want a bloody tonic. I want *her*," he hissed, feeling like a child denied his favorite toy—and not giving a damn. Not with the memory of dark eyes and a mouth so hot it melted him from the inside out. "What you can do is fetch me the woman from last night."

"The w—"

His swift glance silenced Frank from echoing his words yet again.

Clearing his throat, his valet began again, "Of what woman do you speak, Your Grace?"

"Last night. The girl from last night."

"Ah. You mean Lord Hunt and his guests."

"Yes," he snapped, slicing a hand through the air. "Where are they?"

Frank's lanky frame straightened a bit, and a bit of color returned to his cheeks. The familiar spark entered his eyes as he announced, "I sent them home."

"You sent them home?"

"Indeed. You were unconscious. I did not think you would mind . . ."

"Clearly, I did. I *do*."

Frank cocked a reddish-brown brow, murmuring drolly, "You were snoring. And drooling as I recall." The latter he added with a fair amount of satisfaction. "I did not think you in any shape to entertain."

He scowled at Frank, suspicion settling heavily in his gut. Dominic stepped forward, wondering what it was about that cocked brow, that droll tone that got under his skin. In short, what was it about this lad that aggravated him? And yet . . . he was not inclined to dismiss him. Most baffling. "Allow me to explain that your duties do not go so far as to rush off my guests. Understand?"

"Quite so, Your Grace." Frank nodded, his voice very correct, very punctilious very . . . aggravating.

"I'll have to ask Hunt about her now," he muttered, looking from the impertinent valet as he dragged a hand through his hair.

"I beg your pardon, Your Grace?" Frank inquired, his voice emitting a heavy dose of virtuousness. He glared at the valet. *Bloody hell.* It was like having the archbishop for your personal valet.

"None of your concern," he snapped.

It occurred to him that he *should* dismiss him. In his position, other men would. And yet he couldn't. Perhaps he was letting Adams's recommendation blind him. Or there was a more obvious reason. Frank had disarmed old Foley, likely saving his life. While Diddlesworth fled the room, the lad had shown surprising mettle. He could hardly sack him.

And yet none of those reasons moved him. He did not know, however, what did. Dominic drew a calming breath into his lungs. "I'm confident we have reached an understanding."

"Of course. It won't happen again, Your Grace."

Was that condescension he heard? And there was that *look* again. His valet looked him up and down in a swift, no less thorough survey. As though he had assessed Dominic and decided him lacking. The look seemed to convey . . . disappointment. As if Dominic fell short.

Determined to insert the proper distance between them, to reestablish their prospective roles as master and servant, he intoned in his most ducal manner, "See that it does not or you will find yourself seeking a position elsewhere."

A dull flush crept over Frank's cheeks. The slightest quaver shook his voice as he asked, "Is there anything else I can do for you, Your Grace?"

He took his time replying, tearing his shirt free of his trousers as he moved across the room toward his dressing room. "Send for my breakfast. And have my horse readied." For once, he did not feel like sleeping the morning away. Or struggling to paint the portrait of a woman that eluded him . . . in reality and on the canvas. Elusive women appeared to be his forte of late.

"Yes, Your Grace." Frank turned, but not before his eyes flicked to the serpent tattoo on his chest. Color nipped his cheeks. No doubt he condemned Dominic for that, too. His narrow back disappeared into his room. Uncannily, the sight of that unyielding back brought to mind his grandfather. Another judgmental man. He grimaced. He had long quit caring what his grandfather thought of him, but for some reason, the opinion of his valet mattered. Almost from the start it had. Even when he was a mere footman. Damned bothersome. And . . . *strange*.

He had managed to live conscience-free for

most of his life. He had no desire to grow scruples now. Especially because of a wet-behind-the-ears lad who seemed to know everything about being a man—an honorable one, at any rate. He shrugged, directing his thoughts away from Frank and back to the woman from last night . . . and how soon he could finish what they started before his interfering valet sent her home.

# Chapter 16

"**S**tay *in*? What do you mean you wish to stay in? Have you played so hard in my absence that you've overtired yourself?" Hunt swung his leg over the arm of the wingback chair in a leisurely manner, twisting his cravat lose as he did so.

"No." Dominic stared out the window at the darkened square. The fire popped and a log crumbled in the massive hearth.

"What's wrong with you, then? You should be chomping at the bit for a little diversion."

"I venture out often enough. Stay occupied. Ride in the park. And last night I played cards at the club."

"That doesn't signify. I'm talking about women, Dom. Nearly a week and no women." Hunt shook his head. "That's not like you. And it's certainly not like me. I've been a week in the country, staring at ledgers and account books and tolerating my beyond silly mother—hell, I need some female company. The *right* sort of female company. I thought for certain you would join me."

Dominic shrugged, his finger idly tracing the rim of his glass. He brought it to his lips and took the barest sip. The contents held little appeal.

"This is special invitation only," Hunt's voice continued. "You don't want to miss it. I have it from an excellent source that Madame Fleur will be unveiling some new lovelies tonight."

Dominic shrugged yet again, grunting a noncommittal response. Since the morning he woke to a cold bed and aching head—not to mention the fuzzy recollection of a woman he desperately wished to remember—he had felt strangely disinclined to indulge in his usual pursuits, namely hard drink and harder women.

"What will you do?" Hunt waved a hand. "Stare at the walls?"

For some reason his gaze sought out his valet, moving silently about the room, his movements swift, no doubt eager to be gone from the room and the talk of sampling savory lovelies.

"What about returning to Fatima's?" he suggested, his request, hopefully, innocuous.

"Again?" Hunt frowned. "I've tasted all I want to from that particular garden."

Dominic suppressed a sigh of impatience. He had returned to Fatima's twice in the past week—a fact Hunt need not know. He had searched among the rouged faces, trying to recall which woman inspired memories of sweet lips and even sweeter-smelling flesh. All to no avail. Perhaps if Hunt returned, he could identify which woman haunted Dominic's every thought.

Deciding he needed to be more forthright if he was to learn anything at all, he cleared his throat. "Now that bit of skirt from the other night might be worth revisiting."

Hunt's brows pulled together. "Which one?"

"The one from Fatima's."

"You mean the other night when your prig of a valet chased us off?"

He sensed Frank's reaction before he looked. The lad straightened from where he bent before the hearth, stirring the fire. Stiff as a poker, he turned and glared at Hunt. His friend did not even cast him a glance, merely stood and helped himself to more brandy from the tray.

"Yes." Dominic scratched his jaw, striving for an air of indifference. Hunt could not know how serious his interest ran. How desperate. "What was her name?"

Out of the corner of his eye he noticed Frank pausing as he straightened the papers and ledgers on his desk, his gangly frame stilling with the suddenness of sighted prey.

"Jenny, I believe."

"Jenny," he murmured, testing the name. And still not liking the sound of it on his tongue. It wasn't right. The name didn't fit with what he recalled of her, vague as the memory was.

"You liked her, eh?" Hunt smiled. "She was a nice piece. Had a taste of her myself when you expired so soon that night. She and Dottie both. Couldn't disappoint them."

Dominic clenched his teeth and fought to look unaffected, even as the thought of the woman in Hunt's bed made his hands curl into fists. Made him want to lunge from his seat and tear into his friend.

He shook his head, ridding himself of the impulses. Mad as they were. What was he doing feeling so possessive? And for a woman he scarcely remembered. A woman who made it her business to entertain men. *Many, many men.* Hell, no woman was worth coming between him and one of the few friends he could claim.

"I suppose." Dominic shrugged, trying to appear unmoved.

"Well, if you insist, we can drop in at Fatima's before we head on to Madame Fleur's."

Frank began moving again, his movements stiff, quick, lips pulled into a tight line. The sight of his evident censure pricked deep at the center of Dominic's chest. The location of his conscience? Impossible. What his valet thought of him did not bear significance. He didn't care what anyone thought of him.

Perhaps it was Frank's hovering judgment. Or perhaps that Hunt had gotten to his fantasy woman first. Whatever the case, his mood soured considerably and he craved nothing more than solitude. "No. You go on without me."

Hunt set his glass down with a clank on the side table. "Very well. Stay in, old man. But tomorrow, you're going out if I have to drag you myself."

Dominic waved a hand in mock salute, watching Hunt as he departed. His gaze then sought out his valet, observing him beneath hooded lids as he gathered Hunt's glass and set it on a tray.

"Frank," he murmured.

The lad's gaze flew to his, and the chilliness in that brown gaze was precisely what Dominic knew he would find. Even expected, it annoyed him to no end. He held his half-full glass in the air, proffering it with a slight shake.

His valet approached, lips a hard, unbending line as he reached for the glass, fingers circling it. For a moment, that hand caught his attention. Far from lily-white. It bore the evidence of hours out of doors. Still, it was an elegant hand. The fingers long. Refined. Dominic's lips curled in a smirk and he wondered if he soaked them in rosewater like half the fops of the *ton*.

When Dominic failed to release his grip on the glass, Frank looked at him questioningly. "Your Grace?"

Opening his hand, he released the glass. Frank set it on the tray, watching him warily. Deserved, Dominic supposed. He felt particularly volatile tonight.

"Go. I have no need of you tonight."

The valet marched from the room in a straight line, no mincing steps about him, and Dominic wondered why that sight should displease him only more.

Fallon strode swiftly down the corridor, the contents of Dominic's glass sloshing wildly on the tray. Her face burned uncomfortably hot. She didn't know what bothered her more. Enduring the sound of Hunt's voice and crude remarks . . . or that Dominic was on a quest for some tart he believed to be her!

The sound of muted laughter stopped her in her tracks. A door to the left stood slightly ajar. Frowning, she approached, peering inside, instantly recognizing Lord Hunt's blue jacket as he backed a woman against dark drapes. Fallon could not see past the viscount to identify her. She stepped deeper into the room, her steps silent on the plush Persian carpet. Hunt dipped his head then, suckling at the female's bared breasts. Familiar gray skirts—worn by all the women on the duke's staff—bunched at her waist, below pale breasts and Hunt's dark head. Her neck was arched, face buried in the drapery. Fallon inched closer, squinting in the gloom.

The servant moaned, weaving her fingers in Hunt's rich brown hair. "You shouldn't—" Her words broke on a sharp cry and her face lowered then, granting Fallon full view.

Naïve, flirty little *Nancy*? Fallon shook her head. Clearly her interest in *Francis* had not withstood a viscount's persuasions. The dear, stupid girl. Didn't she know she played with fire?

"Oh," she gasped, her head lolling against the velvet drapes. "Lord Hunt! What are you doing to me?"

His low growl floated on the air. "Giving these sweetcakes what they've been begging for, my girl."

"You shouldn't! I'm a good girl—" Her words were cut off again as he hand delved beneath her gray skirts. She squeaked, but then her cry altered, swung into a low moan.

"*Yessss*," she sighed. Apparently his hand was doing something that met with her satisfaction.

"You like that, eh?"

Nancy tugged his head back to her breasts, hardly a sign of protest. Disgust rose high in Fallon's chest. Eager to leave them to their amusements, she shifted her weight, ready to turn . . . until the floor creaked under her. Hunt swung around, his annoyed gaze narrowing on Fallon.

"Francis!" Nancy pulled up her dress, cheeks burning brightly.

"Ah, our young sentinel has arrived." Hunt stepped back from the maid, wiping his lips as if clearing the taste of Nancy from his mouth. "The guardian of all that is Right. Come to break up the little fête?"

"I heard a sound," she said lamely.

"Yes, well, that happens when you pleasure a woman." He cocked his head to the side. "Something you probably know nothing about. Is that it? Because you've never had a proper frigging, no one else can? Nancy, dear, perhaps you should take pity and entertain the lad here."

Fallon's hand curled into a fist. She was right to dislike him. Her abhorrence for his father had nothing to do with it. He was a cad.

If possible, Nancy's cheeks grew even redder. "My lord!" She darted Fallon an embarrassed glance. "Please!"

Fallon turned, ready to flee.

"Francis, please!" Nancy cried. "Let me explain."

Fallon did not stop. Clutching the tray, she strode hard ahead, steps brisk, convinced that her deception was the smartest decision she had ever made if it put her beyond the attentions of men like Hunt.

*And what of the duke?* Would it be so terrible to

have his attentions? For him to learn she was a woman?

*So I could be another Nancy? Used and discarded like common refuse?*

Shaking her head, she vowed she would never find out.

# Chapter 17

Thal night Dominic dreamed of Wayfield Park.

The grim visage of Mrs. Pearce rose in the gray of his sleep. She looked on, eyes as bleak as a stormy sky as she forced a scalding poker to his palm. Then he was running, racing down corridors, the faces of his long-dead ancestors watching, judging, condemning.

Suddenly he left them all behind, finding himself planted in a carriage, soft squabs at his back. Fallon O'Rourke sat beside him, her eyes warm and glowing. Inviting. Her face was a hazy blur like in his portrait, features not quite distinct. But there was her hair. That he recalled perfectly. The glorious mane floated around her in a luxurious sun-tinged cloud. Her hand took his, fingertips a feather's stroke on his scarred palm. Her lips curved, seductive as he slid the sleeves of her gown down, down . . . .

Dominic was jostled rudely awake, ripped from the dream that had taken a decidedly delightful turn.

"I brought Jenny for you. Wake up, Dom!"

Blinking, resentment sharp pinpricks in his chest, he craned his head around. Feminine giggles filled the room. Before he could push off his stomach, a warm body dropped down on the bed beside him. A soft arm slid around his waist.

"Hello, love," a voice cooed near his ear in a rush of hot, gin and tobacco-laced breath. "I hear you missed me."

A hand slid between his chest and the bed, past the sheets bunched at his hips, seizing his manhood in an ungentle grip. He shot up in bed with a stifled yelp, disentangling her hand from around him.

Hunt's laughter filled the room. "Easy there, Jenny. Give him time to wake up."

Dominic rubbed his eyes, following the shadowy figure of his friend as he strolled across the room and pulled open the drapes. Moonlight shimmered into the room. "Hunt? What the devil are you doing here?"

"I let myself in."

Dominic frowned. He was going to have a talk

with Adams. And where the hell was the usually vigilant Frank?

"I brought you a present. I knew you would be glad to see Jenny again."

Dominic eyed the female closely, from her rouged lips to the cheap, decadent gown. Her lips were full enough. But the same mouth he had kissed?

Grinning, Jenny snuggled closer, her hand drawing ever-widening circles over his tattooed chest and shoulder as a slight knock sounded at the door.

"Your Grace, are you well? I heard a sound—"

Dominic stilled as his valet entered the room. Their eyes locked across the distance. For some mad reason he felt like a boy caught at mischief.

Hunt planted his hands on his hips. "Ah, your keeper has arrived, Dom."

Frank's face reddened as he absorbed the scene before him. "Forgive me for disturbing you, Your Grace. I'll leave you to your . . . company."

"As will I," Hunt declared, dark cloak swirling around him as he moved toward the door. "You're going to be occupied for the remainder of the night." He winked over his shoulder. "And perhaps tomorrow, too, eh?"

"No *perhaps* about it," Jenny chortled.

The door clicked shut behind Hunt, leaving Dominic, Jenny, and Frank alone in the room. Frank's eyes shined darkly in the gloom. The flesh at the back of Dominic's neck tingled as their gazes locked. Something *odd* lurked in that gaze. An emotion Dominic couldn't quite identify. *Sadness? Hurt?* Perhaps it was just odd that emotion lurked there at all. Why should it? Why should a bloody valet care how his master occupied himself? It was deuced strange.

Then, like a fire doused, the emotion vanished, banked within a flat, dark stare. Frank departed the room in a hasty retreat. Dominic stared at the closed adjoining door for some moments, long after Frank had passed through it. A deep heaviness settled in his chest. He did not move, even as Jenny rubbed herself against him.

"Come, my fine duke. Lord Hunt told me how eager you've been to see me again."

True. He'd thought of her for days. Traipsed to Fatima's searching for her. And now, with her in his bed, he wished her gone. He could only credit his fascination with her to alcohol-induced madness. Because the cloying chit in his arms failed to rouse him. Not as she had a week ago. Not as she ever would.

*   *   *

Fallon poured the last kettle, nodding in satisfaction at the plumes of steam wafting over the tub. Her hands trembled as she lowered the kettle to the floor beside an empty bucket. They had trembled since she left the duke's rooms. The heavy, gnawing ache beneath her breastbone had not lessened either.

With one last glance over her shoulder at the door, she stripped off her clothes, confident that the duke would have no need for her the rest of the night. Not occupied as he was.

She carefully eased one foot in the water, sighing in gratification. *Bliss.* It was worth lugging water up the stairs—not that she hadn't become particularly equipped at lugging buckets of late. Mouth twisting wryly, she leaned back in the copper tub, sliding down until she was completely submerged. Rising, she wiped water from her face and began scrubbing her hair, scratching her scalp with her fingers, ridding herself of every last drop of the oily pomade she applied before donning her wig.

That done, she washed all of her body until it glistened pink. Thus far, she had made do cleaning herself from the basin in the room's washstand. Dropping her sponge, she released another sigh and leaned back again, propping one foot over the tub's edge.

Fortunately no sounds carried from next door. That she couldn't have abided. To actually *hear* him with another woman. A woman he believed to be the one he kissed senseless a week ago. *Her.* Still, the image of him in bed with Jenny lingered, tormenting her. The tart possessed curves enough for two. And her breasts . . . Fallon snorted. It was almost too funny to think that they could have been confused for one another. No doubt Dominic was having a fine time with her. Her chest tightened and she rubbed wet hands over her face as if she could wipe free the images from her head and ease the itchy ache from her eyes.

Jamming her eyes tight, the images stayed, twisted and turned, taking a life of their own. She saw Dominic in his big bed, kissing, loving . . . the serpent tattoo rippling, *alive* with the movement of his body as his broad hands roamed over yielding, female flesh. Only the woman was no longer Jenny. She changed. Became Fallon. As she once looked. Her hair long, the gold-red tresses tangled between them. Instead of Jenny, *her* hands stroked his chest, following the twist of that serpent across his flesh.

She rubbed the base of her palms into her closed eyes, pressing hard, but it did no good. The vision clung, tenacious as a root, unfolding itself in startling detail. Heat scored her face, working its way down her body.

She saw Dominic perfectly in her mind. His strong hand dove into her hair, twisting the strands around his fist, forcing her closer as he bent her backward for his kiss. A kiss she remembered only too well. A kiss he gave to another even as she entertained sordid thoughts of him. She slapped a hand on the water's surface, spraying droplets in her face.

Blast him! Was he so jaded he could not differentiate between women?

Lurching to her feet, she stepped from the tub, water sluicing down her body and forming a puddle at her feet. She snatched her towel from a nearby chair. Muttering, she roughly chafed herself with the linen.

Foolish as it seemed, she wanted to march next door and correct him of his misapprehensions. Invite herself into his bed instead. *Don't be ridiculous, Fallon.* Let him slake his lust on another. She wanted nothing to do with him. Her hands slowed, her movements gentling, becoming less punishing. Inhaling deeply, she gathered her composure.

At her current wage, she need only continue her deception a while longer. A few months at the most. Then she could move from Town. Away from the noise, the fog, the smell. She could escape it all. Sequester herself in the country. A small cottage. A simple, humble living. She could teach music or French, even rudimentary Latin. Any number of things she had learned at Penwich. It might have been a grueling existence, but she had received an excellent education. And then there was what her father had passed along to her. With her knowledge of gardening, she could grow and sell flowers or vegetables. All enough, she was convinced, to get by.

She could forget all about the demon duke and focus on carving out a home for herself. The only thing she ever wanted. The only thing that mattered.

Grumbling under his breath, Dominic stood and donned his robe, yanking the belt tight in an angry motion.

"Sorry," he grunted, not sorry at all. He sounded angry. And he was. But not at Jenny—the girl had tried mightily to kindle his interest.

He handed her several notes. "Here. Take this."

Rising from the bed, she took her time putting her dress to rights before snatching the money, counting it in front of him with agonizing slowness. Her gaze slid over him with narrow-eyed cunning. "And what do I get for my pride? It's twice now you've sent me away . . ." Her gaze flicked over him. "Unsatisfied."

Instead of arguing, he handed her more. "I'm certain there are finer gentlemen to appreciate your charms."

A slow smile spread across her face. "Thank you, milord." Stuffing the notes into her gown, she shook her head ruefully, looking him up and down as though he were a piece of horseflesh to be assessed. "Don't have a go with too many nobs that look as you do, though. A right shame." She stepped closer with a conspiratorial air. "You know, I've a friend good with herbs. She might have a remedy for what ails you."

His forehead creased. "Ails me?"

Jenny held one finger straight in the air and then let it fall limply, the digit waving listlessly toward the floor.

Dominic stifled a snort, more amused than he perhaps ought to be over the slight to his virility. Better she think the fault in him than her. No sense pointing out that her sour breath may have had more to do with his disinterest.

"Thank you for the suggestion," he murmured.

Nodding, she departed the chamber.

He shook his head. Sour breath aside, she was a pretty bit of skirt. But not the woman he kissed the other night. And that was the crux of the matter.

Strolling across the chamber, he dropped down into a plush armchair near the window. He stared out at the night. A waxing moon peered down through a latticework of branches.

A heavy mist hung on the air. The light from the square's lamps fought to penetrate the opaque fog. He heard the clattering of hooves below and imagined Jenny departing below, courtesy of one of his coaches. He beat his head against the chair's back once. Twice.

*Bloody hell.* What was the matter with him? He should be out on the Town with Hunt. Or enjoying himself in bed with a lively bedmate. If not Jenny, some other. Instead he languished away like a lovesick fool, yearning for a woman he had evidently dreamed up.

The restlessness that had plagued him while abroad, following him across a myriad of countries and chasing him all the way home, still lingered. Like death's hand, it crept silently through the night, reaching for him even now, preventing him from enjoying his usual pursuits. Women, drink, cards. None enticed him.

Pity Frank had come in when he did. Now the lad went to bed thinking Dominic was engaged in all manner of vice. The young pup had looked at him with such disappointment that Dominic almost felt inclined to knock on his door and correct him of his misapprehensions. His lips thinned and he clutched the arms of the chair firmly. *Almost.* He did not care what one wet-behind-the-ears boy thought of him. He did *not*.

He thrummed his fingers over the padded arm, his gaze moving toward the door, to the thin glow of light peeping beneath it. From the door, his gaze moved to scan his room, alighting on the nearly empty decanter of brandy.

With a muttered curse, he surged to his feet, snatched the decanter and stalked toward the door. Clearly, his young valet was still awake. Why not make use of him?

"Frank," he called, giving the door a swift, angry rap before closing his hand around the latch—and telling himself it was to simply request more brandy. Not because he gave a damn about what the young prig thought of him.

Opening the door, he stepped inside the smaller room, his gaze sweeping the dim interior, lips parting, readying to speak.

A soft glow of lamplight permeated the room,

lending everything a soft haze. Then he realized some of the haze was in fact a vapor on the air. Steam rose from the copper tub on one side of the room.

His gaze landed on the tub . . . then drifted to the figure standing beside it, a female, so still, frozen like one of the marble statues in the garden at Wayfield Park. Something froze inside him as well. They stared at each other for an interminable stretch of time, gazing at each other as two enemies coming face-to-face on a field of battle. She with a towel clutched to her bare body.

Her eyes flared wide, enormous and frightened as any animal caught in a predator's sights.

The decanter slipped from his fingers, the dull thud barely registering. His gaze dragged over her, feasting on moist flesh. The wet towel did little to conceal all that pink, glistening skin— the endless legs . . . an amazing stretch of well-shaped legs. More legs than he remembered ever seeing on a woman. His gaze roamed upward, sliding over long lines and gentle curves until he encountered her face—and gave it his first hard look.

The truth struck him in a blazing flash, knocking the wind from his lungs as effectively as a fist to his chest.

His heart pounded fiercely, blood rushing his veins in a searing burn. The air crackled as he fought to swallow past the thickness in his throat. Oddly, he felt more awake, more alive than he had in years . . . ever since he became a dead shell of a man . . . alive only when he lost himself in a woman's heat or when he lost himself in his painting, in the colors, in the flying stroke of his brush on canvas.

Staring at her, he felt alive. Awake.

Staring at her face—a woman he never met, yet *knew*—he grasped the astounding truth. This was the woman he had kissed. The one to fill his head all week. Not a figment of his imagination. Not wishful thinking. A wholly flesh-and-blood woman. She was real. She was here.

And she not a *he* at all. She was Frank.

A fact that did not shock him nearly as much as it should. Strangely, it fit. Made sense. More sense than his obsessing over whether his wet-behind-the-ears valet *approved* of him. All her disdain and haughty regard made perfect sense now. *How like a woman.*

Fury spiraled through him, threatening to spill forth and devastate all in its path. Including the wide-eyed female before him.

Especially her.

His hands flexed at his sides. He flicked a glance to the floor and the decanter of brandy. The last of its contents seeped into the carpet just as the last drop of his control evaporated, a fast-fading curl of smoke on the air. Gone. With the last of his restraint.

# Chapter 18

"**F**rank?" he drawled, his mind grasping what his eyes already recognized . . . what perhaps he had known all along, buried somewhere deep inside him.

He stepped closer, bare feet sliding over the carpet as he contemplated why he had not faced the truth sooner. Why he had not *seen* her? He assessed her. Even tall as she was, she was undeniably female.

Her mouth worked, but no sound came.

"Frank," he repeated, his voice hard as ground glass.

She shook her head. *Stubborn chit.*

"But then I suppose that's not really your name, is it?" He subjected her to another thorough, insulting examination, his stare lingering on her poorly hidden breasts. Small but pert.

Her gaze darted left and right as though seeking escape. Moistening her lips, she finally found her tongue. "How dare you barge in here? Even a servant is entitled to a modicum of privacy."

"Indeed." He cocked his head as he advanced on her. "Especially a servant with something to hide."

Her expression tightened as he came closer. She shook her head in desperate denial, her damp hair tossing, skimming smooth, well-rounded shoulders. Shoulders well toned with muscle. A testament to her working-class life. His gaze skimmed her body again, and he blinked, distracted. None of the ladies of his acquaintance could boast such a fine, strong body. *A woman built for pleasure, for taking a man deep inside her.*

He forced the thought away. Perhaps he had been so able to reject her as a woman because he had never met a woman like her before.

"That's not it at all," she denied hotly. "I—"

"Yes. It is." He nodded slowly. "Cease your denials. You're simply angry because you've been caught at your charade."

Now he understood why he'd always felt slightly on edge around her. Especially curious when he scarcely noted the servants around him before. Certainly none had ever gotten beneath his skin before. None save her.

She stopped her retreat, her back against the wall. She held up one hand as if that alone could ward him off.

A savage smile twisted his lips. Anger burned in his blood. Dark and dangerous. He flattened both hands on the wall, one on either side of her head. Damp heat emanated from her body, drawing him in. Leaning closer, her palm rose up to flatten against his chest, clearly thinking to stop him.

Blistering heat sparked where they touched. Her gaze flared wide, almost directly on level with his. But she did not withdraw. Not as she should.

Something held her hand there, a will that matched his own, a determination to show control. Dark desire flared within him. Primitive and fierce as any wild animal bred to take and conquer what he craved.

He studied the brown depths of her eyes, truly seeing them now. The amber hue glowed like fire. He read the fury trapped there, as trapped as she was. And something else stirred there. Awareness of her defeat.

His slow smile curved his mouth. He dipped his head, grazing her soft cheek with his own. Her indrawn breath hissed near his ear and deep satisfaction smoldered through him.

He breathed directly into her ear, "Game over. Time to pay the piper."

She shoved hard at his chest, harder and stronger than he would have thought a woman capable. He stumbled back. She darted past, fast as a hare.

He surged forward with a growl, a predator set loose. He caught her just before she reached the door. His fingers tangled in her hair. She cried out.

With a jerk, he hauled her to him, her back colliding with his chest. Releasing her hair, he folded his arms around her, sliding his fingers over the soft flesh of her throat, skimming the delicate line of her collarbone until he grasped her shoulder and spun her.

Instantly, he was aware that the towel had disappeared—a casualty of her foolish attempt to escape. Her chest heaved with ragged breaths, and he was acutely conscious of the nipples beading into hard points against him. Scarlet stained her cheeks. "Shall we finish where we left off the other night?"

Her eyes widened.

"Oh, yes," he growled with a brutal nod of his head. "That was you. Don't think I don't know it."

"My towel," she bit out, looking to the side

where the towel sat in a crumpled pile on the floor.

He shrugged. "A good place for it."

Her eyes glittered with defiance, widening in outrage as he grew hard and insistent against her. With a rocking motion of his hips, he nudged the warm juncture of her thighs.

"Wretch!" Her bare heel slammed down and ground into his foot.

"Bloody Amazon," he cursed, hopping back, still holding on to one of her arms.

She struggled, straining to reach her towel on the floor.

With a quick twist, he snatched up the towel himself, never releasing her arm.

"Bastard," she hissed. "Hand it over! Don't you have a tart next door ready to prance naked for you? What do you need me for?"

"I sent her home." His gaze dropped to her body. Quivering with rage, he had a fairly good idea how those breasts would look perched above him, shuddering as he moved inside her. His mouth dried, and, suddenly, her punishment had become his. Those small perfect breasts, the high-tipped nipples, pink as freshly picked raspberries, ensnared him. So much so that he didn't see her tightly wound fist coming.

Pain exploded in his right eye.

Releasing her, he covered his eye. "You bloody hell *hit* me!"

She didn't answer, simply grunted as she fought to grab the towel back.

Dropping his hand from his stinging eye, he held the towel high above and wrapped an arm around her waist, crushing her to him. Still trying to reclaim her towel, she hopped on her feet, her nipples chafing his chest.

He hauled her even closer.

Her eyes clashed with his. She ceased moving. Indeed, it seemed she stopped breathing.

His gaze roamed her face, taking it in, seeing *her*. For days, weeks, it had been Frank. His anger returned, flared anew at the reminder. "Did you have a good laugh?" He tightened his arm around her waist. Surprisingly small for a woman of her size.

"Astonishing as it may seem, not everything is about you." She fell still as stone in his arms. And yet she was as soft and warm as any woman, her nipples burning into his chest. Heat radiated from the apex of her legs, almost in perfect line with his throbbing cock.

He stared hard into her face, his gaze skimming

over the strong angles, the strong nose, the full mouth. No beauty to be sure. She failed to possess the petite features and delicate bones that marked a woman as truly beautiful—at least by the *ton's* standards—but she was no less striking.

"Then why did you do it?"

Her lips pressed together in silent mutiny.

"Tell me," he demanded, determined to have the truth. "Speak—" he broke off, about to say "Frank." The near slip only made his blood churn hotter.

Air escaped her in a hot rush. "It's about *me*. About keeping a bloody position for longer than a fortnight."

"And you need to live as a man in order to do that?"

"Apparently," she snapped, renewing her struggles. "Otherwise I risk being molested." Her fiery gaze snapped to his, the accusation hot as smoldering coals. "As now."

"I don't molest the women in my employ."

"You are now! As a woman in your employ, I would be at the mercy of your desires."

"Are you female? I can't be sure," he snarled even as his blood thickened at the feel of her pressed so intimately near. *Definitely a woman.*

Fire lit her cheeks and her eyes glowed an even brighter amber, like flame trapped in polished glass, fighting to escape. And, God help him, he wanted it to.

"You bloody well know I'm a woman. Now unhand me."

Even in his fury, something stirred in his gut. A quiet thrill at her boldness, at her audacity to dare such a deception, to talk to him in such a manner—as no man did—*to strike him in the face.*

"And what should I do with you, fraud that you are?"

"Send for the watch. I'm certain that is what you will do."

He arched a brow. "And why are you so certain?"

"Because that is what toffs do, *Your Grace.*" His title, she sneered like an epithet. "Suppress and abuse all beneath them."

Dominic jerked as though he had been struck. *Again.* "You are the one who committed the offense here."

She shook her head as though she did not hear him. "What are you waiting for? Get it over with."

An idiot could not miss the bitterness in
her voice. "What happened to you?" His gaze
skimmed her shorn hair. "Some fine lord cross a
line he should not have?" Even as he posed the
question, an odd tightness gripped his throat at
the prospect, and he knew with absolute certainty,
that if that were the case, he would find the man
and kill him.

Splotchy patches of color broke out over her
face. "No!" The word shot from her lips as if such
a thing were utterly impossible. "Do I look like
I would let a man take advantage of me? I'm no
one's plaything. I resisted the allure of your web,
did I not?"

He blinked and gave a small shake of his head.
"I thought you a man. I never propositioned
you—"

"Oh, we've met before." Her words cut into
him. She arched a brow, waiting, it seemed, for
him to remember.

He stared at her for a long moment, absorbing
the features of her face, the aquiline nose, the full
mouth, the proud, high arching brows. And the
hair. *The bloody hair.* While still mostly wet, several dry wisps floated around her face. *The color
of a Spanish sunset.* Even in the room's muted glow,

the strands glinted fire—a myriad of red and gold. The memory of a carriage ride with Fallon O'Rourke slammed into him. A portrait sat two doors over of this very woman. And she had been beneath his nose for weeks!

"You," he breathed. "I took you to the Daventry Hotel." Instead of feeling pleasure at seeing her again, his sense of betrayal only intensified. *At least you can flesh out the face now.*

"Indeed," she replied in a clipped manner that reminded him of Frank.

Bile burned at the back of his throat. "Did I offend you so much that you decided to make a fool of me with this little charade?"

"The agency referred me. I needed the work. It wasn't personal."

"No?" He palmed her waist, sliding down to cup one smooth cheek, round and firm. "It feels quite personal to me."

Air hissed from between her tightly clamped teeth. "Stop."

The dark pupils of her eyes dilated as he fondled the warm flesh. He knew desire when he saw it. Recognized when a woman slipped to that place where she scarcely remembered her own name.

He released her derrière to trail his fingers around her hip, his touch feather soft, sliding inward, seeking her heat. Her flesh quivered beneath his hand. Gently, he teased the tender skin of her inner thighs. She grew heavy in his arms and he tightened one arm around her waist to keep her from falling.

Her thighs parted for him.

"That's it," he murmured, sifting through springy-soft curls. He groaned as his fingers met moist warmth. Never had a woman felt more ready. More willing.

Her eyes drifted shut and he jostled her in his arms, passing his fingers over the core of her. "Watch me," he commanded.

Eyes wide, she held his stare as he toyed with her, finding that tiny little nub, rubbing and squeezing it until she panted hotly in his ear. He eased a finger inside her. Her slick channel closed tightly around him. He pressed a thumb against her nub, rolling it as he stroked in and out of her in deep penetrating glides that left his cock aching to be free, aching to feel her clinging warmth surround him. To put his stamp on her.

Fallon shuddered and cried out, her thighs clenching around his hand. Eager to join her in her climax, he moved a hand to the front of his trousers, confident that he would have her on her back beneath him in moments. He could think of no more fitting punishment than hearing her cry out his name in pleasure.

*Except that would make her right*. And Dominic as bad as all the other blue bloods she measured him against.

Her words came back to haunt him. *A female in your employ, I would be at the mercy of your desires.*

Cursing, he released her.

Suddenly having to stand on her own, she nearly collapsed. Staggering back, she collided with the small bed. For a moment, he allowed himself to feast on the naked sight of her, the long stretch of legs, the perfect thatch of tawny hair between her legs that he had touched moments before . . . that he ached to touch again.

He burned to possess her, to take her. But he would not. Not because he was good or kind or, perish the thought, a gentleman. He was none of those things. Nor did he aspire to be.

"You're welcome," he snarled.

She shook her head, clearly confused.

"I'd say that just about nullifies your certainty that *all* toffs abuse those beneath them. I've taken nothing from you. I've only given." He raked her with a carefully neutral stare, trying to ignore her flushed skin and overly bright eyes . . . or the agony ripping through his unfulfilled body "And left you quite satisfied."

Her mouth sagged, color suffusing her face. Her hands fluttered over her body, trying to shield herself.

Crossing her arms over her chest and pressing her thighs tight in a protective gesture, her square little chin lifted. "What now? What will you do with me?"

He knew what she *thought* he would do. What he likely *ought* to do. Certainly other men in his position would call the watch on her. Impersonating a man and passing himself off as a duke's valet certainly bore penalty.

"What should I do with you?" He slid his gaze over her in slow perusal, suppressing the thoughts of what he'd like to do . . . all that his base impulses commanded he do.

"I'll be gone in the morning."

"Very well." He nodded and moved toward the door.

Her leaving would be for the best. He didn't need a fraud beneath his roof. No more than he needed a woman he ached to possess. A woman that wanted nothing to do with him.

# Chapter 19

Fallon started at the knock on her door. She had scarcely slept a wink all night, too anxious over the duke sleeping one room over, an unlocked door between them. Not that she feared ravishment. If he was bent on that, he could have had his way with her easily enough. Her cheeks burned as she recalled her ardent response to him. Her desire to run her fingers over that tattoo of his. Her willingness to give herself to him entirely.

Clutching her neatly folded nightshirt to her chest, she faced the door, half expecting it to swing open and the duke to storm inside the small room as he had done the night before.

Instead, his voice carried through the door, without the slightest inflection. "Five minutes. My study."

Nothing more than that. She bristled at the tersely worded command. Turning, she stuffed her nightshirt in her valise, no longer caring at keeping it neatly folded.

He need not speak to her in that high-handed manner anymore. Hot air puffed through her lips. As of last night, she was no longer his servant.

Still, he had not kicked her out into the night the moment he uncovered her deception. Nor had he called the watch on her. She supposed that was something to accord a little gratitude. A gentleman in his position could—*would*— have done that very thing. It certainly matched every notion she ever harbored of overprivileged noblemen.

Shaking her head, she scanned the room, making sure she had not forgotten anything. She snorted. She scarcely need worry about leaving anything behind. Since the day she arrived at Penwich's, she owned nothing more than the clothes on her back.

Wrapping her fingers around the handle of her valise, she departed her room with her chin high, prepared for the stares of any servant she might pass in the corridor.

She would leave after he said whatever he had to say. She doubted it would take long. After last night, what more was left to say?

Striding down the corridor, she smoothed a hand down her serviceable frock—the same blue dress she wore when she met Marguerite in the park, the only one she risked including among her things.

Moments later, she stood before the duke's study, grateful she had not happened upon any of the other servants. With luck, she could avoid them altogether and avoid the potential awkwardness. They had all been so kind to her, far more accepting than the staff of any other household. Revealing her deception would give her no small shame.

Patting the hair she had managed to pin back—save the wisps falling at the back of her neck—she rapped her knuckles against the door.

"Come in."

Posture stiff, she entered the room, her right hand clutched tightly about the handle of her valise. Strangely, she felt as if she were back at Penwich, called into Master Brocklehurst's office for the beating the school mistress claimed she deserved for her impertinent tongue.

Sucking in a deep breath, she reminded herself that she wasn't that girl anymore, that no man had the right to beat her. Not then. Not now.

He looked up from his desk, his face a perfect study in stone. Papers that he actually appeared to be reading were scattered before him. It was the first time she had seen him preoccupied in a task and not pursuing vice or leisure. The sight unsettled her further, challenging her opinion of him. Making him appear somehow decent and industrious, not the libertine she first judged him.

He did not speak for some moments. Those smoky blue eyes of his slid over her in slow appraisal. Her thoughts turned to last night, when she had stood before him naked. Heat scored her cheeks. How is it that dressed even in her shabby gown, she felt naked before him?

*Because that was what he did.* Scoundrel to the core, he knew how to unnerve a woman with a single look.

Duly reminded, she resisted the urge to fidget. Holding her spine straight, she ground out, "Yes?"

He leaned back in his chair. "A dress suits you. Now I recall what motivated me to try and seduce you that first night."

The heat searing her cheeks intensified at his bluntness. "Was your lewd behavior that night your idea of a seduction?" She sniffed. "Then I have no fear that I shall ever succumb to you."

Something glinted in his eyes, the gray lightening until his eyes gleamed like polished pewter. "I've evidence that you are not immune to me. Shall I prove it?"

A tremor skated her spine. "Of course not."

The last thing she needed was a repeat of last night. Even before her humiliating surrender, time spent as his valet had taught her she was not immune to him.

With a blink, the cold duke was back. "Pity you cut your hair," he remarked. "It was quite lovely."

Her hand flew to her hair self-consciously. In spite of herself, her vanity smarted at the comment and she wished for her long hair again. *Wished for him to still think it lovely.*

His gaze moved then, dropping it to her valise. "Going somewhere?"

"I would think that obvious." She had declared her intention to leave the night before, and he had seemed vastly agreeable at the time.

He shrugged. "Yes, well. Perhaps an unnecessary measure."

Certain she misunderstood, she gave her head a small shake. "Begging your pardon?"

"You're educated," he announced, seemingly off topic.

She blinked, a bit startled at the sudden proclamation. "Yes." It was the one thing Master Brocklehurst saw to . . . perhaps the only thing for which she could accord him any gratitude. "My father died when I was thirteen. I was then sent to the Penwich School for Virtuous girls."

"I see." Nodding, he motioned to her person. "And now, correctly attired, you are a suitable addition to any household."

She moistened her lips. "What are you saying?"

His mouth twisted. He steepled his fingers together and studied her for a long moment. "You may stay on here."

She narrowed her gaze on him, instantly wary. "Why would you want me to?"

He arched a dark brow. "You question my motives? I would think you merely happy to keep your post."

"Everything comes at a price." She had learned that long ago.

"My, so jaded for one of such tender years."

"Why would you let me remain here?" She tightened her palm around the handle of her valise.

Leaning back in his chair, he folded his hands behind his head, surveying her with hooded eyes. "You claim you only wish to earn a living, that you've been unfairly treated in the past." He shrugged as though he were not convinced of that. Indignation swirled hotly in her belly. "I'll give you your chance, then. You may stay on. As a woman. In whatever capacity Mr. Adams deems suitable. I shall leave that for him to decide."

She stared at the face that had become so familiar . . . and longed to issue a refusal. Her pride wished to decline his offer and march from the room. But logic held her in check. And self-preservation. Always self-preservation reared its head, guiding her when pride would have her starving and sleeping in a gutter.

"Agreed?" he asked with that maddening lift of his brow.

She gave a small nod, uncertain that she had not just made a pact with the devil.

He nodded in turn. "You shall see that not all gentlemen are the dishonorable lot you believe them to be."

"Oh?" she heard herself mutter before she could think better of it, her smart mouth running away with her. "You claim to possess honor now?

I thought you eschewed such lofty ideals, relishing your role as a libertine."

"Let it never be said I *abused* a woman . . . especially one in my employ. You'll be safe under my roof, have no fear on that account." His eyes gleamed, lips twisting with mockery. "Last night should attest to that." His fingers drifted to his mouth then, the blunt tips stroking his upper lip with indolence . . . and she remembered those marvelously wicked fingers on her. *Inside her.* Wretched beast of a man.

"Safe from you? How singular." She shook her head, her short waves tickling the back of her heated neck. "I did not feel safe from you last night." No. She had felt a myriad of emotions. Chiefly desire. But never safe.

"You've your virtue intact."

"You"—embarrassment roasted her cheeks— "touched me." Was she discussing this? With him?

"I did more than that." His mocking smile faded, his lips forming a humorless line, a perfect match to the flat slate gray of his stare. "But it won't happen again."

"How can I be certain? How can I trust that your intentions—"

He rose in one swift motion, the action silencing her. His jaw hardened as he rounded his desk. Her heart hammered wildly as he leaned against its front, crossing his feet at the ankles. "You think a great deal of yourself. You're not so irresistible, you know." His gaze skimmed her. "And I've never been partial to Amazons."

Heat scored her face. She bit back the slew of stinging retorts that rose on her tongue. All silly considering she *wanted* him to leave her be, to see her as merely another servant in his household. She should hope he found her unappealing.

"Excellent, then," she said briskly. "I shall be happy to stay. Thank you, Your Grace. I will report to Mr. Adams."

Turning, she strode from the room, wondering at the tightness in her chest that felt oddly like regret.

Last night, when he had put his hands on her, she had imagined he desired her. Imagined that he craved her more than any other woman. No matter how many scores preceded her, he made her feel special. Therein rested his power . . . his ability to seduce anything in skirts.

Not her.

*Not me, by God.*

No matter how irresistible she found him, resist him she would. She would not fall into his web. She had spent too many years avoiding the traps of men. She would not stumble now.

# Chapter 20

**F**allon stopped abruptly at the top of the stoop, staring at the small form blocking her descent. With the afternoon free, she had intended to spend it with Marguerite, to apprise her of all that had happened—*most* of what had happened, at any rate. Yet the sight of the slight, bone-thin shoulders shuddering with tears halted her in her tracks. Suddenly her wish to be free—to escape the indiscreet whispers and hot-eyed speculation of everyone in the house—withered to a swift death.

Bending from the waist, she surveyed the profile of a grimy-faced youth of no more than ten years. Tears left shiny tracts down cheeks that had not seen a good scrub in as many years. Clearly one of the duke's urchins.

Descending another step, she settled herself beside him on the stoop, folding her hands carefully over the skirt of her dress.

She leaned her shoulder against the iron railing to her right. "Mind if I sit here a bit."

He shot her a startled look and dragged his sleeve across his nose with a loud, wet sniff. For some moments they sat side, by side, saying nothing, the hawking calls of the vendors out in the square the only sound on the air.

The lad continued to send her several surreptitious looks, without quite turning his face to look at her person. "You're the one they're all talking about."

She lifted a brow at his abrupt announcement, her fingers clenching tighter about her reticule. It was one thing to suspect yourself the subject of gossip, another to know. "Am I?"

He nodded. "I 'eard them. In the kitchens. You're the one that thinks she's a man."

Fallon's mouth turned a bit at that. "I don't *think* I'm a man."

"You dressed like one, though?"

"I did."

"And let everyone think you were one."

She winced and gave a single nod.

"Why?"

Her fingers tightened around her bent knees. "I guess it seemed easier than being . . . well . . . me."

He nodded again, his manner strangely wise for one of such tender years. "Wish I didn't 'ave to be me."

"What's wrong with being you?"

"Today I'm to be sold," he replied in peevish tones, glaring straight ahead.

"Sold?" Fallon blinked. "Surely not."

"Aye, the 'igh master in there found a position for me." He thumbed behind him, the gesture brutal and savage. "But I know what that means."

"You do?"

"Aye, 'e bloody well sold me. Like my uncle sold me to the workhouse when Mam died. I'll not go back to a place like that again. I'll take to the streets first."

Fallon frowned. "I can assure you His Grace does not intend to *sell* you."

The boy thrust out his bottom lip in mutiny. "How do you know? You know 'im?"

Fallon thought for a moment before replying. "Yes. I know him well enough." And she supposed she did. Her cheeks warmed as she thought about just how well he knew her. She hadn't seen him since the morning in his study, but he haunted her thoughts . . . as did the memory of those magical hands on her. On her body.

At the boy's expectant gaze, she cleared her throat and elaborated, trying to offer him the reassurance he so clearly craved. "His Grace would never sell you. He is a good man. A kind man."

"Indeed?"

At the gravelly voice, she lurched to her feet, one hand clutching the steel railing edging the steps. Dominic stood framed in the doorway, studying her intently. *How long had he been there?*

"A good man, you say? Kind? How interesting to hear you say that."

The boy darted uneasy glances between Fallon and the duke.

"Nonsense," Fallon said tightly, looking meaningfully at the duke. "I was just assuring your young charge here of how very good you are."

"Ah." He descended a few steps. "Well, good enough to escort you to your new home." He ruffled the lad's wheat-colored hair. "What say you to that, Andy? Ready?"

The lad's face paled and he looked with entreaty to Fallon. He inched close enough for his arm to align with her side, his hand brushing hers.

The duke studied them for a long moment, noting Andy's closeness to her with a keen gaze. "Perhaps you would care to join us, Miss O'Rourke. After we've secured young Andy, I can deposit you wherever you wish." His gaze skimmed her. "Clearly you have plans for your afternoon."

"Yes. That should be satisfactory," she murmured, nodding in agreement even as she balked at the thought of spending time with the duke. She had vowed to avoid him, to prove not only to herself but him that she could be a model servant—one who went about her duties attracting as little notice as possible. One who did not crave her employer as might an idiot female with aspirations above her station.

She knew her place in the world. And it was not with him.

Dominic stared openly at the female across from him. *Female.* It *still* rankled. Dressed in her drab blue dress, he had difficulty reconciling her with Frank—the fierce-eyed valet with an impertinent tongue whose approval he had, absurdly, sought. The fierce eyes were still there. As was the boldness . . . however much she attempted at an air of meekness.

The boy sat close to her side, shooting Dominic narrowed glances. Natural, he supposed. Dominic had rescued him from a beating, after all. Likely every man struck a note of distrust with the boy.

Interesting Andy should like *her* so much. He had overheard their conversation, eavesdropping shamelessly when he found her sitting with him on the stoop. Her compassion surprised him. Nearly as much as her endorsement of him. And why would she waste her free afternoon on some street scamp?

At Dominic's continued stare, the boy stuck out his tongue and slid a bone-thin hand around Fallon's arm.

She looked startled for a moment, and he waited, lips twisting, ready to see her remove the urchin's grimy paw from the well-pressed sleeve of her dress. Instead, she relaxed back into the seat and covered his hand with her own, her long elegant fingers wrapping around his thin hand, her shiny, clean nails a marked contrast next to his dirt-encrusted ones.

Something loosened inside his chest and he turned abruptly, looking away, staring crossly at the drawn curtains. *Bloody hell.* She possessed a tender heart. Not a particularly welcome insight. Given the chance, the wolves would gobble up a morsel like her. *And are you not the greatest wolf of them all?*

Grimacing, he parted the curtains just as the carriage rolled to a stop. Gratefully.

"We're here?"

Nodding, he stepped down from the carriage. Turning, he assisted Fallon from the conveyance, his hands lingering longer than they should on her waist. Her cheeks pinkened but her eyes did not lift to his. She avoided his gaze. Clearly unwilling to acknowledge the spark of connection between them. A spark he was beginning to suspect could not be avoided. The predator in him purred to life, eager to dominate, to feel her eyes on him, feasting and absorbing in the same manner his gaze devoured her.

He gnashed his teeth. Was she playing at the docile maid now? He wouldn't have it. He wanted her alive and spitting as before, when he held her against him—naked, her skin hot from her bath, her moist woman's flesh milking his touch.

She stepped free of him and faced the shop, blinking at the Confectionery before them as young Andy hopped down. She looked to her left and right, clearly uncertain.

Shifting against the sudden tight fit of his breeches, Dominic gestured before them, opening the door. With the door's bell tinkling over their heads, Fallon and Andy stepped inside, their eyes rounding in unison at the sweets on display in glass counters.

All manner of aromas assailed the nose, sugar and cinnamon and spiced fruits. Fallon glanced at him, one brow cocked in question. Andy had yet to reclaim his composure. He slid his hand from Fallon's and pressed himself to the display of goodies, fogging the glass with the close press of his open mouth.

"Ah, Your Grace!" A ruddy-faced man bustled from around the counter, his belly swaying side to side against his striped apron. "We've been expecting you. You'll have to forgive that Mrs. Applebaum is not here to greet you . . . she is still preparing for the lad at home. Mentioned something about meat pasties for lunch . . ." The proprietor winked broadly at Andy. "You'll see. Mrs. Applebaum makes the best pasties." He rubbed his considerable belly. "Believes in feeding the working man, she does."

"Mr. Applebaum." Dominic settled a hand on Andy's slight shoulder. "This is Andy, the boy I told you about."

Mr. Applebaum nodded, looking the lad over with deep consideration. "Looks wiry enough. What say you lad, willing to earn your keep?"

Fallon's hand drifted to Andy's other shoulder, the gesture inherently maternal. Suddenly a flash of her with a babe in her arms and another clinging to her skirts filled his head. Shaking the domestic image from his head, he focused on Applebaum.

"'Fraid the wife has notions of coddling and cosseting you. You'll have to bear it, lad." Despite the gruffness in his voice, something tender crossed the man's eyes. "We never had offspring of our own." With a sniff and swipe of his bulbous nose, he added, "I confess, I'll be glad for a helping hand in the shop. And the company."

Andy found his voice at last. "I'll be living with you? And I'll be working here?" His head turned, sweeping the shop, his gaze not missing a single licorice stick, gumdrop or rum-candied tart.

"Yes, and I'm afraid my taste buds have become a bit jaded over the years." He patted his stomach. "I'll need you to help with the sampling."

Dominic suppressed a smile at Andy's animated nod. "I won't mind at all, sir! Not at all!"

Dominic felt it then. Felt *her*.

Without looking, he knew she gazed at him.

The curious heat of her stare roamed his face. Turning, he met her gaze. She looked at him as though she had never seen him before. Something indefinable glowed in her eyes. Something that made his chest tighten almost painfully.

Already, Applebaum was leading Andy away, talking animatedly of the day's plans . . . something about frosting a seven-tiered cake for the Mayfair's Ladies' Horticulture Society.

"Andy, wait!" Fallon swept forward. Crouching, she folded the soot-faced lad in her arms. She smoothed a hand over his head, rumpling the wheat-colored hair. Her hand slid down, fingers trailing his grubby cheek fondly. Dominic's chest twisted and he looked away, suddenly wishing himself a nine-year-old orphan. *Bloody hell.*

Applebaum stepped forward to offer a hasty farewell, thanking Dominic for placing the lad with him, and thrusting a white paper sack in his hand. "Dark chocolate fudge. I remember how much you like it, Your Grace."

Nodding his thanks, he glanced at Andy again. "I only hope you find satisfaction in the arrangement. If the situation proves untenable, send for me. I can make other arrangements."

Applebaum shot a quick look to the boy, presently being fussed over by Fallon. "I think we shall get on very well, Your Grace."

Dominic waited as Fallon finished with her farewell. He caught her whisper to the boy. "Be happy."

The tightness unfurled from his chest with the suddenness of a balloon bursting. Fallon O'Rourke, he grimly accepted, was a creature unlike any other. A scant hour with Andy and she had taken him into her heart.

A desperate urge to be that liked—*by her*—ignited a slow burn inside him.

He led her from the confectioner's shop, his hand on her elbow, scarcely recalling his steps or climbing inside the carriage or popping a piece of fudge in his mouth. As the rich creaminess dissolved on his tongue, he offered her the bag. She accepted it. He watched her take the chocolate into her mouth, place it upon the pink tip of her tongue, and arousal stabbed through him.

For some moments they sat in the still carriage, he staring darkly at her.

Her voice penetrated the thick air between them. "The park. Would you not mind taking me there?"

He would not mind *taking* her. *Here. Now.*

At his mulling silence, she slid closer to the door. Almost as though she contemplated jumping. "Or I can walk the rest of the way."

He rapped abruptly on the roof, calling out their destination in a barked command.

With hooded eyes, he continued to watch her. She settled deeper against the squabs, her fingers worrying the strings of her reticule.

"I hope Andy likes his new home."

"Why should you care after a boy you just met?" he demanded, his voice coming out cross and accusing. He did not want to like her . . . did not want to imagine she had a good reason for her deception. For making a fool of him.

She blinked. "I could ask you the same."

He started, unaccustomed to wondering why he plucked urchins from the streets with regular frequency. He just did—had for quite some time. *Because you see yourself in their hopeless gazes.* His jaw tightened against the unwelcome answer whispering inside him. "A hobby."

"I thought you already had a hobby." Her eyes glinted and he remembered their earlier conversation when she—*Frank*—had demanded to know why he seduced everything in skirts, in specific married skirts. *Everyone needs a hobby*, had been his pithy reply.

"One can have multiple hobbies." Shrugging, he added, "I stop in at Applebaum's often. Love their fudge." He looked pointedly to the white paper sack. "Applebaum mentioned needing help . . . and I knew he and his wife lacked offspring."

"So you appointed yourself their benefactor and decided to find them a ward?" She snorted. "Not likely. Say whatever you like, but I'm afraid you've been found out." That square chin of hers lifted in a haughty angle. In that moment he had a flash of Frank again, all cheek and insolence.

"Oh? Do share your discovery."

"You, Your Grace, are not nearly as wicked as you would like the world to think." Her words did not rankle so much as the little smirk playing about her mouth. A wide-lipped virago's mouth.

"What do you know of wickedness, Miss O'Rourke? You who hides behind disguises, leading a half-lived life?"

Hot color licked her cheeks. "My life is *not* half-lived. I've lived plenty. No coddled existence, to be sure. And I've seen my share of truly wicked—"

"Is that so?" He moved across the carriage, dropping down beside her. "And what would truly wicked be?" Before she could respond, he ran a finger down her bare neck. The stiff collar of her dress stopped him from going further, from descending, as he wished, to those perfectly formed breasts burned in his memory. He pressed his open mouth to the warm skin of her neck, touching where he could. Tasting.

She stilled, all warm, pliant woman against him. Gripping her chin, he turned her face to him and breathed in the chocolaty hint of her breath. "Like kissing a man in a moving carriage in the middle of the day? Would that qualify?"

Her gaze dropped, fell on his lips, and her head gave the barest nod.

He brushed his mouth against hers, enjoying the softly parted lips, the moist breath slipping into his hungry mouth, the feel of her body shuddering in surrender.

Her eyes remained open. Shocked wide. The taste of her filled him with raw need. He kissed her harder, tasting heat and Fallon and dark chocolate: the sweetest combination. Nothing he had ever experienced.

*Fallon.* So sweet, so uncorrupted for all her claims of hard living. A primitive need to claim her and protect her as his own seized him. The urge sent a ripple of alarm coursing through him nearly as potent as the dark desire smoldering through his veins.

Still kissing, mouths hard and ravenous on each other, he lifted her hand from her lap and pressed it over his bulging erection, determined to teach her *wicked* . . . and watch her fly from him in maidenly outrage. As he knew she would. As he needed her to do in order to stop.

Her hand flinched before settling over him, relaxing, testing his shape with a curious flex of her fingers, and he realized his mistake. He had not thought of what her touch would do to him. A groan ripped from his throat, bleeding into their kiss.

The sound woke her, tore her from him. She snatched her hand back and flew across the carriage to where he once sat, staring at him with the wild eyes of a hunted animal.

She clutched both hands tight in her lap, her thumb rotating rapid circles in the palm he had pressed against his cock. Heat scored her cheeks a deep shade of scarlet. Even her neck burned brightly.

"Why did you do that?" Her gaze lifted, meeting his, holding. The glow of those amber eyes made his stomach tighten.

Jaw clenched, he stared back, devouring the

sight of her. His erection pressed hard against the front of his breeches, aching for her.

"I want you." He would no longer deny it. The wanting prowled like a live beast within him.

She stared. Her breath rising and falling. "You said I would be safe from you."

He nodded fiercely, dragging a hand over his face. His every muscle strained to drag her back into his arms. "I did."

"You lied."

Her whispered accusation knifed through him. "I did not know I would want you so much."

Her mouth parted. Something flickered in her eyes, making them glint red, not brown at all. Perhaps that explained it. She was some sort of angel from hell bent on possession.

The carriage rocked to a stop. He shook his head. A moment later the footman knocked upon the door. Fallon moved like fire licked at her heels.

He curled his hands into fists to stop himself for reaching for her, but it did no good. Before she escaped through the door, he grabbed her wrist. "And now *you* know. I want you. You remain at your own peril."

Her eyes widened and he released her. He watched her go, slipping out the door . . . and he wondered if he would ever see her again.

# Chapter 21

"**A**h, blast." The older maid rattled amid her basket of rags and polishes.

It was likely the first time Martha had uttered a word in Fallon's presence since she had been exposed a woman. She had sent Fallon plenty of disapproving looks, letting her censure be felt, but never deigned to speak. Her behavior was similar to that of the rest of the staff. They did not treat her badly. Just coldly.

"I left the vinegar in the last room." Martha tapped at the side table where candle wax had spilled. I'll be back in a moment." She lumbered toward the door, stopping to shoot Fallon a pointed stare. "Don't"—she gestured around the duke's bedchamber—"touch anything until I get back."

Fallon watched as she swept from the bedchamber, leaving her alone in the duke's rooms. A scenario that might have worried her if she had not spotted the duke leaving the house earlier.

*I want you.* A tremble shivered through her. A man had never said those words to her. Certainly she had endured innuendos and crude suggestions in the past, but a blatant declaration of desire . . . and issued from the lips of a man whose kisses made her toes curl? Her gaze roamed the bed, trying not to imagine herself in its vast space. *With him.* She tried and failed. The wicked way he had touched her—the wicked way *she* had touched him—did not feel that . . . *wicked.* It felt *right.* Sighing, she turned from the bed. She could not go on thinking such thoughts.

Of her own volition, her gaze wandered to the door. The door she was never to enter. The room she was forbidden to see. She could have managed a peek before, when she was his valet, but she resisted . . . somehow thinking it was a weakness on her part. An admission, if only to herself, that the duke intrigued her, that she wanted to know more about him.

Now she didn't care. He interested her. She knew it. Since depositing Andy at the confectionery, how could she deny it? He more than interested her. He enthralled her, mystified her. A demon duke one moment. A philanthropist the next.

Skimming her feather duster along the wall

idly, she inched nearer the door. So what if he caught her? He already thought the worst of her. Thought her deceptive and borderline criminal.

With a quick glance over her shoulder, she closed a hand over the knob and eased open the door. Instantly the smell of charcoal, oils, and turpentine assailed her. The room felt stuffy with only its single window. Several canvases leaned against the walls, too many to count.

Bold splashes of paint met her gaze. Color was everywhere, within landscapes, portraits, still lifes. Even the poorly lit room could not diminish the vibrancy. But unlike anything she had ever seen at Trafalgar Square, this art was savage, wild and unapologetic in a way she knew only one man to be.

Realization dawned slowly. *A painter?* The duke lost himself in yet another exploit that wasn't wholly corrupt?

An easel stood near the window, seeking what little light the drizzly day had to offer. Fallon stepped farther into the sparse room, eyes narrowing, squinting against the glaring colors of the canvas sitting on the easel. The reds and browns and golds gradually took shape and definition. Became—*dear God*—her!

The great mass of her hair was as it used to be,

before she took a pair of scissors to it. Her face peeked out over one bare shoulder the color of an apricot. Her eyes shone darkly, alive, leaping from the canvas. Secrets gleamed in those eyes, warm with seductive promise. Her mouth was parted, lips wide, a deep pink. The mouth of a woman who knew . . . *things.*

*Is this how he sees me?*

She lifted a trembling hand, ready to brush them over the canvas.

"What are you doing in here?"

Her heart lurched. Dropping her hand, she spun around.

Before she could move, before she could speak, the duke was bearing down on her, long legs eating the distance separating them, a brutal gleam in his eyes.

Grasping her arm, he hauled her from the room. He flung her ahead of him as if he couldn't stand the feel of her. "Did I not warn you to stay out of there?"

Rubbing her arm where his touch burned like a brand, she demanded with far more daring than she felt. "Did you paint that of me?"

He glared at her. "Who else would have done it?"

She shook her head. "Why?"

"Why do I paint?" he snapped, his head cocking at a dangerous angle. "Or why did I paint you?"

She shook her head. *Both.*

His gaze blistered. "I like women." He shrugged. "In bed and on the canvas."

Fire lit her cheeks.

He motioned behind him, the gesture violent. "Did you care for the likeness?"

She lifted her chin, still grappling with the notion that the duke occupied himself in such a laudable pursuit. That, however unorthodox his style of art, he painted. *He painted her.* "It looks nothing like me. I'm not nearly so . . . interesting."

His gaze flickered over her. "Not in that ugly sack, true. But I've seen you more *interesting*. Without a stitch on."

"Oh!" Her face burned hotter, cheeks stinging as she recalled his intrusion in her room an instant after she emerged from her bath.

Their gazes locked, and she knew he was remembering everything about that night. He moved closer, his chest a wall of heat singeing her through her clothes. The anger had dissipated from his flushed face, but his eyes still burned on her with even greater threat than moments ago.

*I want you. You remain at your own peril.*

Yet here she stood, reminiscing over how his kiss tasted.

And then she remembered more. She remembered what happened when he had touched her, where—

A swift gasp cut through the charged air. "Your Grace, forgive us. We had hoped to finish before you returned."

Martha stood framed in the doorway, looking back and forth between them. Her gaze skittered to the open door of the duke's studio, and she shot Fallon an accusing glare. With a hard shake of her head, the older maid indicated Fallon should exit the room.

Glad to oblige and relieved at the interruption, Fallon turned, fleeing the room, the heat of Damon's stare following her as she fled.

In the future, until she found a way to remove herself from this mess, she would take care to never find herself alone with him again. Because next time Martha might not arrive to save her.

Fallon stood on her tiptoes, stretching for the canister of walnuts the Cook asked her to fetch. With a grunt, she ceased reaching for the impossibly high shelf. Hands propped on her hips, she fixed a considering glare on the inoffensive-looking jar.

"Let me help you with that."

Fallon turned, finding Daniel, the head foot-man, immediately behind her. She smiled at him, and his grin broadened in his narrow, freckled face.

He had been exceptionally kind to her since her "unveiling," paving the way for the other servants to do the same. That alone endeared him to her. Especially considering the less than warm welcome she had received when Mr. Adams first presented her to the staff. No doubt Mr. Adams's gimlet stare and Daniel's ready acceptance had saved her from total annihilation. Aside of a few snickers and side-long stares, no one treated her outright poorly. Well, no one save Nancy. The maid seemed disinclined to like her, no doubt embarrassed over her infatuation with *Francis*.

Fallon eyed the man who stood several inches shorter then herself. Rather than wound his ego by pointing out she was taller, she stepped aside. "I'm trying to reach the walnuts."

Soon he realized what she already surmised. He could no more reach the canister than she. Shooting her a determined glance, he hopped upon the lowest shelf and seized the canister, dropping back down to his feet with a flourish. With an elaborate bow, he presented it to her.

"Thank you, Daniel." She accepted the jar.

"Always happy to help a lady in need."

"Am I interrupting?"

Fallon and Daniel swung around to face the looming figure in the pantry's threshold. Her heart jumped a little in her chest at the familiar visage of the duke.

His lips barely moved as he spoke. A dark shadow passed over his hard features. "Isn't this a cozy scene."

Daniel made a sound in his throat that sounded like a chicken being strangled. "Y-Your Grace." Clicking his heels together, he bowed smartly.

Without even looking at the footman, the duke bit out, "Leave us."

"Yes, Your Grace." Daniel scurried past, dipping one last bow of deference. With a hasty, apologetic glance for Fallon, he disappeared from the pantry.

Her pulse hammered madly at her neck. She could not—*must* not—be alone with him. She stretched out a hand, her mouth parting, ready to call Daniel back.

"Good riddance," the duke drawled as the door to the pantry clicked shut. He leveled her with his intent stare. "I have you alone now. You may have escaped me earlier this afternoon, but no one can save you now."

She dropped her hand to her side. Fallon inhaled deeply against the sting of resentment his words elicited. "I don't need anyone to save me. I can look after myself."

"Indeed," he retorted, stepping close. Too close. "You're like a cat, is that it? Always landing on your feet. It hasn't taken you long to win over the men on my staff."

A small window high in the pantry's wall offered enough light for her to see the dark ring of blue around his irises. Beautiful and subtle, soft as undulating grass in the glow of moonlight. Ironic considering the hard bend of his lips.

He glanced at the door Daniel departed through, then back at her. His smoky gaze slid over her in a slow drag of heat. "Perhaps there's a reason you keep getting the sack."

Cold swept over her, effectively dousing the heat his gaze evoked. "Meaning what precisely?"

"You do have a way about you . . ."

Indignation began a slow creeping burn up her neck. "What *way* would that be?" Even as she asked the question, she was certain she would not like his answer.

He shrugged one shoulder. "You could be less provocative."

Anger churned through her stomach. She pressed a hand to her belly. "You think I bring unwelcome advances upon myself?" she demanded, the blood rising in her face.

He cocked his head. "Well, you were fending off the attentions of a man the first time I saw you. Every time I turn around, I find you in the same scenario. Even I have trouble keeping my hands to myself."

"You cannot be accusing me . . ."

He took a step closer, an encroaching wall of heat, and she saw from the hard glint in his eyes that he was not jesting. He thought her *responsible* when a man fawned over her?

His indigo blue jacket brushed the starched front of her dress, a bright splash of color against the muted gray of her dress. "Perhaps you should rethink what you *do* around men."

"What I *do* around men?"

As if she did anything deliberate. As if she set out to get sacked and put her livelihood in jeopardy. As if she enjoyed living one step from the streets.

"And what is that?" she spit out.

"Twist them into knots . . . make them want you even when they know they should not."

"Only an arrogant bastard born with the world bowed before him would say such a, a . . . stupid thing!" Her chest lifted on ragged breath, but she could not regret her outburst. Not even at the narrowing of his eyes or the deepening color in his cheeks. She jabbed him once in the chest. "Why not call me a whore?"

His hand closed over her hand, his grip hard, a warm pulsing manacle.

She wrenched her hand free and buried it in the fold of her skirts.

He was silent for some moments, tension emanating from him in waves as palpable as steam. When he at last spoke, his query gouged her, swiping at an already open wound. "I should be glad if you were, then we could stop these games and do what we really want to each other."

She flinched, his words too crude, too rough . . . too stark and thrilling in their honesty. Her palm swung toward him—without thought or deliberation—a blurring arc on the air.

For the second time in one week, she struck a duke.

Or tried, at any rate.

He ducked aside and she missed entirely. Rot! A small sound of distress escaped her tightly compressed lips and she swung again.

This time, he caught her hand.

She gave a fierce tug, but he would not surrender her hand. Anger swept through her in a savage burn. She fought to be free. Beyond control now, she swung again. He caught her other hand, too. Fallon stood there, both hands caught, and felt an utter fool.

With both hands imprisoned, he forced her back until her body met the wall of shelves in a noisy rattle of jars and crockery.

She gasped at the sudden move. With the sharp bite of shelves at her back, the hard wall of his body at her front, she could scarcely draw breath.

Their eyes locked, collided, battled with unspoken words. Tension crackled on the air. Awareness throbbed between them. His eyes smoldered, nostrils flaring.

She opened her mouth, but no words fell. A mistake.

His gaze dropped to her lips. The blue ring around his pupils darkened to near black. Her throat tightened. His head moved slightly, dipping, then stopped with his lips a hairsbreadth from her own.

A shutter fell over his eyes—the fire once there gone, banked.

Her heart twisted even more fiercely as his fingers began to loosen their grip on her hands.

*Now he would stop?*

Her heart sank and squeezed.

She felt his withdrawal, felt his body ease away, saw it in the impassivity stealing over his face. That single realization fired her blood. Before she could stop herself, before she could allow herself to *think*, her head shot forward, neck straining, lips seeking his with a desperation that bordered violence.

Shock rippled through her at the first brush of her lips on his. Warm and firm. Intoxicating. Sweeter, hotter, than even their last chocolate-laced kiss. She gasped against his mouth, taking his breath deep inside her.

One of his hands slid around her nape and hauled her closer yet. His lips stole over hers, moving, tasting, caressing, devouring. His tongue slipped inside her mouth and she knew heaven. On and on, they kissed. His hips shoved against hers. The prodding bulge of him very real, very large. The flat of his palm brushed down the front of her dress, between the vee of her breasts.

*No!* She tore her lips free with a gasp and wedged her hands between them, prepared to push him away . . . when the door to the pantry opened.

Fallon staggered free. Heaving serrated breaths, she covered her mouth with the back of her hand, horrified to have been caught by. . .

Her gaze turned to the door and her eyes settled on Nancy. *Grand.* The girl gaped from where she stood in the threshold, feasting large eyes on Fallon and the duke.

As mortification rolled over her, she considered the irony. She had found Nancy in a similar scenario with Lord Hunt. Heat scored her cheeks as she recalled her opinion of Nancy then. She judged her naïve. Easy prey. *A fool.* All the things Fallon prided herself too smart, too *good* to be.

How little she knew herself. The woman she claimed to be, the woman she *wanted* to be, would never give any part of herself—especially her heart—to a blue-blooded devil who swam in vice and possessed a stone for a heart. Her throat thick with emotion, she averted her eyes from Nancy's smirk.

With the duke's intent stare burning on her, she lifted her skirts and fled the pantry, shoving past Nancy . . . her fingers pressed to lips that still tingled in a manner she vowed to forget.

# Chapter 22

"**W**ho is that?"
Dominic followed Hunt's gaze, spying Fallon gathering flowers in the garden with another maid. He grimaced, preferring not having to explain Fallon's little deception.

With a shrug, he attempted to continue the conversation regarding Britain's war with China. Only Hunt no longer participated. A rapt expression on his face, he rose to his feet and strode to the French doors, peering out at Fallon as she kneeled among bulbs of tulips.

Dominic scowled. "Ethan?"

"Hmm?"

"What are you doing?"

"Simply admiring the view."

Dominic tapped a finger impatiently upon the boot crossed over his knee, clearing his throat a time or two in the hope of regaining Hunt's attention. He wondered if it would be bad form to strike a friend of twenty-odd years for ogling a maid in his employ—a female whose existence should scarcely register upon his consciousness. And yet she did. Painfully so. She haunted his every moment, waking or asleep. As she had for some time. Even before he realized her identity.

"Something dashed familiar about her."

If ever a moment arose to explain his valet's disappearance and Fallon's sudden appearance, Dominic supposed it was now. But for some reason he held his tongue, preferring to keep Fallon's unseemly and fraudulent behavior his affair alone. "I am certain you have never seen her before."

"Likely so." He nodded. "How could one forget someone like her?" Hunt shot him a quick glance. "She must be new, eh." Without waiting for an answer, he asked, "Is she as tall as she looks?"

His lips twisted. *Tall enough to pass for a man.*

"I suppose," he returned, rising to stand beside Hunt at the doors overlooking the garden. "I have never made a study of her." Surprisingly, he did not choke on the lie. If he closed his eyes, he could still taste her on his lips.

Hunt smiled. "No? You never imagined those legs wrapped around you?"

His throat tightened at the immediate image. Fallon's long legs wrapped around his hips as he drove into her had become a favorite fantasy. "I'd appreciate it if you quit ogling the girl."

"Look at her." Ethan waved a hand. "She's a woman that demands a second look." His lips twitched. "And a third."

Wasn't that the problem Fallon had alluded to when defending her charade? The very thing that had prompted her to don a pair of trousers and pretend to be a man? She was just too damn noticeable.

He cleared his throat. "Ethan, I'm aware you've made free with some of the other maids—"

Ethan blinked in a mocking display of guile-lessness. "Me?"

"I would appreciate it if you leave Fallon alone. Leave all of them alone, for that matter."

"Fallon, is it?"

He grimaced, regretting using her Christian name.

"I can't help it if the women on your staff find me charming."

He nodded in Fallon's direction through the glass. "I can assure you that she is one female disinclined to the persuasions of a nobleman." She had made clear her aversion to *blue bloods*.

"Already tried, have you?"

A flash of Fallon as he'd seen her emerging from her bath, a wet towel plastered to her body made his blood burn. To say nothing of how she had *felt*. If he had wanted, she could have been his. He shook his head. Fine time for him to grow a sense of honor.

"No," he murmured. "Believe it or not, I don't dally with the women in my employ."

"How noble of you. Fortunately, I am not held to such restrictions." He fairly rubbed his palms together as he gazed out the window.

"Oh, but you are, my friend," he warned, not caring whether he sounded possessive or not.

With an eyebrow cocked, Hunt cut him a sharp glance. "Am I?"

Dominic held his gaze a moment before looking out the window again, his gaze traveling along the elegant line of Fallon's neck as she bent over flowers. She brushed her face with her hand, swiping ineffectually at the russet strands curling against her cheek. "Leave this one alone."

Almost as if she heard him . . . or felt him, Fallon looked up. Their eyes collided across the distance. Her gaze flicked to Hunt beside him. Some of the color bled from her cheeks. She murmured something to the other maid and rose, hastily weaving a path from the garden.

Ethan's voice dragged his attention from her retreating form. "You sound jealous. Certain you aren't staking a claim for yourself? Just say so. No need to play at the honorable gentleman. We both know you are not." Hunt snorted. "Neither one of us are. That is why we get on so well. Always have."

Indeed. A statement he could not deny for its veracity.

"Claim?" he scoffed and forced himself to move away from the window. "She's not a country to be conquered. Merely a woman. And one of no special interest to me." It was a wonder the words did not choke him.

"On the contrary. I find that a perfect metaphor." Hunt lowered himself back down into a wingchair. "A woman is to be conquered like any parcel of land."

Dominic's hands curled around the arms of his chair. "Remind me why I choose to associate with you?"

Hunt laughed. "We're a pair, you and I. Why else?"

"Hmm." Suddenly being as iniquitous as Hunt did not sit well with him. He flicked a hand in the direction of the garden. "Just keep your paws to yourself."

"Of course." A wicked grin curved Hunt's mouth that did not engender a great deal of faith. "What are friends for?"

Dominic shook his head, disgusted and wondering if he and Hunt were truly alike. And, he realized with a start, when had he cared at the distinction?

"Well. Well. Good afternoon."

Fallon's gaze snapped up, her fingers nearly losing their grip on the pitcher of water she held. Hugging the carafe to her chest, she bobbed a quick curtsey as Lord Hunt approached, his boots clicking lightly upon the foyer floor. Darting a quick glance to her left and right, she tried to judge the quickest escape route. Then it occurred to her that running away might appear a bit odd and attract the close scrutiny she precisely wished to avoid from him. Grinding her teeth, she rose from her curtsey.

He stopped before her and dipped a sharp bow. A bow one might present to a lady and not a lowly maid in a duke's household. Unable to stop herself, she felt her brow wing high.

"Allow me to introduce myself, Ethan Waverly, Viscount Hunt."

Ah, a formal introduction, too. Did he think her like simpering Nancy? Easily impressed and ready to lift her skirts at the slightest acknowledgment from him?

With a deferential nod, she tried to step past, careful to keep her face averted. No longer disguised, she hoped he did not recognize her. Although he certainly never paid much mind to the gardener's daughter. Too occupied chasing after the skirts of older girls. Still, she would prefer not risking him reaching the realization that they once shared a home.

Never a home, she quickly amended. For however safe she had felt there with Da to look after her, it had never been her home. Only Hunt's.

He settled a hand on her arm, pulling her close with the boldness of man accustomed to having whatever he wanted. *Whomever* he wanted. Staring at him, his face blurred and became his father's the day he called her into his study to impart the news of Da's death—so punctilious as he informed her that she would never see her father again.

"Come now, is Damon such a slave driver you cannot . . ." his voice faded. Dread curled in her belly as his dark gaze scanned her face intently, missing nothing it seemed, skimming her features, drifting over her hair until recognition lit his gaze.

"Where do I know you from?"

What could she say?

*I'm the daughter of the man your father killed?*

*I'm the duke's valet you disliked so much?*

Before she had time to formulate a response, his voice escaped in a croak, "Fallon." Shock washed over the chiseled lines of his face, echoing the astonishment rippling through her. "Fallon O'Rourke."

The sound of her name on his lips fed panic to her heart. He should not know her. Should *not* remember her.

Wrenching her arm free, she managed two steps before he forced her around again, his hands clamping down on each arm.

"What are you doing here?" he demanded . . . almost as though she should be someplace else. Almost as if it mattered one way or another to him *where* she happened to be.

"Working," she bit out. "I work for a living, Lord Hunt. Just as my father before me. I am quite certain you remember him," she charged, her voice scathing.

"I searched for you—"

"Why?" she bit out. "Your family washed their hands of me years ago, eased their guilt by putting me through Penwich."

He started at the mention of the school. "Yes, Penwich! I went there."

"Good for you." She struggled against his hold. "You should visit again. Yorkshire is lovely this time of year. Now let me go."

"No. You don't understand. I went there looking for you. Only last year."

"Ethan."

The sound of Lord Hunt's name fell hard as a stone dropping. She tensed, recognizing that voice at once, feeling it vibrate in her very bones. Dominic approached, his boots emitting softly dangerous clicks on the marble floor. "Care to remove your hands from my . . ." His voice faded.

Heat scalded her face at the *"my"* he left hanging in the air. They all three exchanged glances. Tension, palpable and pungent, began a slow churn on the air.

Lord Hunt answered at last. "I will. If she promises not to run away."

"What business is it of yours what she does?" A muscle rippled in Dominic's hard jaw, and she knew he issued no idle threat. "Now unhand her before I mop the floor with you."

Hunt flushed, an occurrence she would have thought impossible in the scoundrel. Of all things, she would never have credited him with any sense of sobriety. He was all snideness and levity. Typical blue blood.

Even with Dominic's threat hovering, he did not release her. Her arms began to hurt where he held her, but she hid her grimace.

"It doesn't concern you, Dom. We have history, she and I."

"History?" Dominic stalked forward. Grabbing her arm at the elbow, he yanked her free. He turned a blistering gaze on her—as if *she* had committed some great sin—before looking back at his friend. "Of what history do you speak—"

"This doesn't concern—"

"Say that again and you'll be picking your teeth up off the floor." That muscle now jumped wildly in his jaw, and in that moment Dominic looked the utter savage, and quite capable of doing precisely such a barbaric thing. And more.

Lord Hunt inhaled, his chest swelling. "Fallon and I grew up together—"

"Hardly," she inserted with a bitter laugh. "You were the master's son. I was but the gardener's daughter . . . too young for your perversions, so thankfully you never attended to me—"

Face ruddy, Hunt spit out, "I'm trying to explain something, damn it. My father made a provision for you in his will. He always felt somewhat responsible—"

"*Somewhat?* Only somewhat? He sent my father to the Seychelles Islands—the blasted ends of the earth! And why?" She felt her lips curl back from her teeth as she snarled, "To retrieve a flower for his blasted gardens!" Tears clogged her throat, but she could not stop herself. The floodgates opened. "Did he ever once think of the risk? The dangers to my father? The long year he would be gone from me?" She snorted and took a steadying breath. "Of course a year only turned into a lifetime."

"I visited Penwich and spoke with a man named Brocklehurst," Hunt went on as though she had not spoken. "He did not know where I could locate you."

She scoffed. "Oh, he knew." The headmaster at least knew he could ask Evie. "Brocklehurst would not relish good fortune falling my way. Would you like to know what he *did* relish?" She advanced a step, Dominic's warm grasp on her arm keeping her from charging forward in full pique. "Beatings. He enjoyed beating us. Teaching us God's word with each swipe of his rod. He enjoyed watching us starve . . . and suffer through the cold of winter with poor shoes and threadbare blankets."

"Fallon, don't," Dominic's soft directive fluttered the tiny hairs near her ear. His fingers roved in small circles against her arm, and even in her anger, she felt a small, unwelcome thrill.

She ignored him, finishing. "Next time you stand over *your* father's grave, thank him for his generosity in sending me to such a place."

A muscle feathered along the viscount's cheek. "I did not know. Nor did my father. I am sorry for that. He wanted to do right by you." Hunt straightened and reached inside his jacket. With numb fingers, she accepted the card he extended. "In any case, keep this should you change your mind. On his deathbed he charged me with the task of finding you and seeing you secured. It is a task I do not take lightly."

Dominic's hand softened where he held her, becoming less a shackle on her arm. Without thinking, she leaned against him, suddenly needing the support and uncertain that she would not collapse in a boneless puddle.

Lord Hunt straightened, rigid as a tin soldier, his dark eyes flinty as he looked down at her.

The sudden fall of footsteps filled the charged silence. Mrs. Davies appeared, face etched in concern. "Your Grace?" Several maids hovered behind her.

"Go away," Dominic barked.

The housekeeper and maids scurried away, leaving the three of them in the vast foyer. *Grand.* More rumors for the servants. Ever since Nancy found her in the pantry with Dominic, her life had been a torment. Nancy had wasted no time divulging all she had witnessed. Every time Fallon entered a room, indiscreet whispers floated to her ears. Words like *harlot* and *whore* were uttered loudly enough. Even Daniel and Mr. Adams no longer met her gaze.

"I am sorry for that," Hunt intoned. "But my father did set you up at the Penwich School. He did not abandon you to the gutter or the wolves of the world following your father's death."

Suddenly Master Brocklehurst's gaunt, pitiless face appeared in her mind . . . resembling very much a ravaging wolf.

Hunt continued, "And he has left you a stipend that should afford you some independence and comfort."

As if that could substitute a father. Her head dipped to hide the angry tears brimming in her eyes. "I don't even have a grave to visit. But you think money will make amends?" So like a blue blood. Throw money at a problem—at *guilt*—and expect it to disappear. Her head shot back up, spine straight. Not this time. "I don't want your money. Stuff it."

Lord Hunt's eyes widened. "I beg your pardon?"

"Don't you understand? You can't make it right." She drew a ragged breath and twisted her arm free of Dominic.

"I am certain I can. Perhaps there is something else I can offer." Hunt's throat worked. "Is it marriage you want?"

"Marriage?" She jerked her head as though slapped.

*"Marriage,"* Dominic echoed.

"Does not every woman long for marriage? A good match, that is? Half the mamas in Town are hounding me for that very thing. I can sponsor you. Rather, my mother can. We can arrange a good match for you. A *beyond* good match. With my connections, I can perhaps even land you a title. It's likely more than you've ever aspired to achieve." He flicked a disdainful glance over her starched gray uniform.

*Of all the arrogance. . .*

"You'll sell her in marriage!" Dominic stared hard at Hunt and took a sudden step his way, dragging her with him. He stopped, his free hand closing at his side in a white-knuckled fist. The incredulity in his voice rankled and she tugged free.

Hunt blinked, clearly befuddled. "It *is* done in our circles, Dom. Plenty of titled lords' pockets run short. And she's fetching enough." His eyes roamed her in appreciation. "A sight more than last season's crop of debs."

*"Her?* Fallon? A maid?" Dominic shook his head.

"And why must you sound so astonished?" she demanded, even though she knew. She was nobody. A servant. The daughter of an Irish gardener.

Dominic stared at her, mouth parted on words that would not fall.

Hunt shrugged. "My family owes her a debt."

"My father's life is a mere debt to be paid, is that it?" She glared at the two men before her, staggering back several steps.

Both men loomed before her, everything she had come to loathe. Overprivileged blue bloods who could never understand where she came from . . . or what she hoped to achieve in this life.

Because they already possessed what she most craved.

Freedom. Security. Freedom from the likes of them. Security in a home of her own where she need never answer to anyone.

Disgusted, she turned and fled.

# Chapter 23

**"H**ungry?"

Whirling around, the bread Fallon clutched slid from her fingers and hit the ground. It struck the stone floor with a thud and rolled several feet, bumping into the tip of one black shining Hessian boot. The bite she chewed turned to dust in her mouth. Her teeth worked faster, quickly chewing the remaining bread.

Her gaze lifted, settling on Dominic's hard face. His eyes, relentless chips of ice, drilled into her through the room's flickering shadows.

She rubbed a sweaty palm against her skirts and swallowed.

He approached, his steps tapping and echoing lightly in the cavernous room. As he moved, orange light from the flickering fire licked his features, lending him a demonic appearance. A dark angel from hell. Fitting, she supposed, for the *demon duke.*

"Did you not eat dinner?" he asked, his voice flat and emotionless.

She chafed one hand against her arm. "I wasn't hungry earlier."

Too many speculative stares. Too many smirks. Even Daniel had muttered an unflattering remark beneath his breath loud enough for her to hear. No one needed to explain it to her. The sudden cold wind that blew through the servants' quarters whenever she entered a room had everything to do with the duke's unprecedented visit to the kitchens followed by the ugly scene in the foyer earlier today. She was mud in the eyes of the staff. Only another reason for her to look to the horizon, to end this and find a situation elsewhere. Somehow.

Dominic stopped before her, his booted feet sliding over the stone floor with a nerve-grating scrape.

She watched with growing dread as he crossed his arms and surveyed her with glittering eyes. "But you're hungry now?"

A shiver coursed through her. Suddenly, she suspected he wasn't talking about food and she could not find the words to answer him.

"I imagine if you accepted Viscount Hunt's offer, you would have your own servants to call forth in the middle of the night to deliver you a veritable feast." A faint sneer laced his voice.

She lifted her chin. "I imagine I would."

His gaze slid over her, dark and unreadable. "Of course, as some lord's wife, you would have to permit him a feast of his own in exchange for the honor of his name." The way his head tilted back to scan her body, she did not mistake his meaning.

"Are you deliberately crude?" she snapped. Weariness swept over her. She tired of the fight. All her life, since Da left her, it seemed she only ever fought to survive.

"I speak only the truth. Of course you could simply take the stipend Hunt offers." He nodded as though she very well should. "You could then raid your own kitchen in the middle of the night and need not share your bed with some fine lord."

"A more appealing circumstance to be certain," she agreed, a scenario she did, in fact, find rather tempting. She had thought of little else. Aside of Dominic's blistering kiss in the pantry. She never thought a man could make her feel as he did. Hot and cold all at once.

She didn't know how large the provision Hunt offered, but she would not require much to achieve her dream of independence. Hunt had promised her a life of comfort. Could it be possible? Could the home she always dreamed of be within her reach? Bitterness coated her mouth. If only she accepted the money. Blood money.

She lifted her chin, but said nothing, merely held Dominic's stare, determined he not know how easily his presence rattled her. The silence in the kitchen was suffocating. He was suffocating, an encroaching wall closing in on her.

She had to get away. Now. Tonight. *Forever.*

"Perhaps this is a good opportunity to discuss a proposition."

"A proposition?" He cocked his head to the side, those gray eyes lighting with interest. "Do tell."

She squared her shoulders. "While I appreciate your letting me remain on your staff—" she broke off. "Truly, you've been more than—"

He held up a hand. "Spare me the platitudes. What do you want?"

"I would like a letter of reference."

His features stormed over. "Why?"

"So that I may . . . move on. Leave."

"Hmm. Should I detail your penchant for attiring yourself as a man and passing yourself off as footmen?"

Indignation swept through her. Would he forever hold that over her?

But of course he would. As long as she resided under this roof, it would forever be there between them. "Let's do be honest, Your Grace. This situation is not working out."

"For you," he rejoined.

Her thoughts leapt to their kiss in the pantry. The kiss *she* initiated. Unlike the intimacies shared in the carriage. Or in her valet's room following her bath. She had been the one to move her head that last inch and press her mouth to his. Shameless. And she feared her resistance may fail her again. He had warned her to leave. Warned her that he wanted her.

"For both of us," she finally answered.

He rocked back on his heels, pinning her with his silvery stare. "Ah, you're concerned for me, then? How altruistic."

"A letter would be vastly appreciated."

"Why not ask Hunt? He would be glad to assist you. His family is beholden to you, after all. For that matter, why not take his offer—"

"I want nothing from him."

"Ah." He nodded, as if understanding, as if *seeing* her. "I never took you for the spiteful, stubborn sort."

"I'm not spiteful! Nor stubborn."

"No? Seems to me that you are. You're punishing Hunt for the sins of his father. Even if it means hurting yourself. Spiteful *and* stubborn."

She ground her teeth together, not liking his words . . . especially as they might have struck upon the truth. "May I have a reference or not?"

He angled his head as though considering her request, then bit out a single, emphatic, "No."

"No?"

"No," he repeated in the most affable of tones. "You claim difficulty in maintaining a position, and yet here you have one you're prepared to toss aside. Not very sensible."

She shook her head, his refusal making her feel very much like a caged animal—robbed of choices and any hope for escape. Her desperate thoughts tripped back over those moments in her room, naked with the duke. His mouth on her. His hands. The intimate press of his fingers on her thighs, sliding *inside* her . . .

She could not shake free of the memory. She could not trust herself. Since discovering her a woman, he had kissed her, touched her, melted her with a look. *Upon every single occasion.* And she had let him. At this rate, she would be in his bed before the week's end.

She glanced around the empty kitchen, acutely aware of their aloneness. Her heartbeat accelerated to a heavy drumming in her ears. *You remain at your own peril.*

The driving impulse to flee, to escape, seized her. She tried to step past him. His arms came up, hands bracing the edge of the table, hemming her in.

"Let me go," she ground out, punctuating each word for emphasis.

His gaze scanned her face. A muscle ticked madly in his jaw. "You're not leaving." His words fell hard, savagely. The pulse at her neck jumped, a wild beast looking to escape her body . . . just as she needed to escape him.

"You don't own me. You can't keep me here." She dragged fortifying air into her too tight chest. "I don't need your letter of reference," she tossed out the last bit with more bravado than wisdom, thrusting her chin higher. Without a reference, she had little hope of gaining another respectable position. Which only left the *disreputable* ones.

*Better than surrendering to him. To losing your pride. Losing yourself.*

"Stubborn wench," he growled. "Can you not *try* to make your life easier? Must you forever take the most difficult path? You won't take the stipend old Hunt left you? Fine. But you have security here, you little fool." He jerked his head hard in the direction of the doorway. "Out there, you don't know what waits you."

"Security?" she snorted, thinking of how unsettled he made her feel . . . and how the other servants treated her as a pariah. She scarcely felt *secure*.

"Yes, security," he shot back. "And you could have more, if you so wished."

"More?" Skepticism laced her voice. "Like what?"

Something flickered in his gaze beneath the fringe of dark lashes. The barest hint of emotion. Vulnerability. Sentiment entirely unexpected from him. Then it was gone, like smoldering embers banked with a splash of cold water. He gazed at her with unreadable eyes.

His lips parted. "You could have me."

Her heart clenched at the stark invitation. Elation swelled in her chest. Dangerously sweet. Elation she had no business feeling. She could not *have* him. Anymore than he could have her.

"Impossible."

"Why?" His lips twisted, eyes storming over a tumultuous gray. "Because it offends your oh-so-*proper* sensibilities?"

"We can't *have* each other. You're a duke. I'm a maid." She swallowed in the face of his darkening scowl. "And we don't even like one another."

He laughed darkly, the menacing sound rippling through her and giving her goose bumps. "Ah, you're going to try and pretend nothing exists between us now. Interesting tact. And so easy to disprove."

He leaned closer, his hard chest pressing into her, arching her back over the table.

"W-what are you doing?"

He scoured her with a fierce glare. "Putting it to the test. Never could pass on a challenge—"

"No," she denied, shaking her head fiercely. "I did not mean to—"

"Too late," he pronounced, his gaze dropping, fixing on her lips with feverish intensity. "I've longed to continue where we left off in the pantry."

Her chest lifted on a sharp exhalation. "You promised I would be safe in your household."

"A promise I seem to recall retracting in my carriage." Still gazing at her lips, he replied distractedly. "I did not take into account that I would not be safe from you."

"Me?" she squeaked.

"You're far too tempting." He shrugged. "So

I changed my mind. Never was the honorable sort."

"Convenient," she bit out, arching her back over the table. An image of the parade of women to breeze through his life since they first met flashed through her mind.

"You were warned."

"Certainly you don't need me to slake your lust. You can find any number of eager females and leave me be. Shall I send for one? Perhaps you've forgotten their names? Celeste, Gracie, Jenny. I confess even I cannot recall the names of the two females in the carriage with you the night we first met, but I'm certain I could try to—"

"Always a cheeky remark." His gaze flicked from her eyes to her lips. "No wonder you've met with such trouble. Your past dismissals must have held some merit."

Fury swam through her at his words. All the more because she feared there was a kernel of truth to them, feared that her bold ways may have resulted in her inability to maintain a post.

"And perhaps," she spit out, aiming for his Achilles, "your grandfather is *right* about you."

His eyes darkened. An utter stillness came over him as he pressed against her. "Tread carefully. You know nothing of what you speak."

Still, she could not hold her tongue, could not stop herself from forging ahead with her final stinging accusation, flinging the very words he claimed his grandfather charged him with: "Perhaps you are the devil."

He moved then, grabbed her by the back of the head, fingers digging cruelly through her hair as he tilted her face toward his. "And what kind of fool does that make you? Toying with such a man as me—*the devil himself*?"

Her heart squeezed in her chest. In a panic, she wondered, indeed, what kind of fool that made her. She tried to speak. Words gurgled at the back of her throat, incomprehensible.

"And have you not toyed with me from the start?" He shoved his hips against her, trapping her lower body between the table and the hard wall of his body.

She gasped. Hot desire licked her body. Her hand fumbled behind her, knocking several bowls aside, closing around an object on the table. She brought it up in the air, only realizing at the last moment it was merely a thick wooden spoon. *Grand.* Unfortunate she couldn't have grabbed a heavier piece of crockery. She swung the spoon toward his head.

The slap of his hand around her fingers echoed

in the cavernous room. His harsh laughter scraped the air, rising to the rafters and infuriating her. His fingers squeezed until she dropped her would-be weapon.

He flicked a disgusted look down at the spoon. "A great fool, it would seem. What were you going to do with that? Serve me soup?"

"I had hoped to crack it over your skull."

His lips twisted in a savage smile. She eyed the arms on either side of her, imposing and hard.

He trapped her so effortlessly against the table. Her eyes moved to his and she couldn't look away. Slowly, she stopped struggling, stilling altogether, forgetting all the reasons she needed to fight him. She saw only his eyes. His face. His mouth.

His fingers in her hair softened, but his grip was no less firm as he angled her head back, up-turning her face for him.

Her breath rattled loose in a hoarse hiss as he pressed the side of his face against hers, his cheek rough and scratchy against her own. "You think running away will make you forget me?" His warm breath puffed against her ear and her belly trembled, tightened. *Remembered*.

No. She knew she wouldn't. But then she didn't have to forget him. She just had to get away.

Taking small sips of air to control her ragged

breathing, she shook her head, which only brought her face closer, rasping against his. Her pulse skittered at a mad rate, her heart thumping hard as a drum in her chest. The barrier of the table dug into the back of her hips.

With a suddenness that made her gasp, his hands circled her waist. He hefted her onto the table, settling himself between her thighs as if it were the most natural thing to do. For him, she supposed it was. And strangely, it felt natural—right—to her, too.

*Thinking*, however, no longer felt natural. Or right. All thought fled as his hands moved from her waist to her skirts, gathering them in his fists and hiking them to her waist in a single rough move. His fingers grazed a searing trail along her quivering thighs. Her breath hitched in a strange little hiccup of sound. Feelings ruled. Sensations sang through her body.

He spread his hand over her thigh, a large searing brand on her quivering flesh. His mouth closed over her lips, kissing her until her hands fell on the table, palms flat on the worn-wood surface. His hands moved between them, fumbling first at his trousers, then between her legs. The sound of tearing fabric rent the air. Then his fingers were on her, playing against her. He found the little nub buried in her folds and rubbed, pressed, squeezed until she bucked against his hand.

She whimpered, thrusting her hips off the table to meet him. He eased a finger inside her, working it slowly in, stretching her until a low moan spilled loose. Ducking his head, he claimed her lips, taking the sound deep into his mouth. He drank greedily from her, his kiss deepening, slick tongue sliding against hers in a sinuous dance.

She groaned as his finger withdrew, her hips moving forward, seeking. Her center burned, ached, clenched with need . . .

He tore his lips from hers with a broken gasp. Their heavy breaths mingled between them, warm as vapor. He dropped his forehead to hers, his silvery eyes clung to hers, probing, seeking, reading in her own unblinking stare what her mind—body—screamed. *Yes.*

Then she felt him nudging at her opening, pushing inside her. Bigger. Harder than the earlier stroke of his fingers. Thrilling. Frightening. Invasive.

She hissed at the burning pleasure, the searing stretch of her inner muscles. Deeper, he penetrated her, until the pleasure ebbed, giving way to pain.

Wincing, she tried to slide back. With a groan,

his fingers seized her hips, anchoring her. Holding her still, he surged against her in a final push, burying himself to the hilt, his member pulsing inside her.

She cried out at the swift and piercing pain, her arms trembling where they braced upon the table. Cursing him, she tried to wiggle free.

One of his hands flew to the back of her head. His mouth was on hers again, feverish and hungry. He kissed her until the pain dulled, eddied. A low-throbbing ache started between her legs, matching the pulsing rhythm of his member buried there.

He slid himself out, nearly withdrawing completely before easing inside her again. She whimpered, a long mewling sound that did not sound quite human. Something else burned at her center now, and her legs parted wider without will or volition. Her pelvis turned upward on the table, seeking with an instinct she did not understand.

He held himself still inside her, kissing her until she could no longer feel her lips. Until breath eluded her, unnecessary fuel to her lungs as long as she had him. His mouth, his hands . . . his body fused with hers.

His hand fell on her breast. He palmed the mound through her gown, his fingers finding the peak, rolling and squeezing her nipple until it poked against the front of her dress in an aching little point. Moisture gathered between her legs, but still he did not move.

She writhed on the table beneath him, dark, desperate sounds escaping her lips. She tangled a hand in his hair, pulling roughly on the strands. He awarded her the barest movement, grinding himself in little circles inside her, rubbing the sensitive little nub. She broke free of his lips, hissing her need with a sharp cry. She lifted her calves and locked her ankles around his hips.

"Please," she begged, rocking against him.

His eyes stared down at her, silvery as the moonlight streaming from the window far above.

With a knowledge she did not know she possessed, she clenched her inner muscles around him in repeated clutches.

Moaning, he dropped his head to the crook of her neck and began moving. Fast and fierce, thrusting in and out of her, pounding with unchecked savagery. And still she wanted more. Wanted all. Head tossing back, a scream poured from her lips, drowned out as his mouth covered hers. She shattered inside.

Ripples of delight washed over. She trembled as he pumped into her, the smacking sound of his body against hers thrilling and primitive in a way she never imagined. With a shudder and deep groan of his own, he finished, pouring himself deep inside her.

Panting from exertion, she flexed her fingers where they clutched his head, holding him close as realization slowly dawned. *The demon duke had just ravished her atop the kitchen table.* And she had loved—*exulted*—in every minute of it.

The remnants of desire gradually ebbed from her body, faint tremors playing out along her nerves. She trembled as he lifted his head, his gaze colliding with hers. Still lodged inside her, she felt him pulse, twitch. The sensation was surreal and not a little intoxicating. It was almost as though they were one being. Connected. A bond she had never felt before. From the intense gleam in his eyes, he did not appear any more eager than she to sever that connection.

For moments, they did not move, did not stir beyond their chests rising and falling with matching breath. Staring into his eyes, her fingers curled in the silken strands of his hair, she wished that she never had to move, never had to break the magic of the moment. She closed her eyes in a pained blink. An impossible dream.

He must have reached the same conclusion. Mouth pressing into a recalcitrant line, he withdrew himself from her body, leaving her bereft, empty. The same as before. And yet not.

Different because she now knew what it felt like to lie in his arms and hold him so tight that she did not know where she began and ended. To feel him move over her. In her. A bloody *duke*. A man she could never have.

But one she would forever want.

# Chapter 24

**D**ominic quickly rearranged his clothing, his gaze never straying from her. Taking her hand, he helped her slide from the table. On her feet again, she wobbled, her legs clearly unsteady.

He cursed himself for taking her on a kitchen table with all the finesse of a thoughtless bastard. She had been a virgin, for God's sake. *A virgin.* She deserved more. Better. He would give her that still. He tried to convey this with his eyes . . . while not uttering an apology. Because for all his lack of finesse, he did not regret making love to her. Virgin or not. Kitchen table or not. Selfish bastard or not.

"Come," he murmured, leading her from the room. She followed, readily, willingly. Without question. Surprising perhaps for her. He led her silently up the servants' stairs, down empty, hallowed corridors of flickering light and shadows. Directly to his bedchamber.

At the foot of his bed, he turned her to face him. Her wide amber eyes gazed up at him and his gut twisted. A single gold-streaked lock of russet hair fell over her forehead. He brushed it back, allowing his thumb to trail her cheek. She tilted her face into his touch.

"What you do to me," he whispered.

Slowly, he began to undress her, taking care to kiss her warm flesh as he exposed every delectable inch. She quivered beneath his mouth, his hands. Naked, he eased her back on the bed. Sprawled on the counterpane, her skin was a pale peach against the stark white—the most enticing display of womanhood his eyes ever feasted upon. All long lines and gentle curves. He could scarcely tear his gaze away as he moved to the basin. Returning, he parted her thighs. She sighed as he pressed the wet cloth between her legs, cleaning her with leisurely swipes, unable to stop himself from caressing the creamy skin as he did.

Moaning, she arched her spine off the bed. Dropping the cloth, he stroked her with his fingers until she grew frenzied beneath his touch. Standing over her, he hastily shucked off his clothes and joined her on his bed.

He roamed hands over her legs. "I've dreamed of these," he muttered between nibbling kisses along her calves and thighs.

She released a sharp giggle when his lips brushed the side of her knee. His chest swelled at the sweet sound. He curved a hand around one knee, then the other, tickling the backs, enjoying the sound of her laughter. His chest tightened and he vowed to hear it more often. Twisting, she snatched hold of his hand, ending his tickling.

She held his hand closely to her breasts, her laughter fading as she looked steadily into his eyes. Her thumb roved small circles inside his palm, caressing the raised ridge of his scar, sliding over the bumpy line. He tensed. She dropped her gaze to his palm. His throat constricted as she studied the evidence of his *privileged* childhood.

Tracing the puckered scar, she arched a reddish brow. "How did you get this?"

"It's nothing. A scar from childhood."

Her brow winged higher, the question still clear in her expressive eyes.

Sighing, he found himself confessing, "My grandfather assigned me to the tender mercies of an overly zealous nanny. This is punishment for playing cards with Hunt and a few of the stable lads." His lips twisted at the memory, wondering what inspired him to confide in her. He'd never shared that particular incident of his twisted childhood with anyone. He fought too hard to forget it all to lend it a voice. And yet he had done just that.

"He let her do this?"

Dominic could still see his grandfather's cold expression in his mind as he assessed Mrs. Pearce's handiwork. While he perhaps did not wholly approve, he had done nothing to remove the woman from Wayfield Park. "Grandfather disapproves of gambling. He might have thought the hot poker to my hand excessive, but he saw Mrs. Pearce's intentions as pure." He smiled grimly. "Neither wanted me to fall victim to the evils of gambling as my father did."

She sucked in a sharp breath. "How old were you?"

"Nine."

"And did you ever play cards again?"

He smiled grimly. "Every chance I get."

With utter tenderness, she pressed her mouth to his palm, tracing the scar with her lips. The gentle gesture undid him.

He cupped the back of her head and brought her to him, sealing her lips with his own in a savage kiss. Rolling her beneath him, he readily fell between her parted legs, entering her in one slick thrust.

He moved inside her, past tenderness, past gentleness. His need for her in that moment put him far beyond the slow, easy lovemaking he had planned for her—what he knew she deserved.

She didn't seem to mind. Her nails scored his back, and she took him in, greedily clenching around him, the perfect glove, milking him as he moved faster, harder, determined to forget the past she had revived, determined to forget everything save her and the perfect fit of their bodies locked together.

Fallon carefully removed the heavy arm from around her waist. Setting it down on the bed beside her, she climbed from what had to be the most comfortable bed she ever slept upon and stood looking down at Dominic. Because it was over. This perfect night, the perfect madness, had come to an end. As she had known it would. As she knew it must.

The night peeked between the drapes an indigo blue, hinting at the approaching dawn.

From the moment he first put his lips to hers, she knew that she would succumb and surrender to the infernal need that burned through her whenever he was near. But no more. Tonight was the last time she would ever permit herself to forget who she was. And who he was.

Doubtlessly, he would lose interest in her now, and she could go about her life, saving her wages for the day she would leave servitude forever behind. The prospect, however true, made her chest tighten almost painfully. She could return to her duties with no fear of losing her way again. Or perhaps he would now grant her that reference. Now that he was finished with her. Now that he'd had his fill.

She quickly dressed, her gaze feasting on the long length of him, hungrily memorizing every detail, memories that would keep her company in the future. Sighing, she finished her last button and turned away, hurrying from his room and hastening to her own before any of the other servants roused.

The night was over.

And a full day's work loomed ahead.

# Chapter 25

**D**ominic dressed quickly, sending several lingering glances to the bed as early morning crept through the small part in the drapery. He had thought to wake with Fallon's warm body snug against him, the first of many mornings to come he had decided some time during the night. He had never entertained the notion of keeping a mistress before, but with Fallon, it seemed a natural solution. *The only solution.* He wouldn't stand for her continuing on as a maid. Nor would he tolerate her sneaking from his bed every morning.

In the event he should ever tire of her—a circumstance hard to imagine with last night still so fresh on his mind—he would bestow a beyond-comfortable settlement upon her. She need never work again. A satisfactory arrangement for both of them. He smiled, suddenly . . . happy. Buoyant. Emotions he could not quite recall feeling before.

Who would ever have thought the demon duke would take a mistress? It was the closest to domesticity he had ever come. Or ever would.

Eager to find her, he pulled open the door and set off at a hasty clip. Servants gawked as he stormed through the halls of the servants' corridors. Maids squeaked and flattened themselves along the walls at his sudden appearance. No doubt the early morning hour attributed to some of their surprise. He rarely roused before noon.

Suddenly, he saw her, turning the corridor, her arms full of fresh linens. She froze at the sight of him. She wore a fresh uniform—the gray skirts peeking around the starched white pinafore not the same rumpled dress balled upon his floor only hours ago. That infernal white cap covered her hair again. He longed to rip the offensive scrap of linen from her head.

Her fiery gaze flicked to the servants cowering in deference. Spine snapping straight, her gaze flew back to him, her amber eyes flaming with ire, the warning there bright and clear for him to read. He scowled, rejecting the message. He was lord and master here. And as of last night, they were lovers. He would not stay away.

"Fallon."

Color stained her cheeks at his familiar use of her name.

Servants snickered. He swept a withering glare along the corridor at them. "I am certain you all have duties to perform that requires your presence elsewhere."

In a flurry of movement, everyone disappeared from the corridor like so many ants fleeing the storm.

Square chin lifting, Fallon attempted to pass him in the corridor as if she were simply another servant and not the woman whose virginity he had taken upon the kitchen table. He grasped her arm and whirled her around to face him.

Her dark brows nearly came together as she glared at him over the neat stack of linens and hissed beneath her breath, "What do you think you're doing?"

"The question better asked is what in the blazes are *you* doing?"

Even though they were alone now, she spoke at a rushed, furious whisper. "What does it look like I'm doing? I'm going about my duties."

"Duties?"

"Yes. I am a maid. I work for my livelihood."

Her lashes flickered, the faintest tremble, the only indication that she was perhaps something else, someone else . . . that more existed between them than that of an employer and employee relationship.

Her lips quivered as she spoke. Her voice, if possible, even quieter than before as she added, "Despite last night. That's all I am."

"You don't have to be," he returned, fingers flexing around her arm, the linen fabric of her uniform soft beneath his fingers but no less loathsome. He wanted her out of it. Wanted her in silks and satins. Or better yet, garbed in nothing at all and flat on her back beneath him. "You are more than that to me."

Some of the anger faded from her eyes, replaced with a sort of grim resignation. "I can't be."

"Yes. You can." He moistened his lips, feeling like a green lad as he stated in a hot rush of air. "Be my mistress."

"Mistress?" Her head pulled back, her eyes widening into luminous pools. "Is that how little you think of me?"

"*Little?*" He straightened to his full height, squaring his shoulders. "I think a great deal of you. Otherwise I would not have made such an offer."

Her lips pressed into a single line. "Indeed. Then as *honored* as I am, I shall have to decline." Pulling her arm free, she stepped around him.

He blocked her. "I've never asked another woman to be my mistress, and yet you behave as though I've delivered a grave affront."

She snorted and tried to step around him again, shaking her head fiercely.

"I should think a girl in your position would—" He stopped cold at the stricken expression on her face.

"What?" she bit out. "Drop at your feet in proper gratitude?" She nodded fiercely. "I suppose a *girl like me* should count herself lucky. A girl like me should gladly say yes."

"Don't—"

"No—*you* don't," she cut in. "Don't expect me to feel honored. It's not a respectable proposition, it's not m—" Her voice died, but he caught her meaning. Perfectly.

"Marriage," he finished, nodding grimly, his throat tightening as though he swallowed something harsh and acerbic. "Is that your price?"

"I haven't a price," she hissed.

He shook his head. "I would not offer *that* to *any* woman, no matter how much I think . . . I care for her." He couldn't. He hadn't a heart to give. It had been killed long ago.

"And I would not expect such an offer from you."

He gazed at her in mute frustration. Stark hunger clawed through him.

His boyhood had left him a deadened shell. Whatever warmth he felt now, whatever warmth she breathed into the cold cavern of his soul, would not last. And he would not force her to spend a lifetime with him knowing one day the cold dead would return. A temporary arrangement was all he could promise.

He flung his arms wide. "Then what do you want?"

"From you?" her voice rang shrilly, color suffusing her cheeks. "Nothing. Merely an honest wage for honest work."

"You think to resume your duties as a maid? Here?" His gaze flicked to the linens stacked in her arms, then back to her face. "By God, you do."

She nodded, her face still flushed. "If you would be so good as to put last night behind us, and let me proceed—"

With all the fury of a child caught in a tantrum, he knocked the linens from her hands and pulled her into his arms. His mouth rasped her cheek as he growled, her skin trembling beneath his lips. "You think either one of us can go on as before?" Just the feel of her body against his told him *he* could not. And damned if he didn't intend to make her see she could not either.

She squeezed her hands between them and shoved herself free, breaking the contact. He advanced on her, determination grinding his teeth together.

She held up a hand to ward him off. "No more. We will go on like last night never happened."

Despite her avowal, her gaze dropped from his, and he knew she was not as determined as she wished to appear. Crouching, she quickly gathered the linens with shaking hands, face averted. As though she could not bear to look him in the eye. Straightening, she held his stare with the icy hauteur of a queen, the doubt nowhere in evidence anymore.

"I merely wish to resume my life. Continue with my duties until I can put away enough for a home of my own."

"A home?"

"A simple matter to you, seeing as you possess several, but I have only ever wanted security—a home."

"I can give you your own house—"

"It would belong to you."

"You would earn it."

Fire lit her cheeks. "On my back."

He flinched, then shrugged. "A task you did not find so reprehensible last night."

If possible, her face burned even brighter. "I would be no more than a well-paid whore." She drew a deep breath. Pressing her fingers to her temple, she shook her head as if suffering a headache. "Let us stop this. Please. Last night was lovely, but it's over." *Over.* The word hung in the air, sagging, suspended for a long, tired moment before she added, "There are countless women out there eager for your attentions, wouldn't you agree?"

Dark anger washed through his veins. Was she actually thrusting him into the arms of other women?

Dominic was quite certain this was the most singular event in his life. Generally, women were greedy for him, unwilling to share him and possessive of his attentions. Never mind that he never made them promises—or offers such as the one he just extended Fallon. Females tended to be capricious, irrational creatures. Nothing like this one who looked at him with defiance in her eyes, her rejection fresh and stinging as a slap to his face.

"Yes," he heard himself agree, pride surfacing at long last. "I shall have no difficulty finding another to warm my bed." He snapped his teeth together so hard they ached.

The color bled from her face. She stared at him with stoic acceptance. "Such is your life."

"Quite so." He nodded once. "I'll let you get back to your duties." Turning on his heels, he strode away, damned if he would beg. Damned if he would let her see just how desperately he longed for her in his bed.

She and no other.

Fallon watched him storm away, her heart in her throat, blocking her breath. She bit her lip to keep from calling him back, to accept the offer that went against everything she was, everything she ever wanted to be.

And yet, suddenly, the role of mistress—*his* mistress—did not horrify her as it should have. She could only think of the benefits. The temptations. Chiefly falling asleep in his arms and waking up in them each morning . . . and in a home that he would provide. A home of her own. The prospect nearly made her dizzy. The duke and a home.

But at what cost? The coppery tang of blood washed over her teeth and she quickly released her lip.

Shaking her head, she entered the guest chamber requiring fresh linens, vowing to forget the simple thrill of his touch and recall that she was nothing more than a maid. A servant in his household. At least until she saved enough for her own place. Da had not raised her to become a rich man's mistress. A toy to be played with and discarded when he tired of her.

Dominic would find another to take her place. Several, if his past habits were any indication. She need merely to brace herself for the day she saw him with another. An eventuality. Nonetheless, pain lanced her heart at the likelihood.

Legs suddenly weak, she sank onto the bed, staring ahead, not seeing the fine pinstriped papered walls at all. Instead, she saw herself. Struggling day in and day out to remain unaffected in the duke's household—to act as a shadow when her heart was irrevocably bound to him.

*Grand, Fallon. You perfect idiot. You've fallen in love with the wastrel.*

She rubbed the side of her face. What an impossible situation. Had she truly thought she could go on as before, blithely unaware of the duke? She had *never* been unaware of him. On the contrary. And now . . . given the intimacies they had shared, her carnal knowledge . . .

She blinked, heat flooding her face.

In that moment, she knew what she had to do.

She would accept Lord Hunt's stipend, however insulted she felt upon first hearing it. A dull ache grew beneath her breastbone. She pressed a hand there, rubbing in small circles. Her very survival dictated it. Better a dent to her pride than her heart.

# Chapter 26

**D**ominic ignored the gentleman who stopped before his chair and continued to stare into the hearth's flickering fire as he raised his glass to his lips. At least until the fellow cleared his throat so many times he begged notice.

"I'm busy," Dominic ground out, lips hugging the edge of the glass.

"I'm sorry to disturb you, Your Grace. Your butler directed me here."

"Adams?" He was going to have a word with the man about giving out his whereabouts to anyone who came calling.

"It is a matter of some urgency."

Dominic snorted and sent a quick glance to the man, surveying him with a sweep of his eyes. "Have we met? You look familiar."

"I'm John Meadows. Your grandfather's secretary."

Dominic grunted and finished off his brandy.

With a motion of his hand, he signaled a server to bring him another drink. Leveling a ruthless glare on the man, he spoke evenly, "This is a private club."

"Quite so, but given the nature of my business, they permitted me a brief word with you." He glanced down at his rumpled attire, brushing dust from his trouser leg. "Forgive the late hour and my appearance. I rode all day to reach here."

A quick glance around the room revealed that they were the subject of some interest. Several gentlemen peered at them from their seats, gazes lifting from their newspapers or cards.

"Convey your message and be gone, then." A footman hurried over and deposited a tray with a fresh decanter upon it. Dominic held out his glass to be refilled.

In the last few days, he had spent more time at his club than home. Absurdly, he was hiding from Fallon. Unable, unwilling, to see the very thing— the woman—he most wanted and couldn't have.

The secretary cleared his throat again, tugging at his cravat.

Leaning back against the plush cushion of the chair, he stretched out his boots before him. "Out with it? What's the message?"

"Message?"

"Yes. From my grandfather?" He paused to take another lengthy sip, replying drolly, "What does the old bastard want?"

Meadows's eyes bugged behind a pair of spectacles. "You refer to him thusly?" His shoulders pulled up in clear affront, nearly reaching his ears.

"Know any other old bastards?"

Meadows's mouth worked, clearly beyond speech. The secretary had not been around when Mrs. Pearce reigned supreme at Wayfield Park. Dominic waved his hand impatiently. "Spit it out."

"Your grandfather is . . ."

"Yes." Despite his air of indifference, a certain tightness gripped his chest as he prepared himself for the words to come, already guessing what they were.

"Declining."

His hand stilled for a moment, pausing in bringing his drink to his lips. Not dead, then. *Declining.* He took another sip.

"I see." He lowered his glass to the small rosewood table at his side. Absently, his fingers bent inward, curving to stroke the scarred flesh of his palm. "That last time I saw him he was declining. Isn't that what old men do?"

"Yes, well, he has worsened. I fear he will soon expire."

Dominic's lips twisted in a savage smile. "That also tends to happen when one is old. You die."

"Have you no desire to see him?"

"I already did."

"Perhaps again?"

"He's not dying," Dominic announced baldly, the proclamation earning a few more stares. He forced his eyes wide with feigned guilelessness. "He told me himself that he would not breathe his last breath until satisfied that I am well and settled, married and living a virtuous life."

Meadows's eyes skimmed him with some skepticism. "Indeed. Well, I fear he cannot live forever. Much as some would like."

Dominic chuckled, not missing the secretary's insult. Not missing it, and not caring. "Don't put it past him."

"I know there is some discord between the two of you—"

Dominic stopped from biting out that he didn't know a damn thing. About him, at any rate. And likely he didn't know anything about the good reverend that he appeared to hold in such esteem.

Instead, he only chuckled harder. "Discord? That's rich."

"I would be happy to accompany you to Wayfield Park to—"

"Now, why would I wish to go there?" He had no intention of stepping foot in the home of his youth. His grandfather could perish and that mausoleum could rot from neglect for all he cared. He had spent enough miserable years in those walls.

"Well, aside from seeing your grandfather, there is the matter of Wayfield Park, its rents and tenants—"

"All of which ran smoothly these last years in my absence."

"Yes. Under Mr. Collins's care. Now that he is ill, would you not wish to begin familiarizing yourself with—"

"Not especially. I'll worry about that when I must. After he's dead."

Meadows adjusted his spectacles and angled his head to the side. "I beg your pardon?"

"You heard me."

Meadows gave a jerky nod, the skin of his face suddenly pinched and tight-looking. "I see all that I've heard of you is true."

Dominic shrugged and grunted in a manner that conveyed how little he cared about the secretary's opinion.

Meadows sniffed. "You *are* the devil."

Dominic reached for his glass. "So I've been told."

With a grunt of disgust, Meadows turned on his heels.

Dominic watched the little man flee with a hard smile on his face. He sat for some moments—alone in a room full of people—searching within himself, attempting to gauge precisely how he felt on the matter of his grandfather's impending death. If he felt anything at all.

Nothing, he decided. He found only a dull hollowness within his chest. His usual numbing apathy. *Nothing*. Deadness.

His mind wandered, jumping ahead, seeking, aching, he realized, for the person who brought feeling into his cold life, breathing a warm wind through the arctic void. *Fallon*. For once the thought of her came as a welcome distraction. Fallon—the only person to make him feel he was more than the immoral blot of existence the world perceived. The only person to make him . . . feel. And not just when his body joined with hers. Every time he saw her. Every time he talked to her. Every time he *thought* of her. With Fallon, he felt right, good, *whole*.

And she wanted nothing to do with him. *Damn her*. She wanted to live her life, devotedly saving every halfpenny. For a home. *Home*. What was that anyway, save walls and a roof? What was so important about a bloody home? He possessed several, and none of them meant anything to him.

Finishing off his brandy, he pushed to his feet, suddenly craving solitude. At this late hour, he could return to his townhouse with no fear of facing anyone. Namely her. She would be safely tucked in bed in the servants' quarters. Living the life of a maid. An existence she preferred to that of one with him.

Fallon stared at her small valise, packed with all she possessed in the world. Paltry in sum. A sad testimony to her life, but an accurate reflection nonetheless.

She inhaled a deep breath, her chest expanding as she examined its contents a final time. But no more. She would begin living for herself. Soon her life would be impossible to stuff within one small valise. It would brim full and spill out over the edges. Even if it meant swallowing her pride and accepting the provision Lord Hunt offered.

It mollified her somewhat to know Da would want her to take the help. In fact, he would be annoyed if she did not. She could almost hear his voice now. *Stubborn lass, take the money. I bloody well earned it for you.*

Dominic's face floated before her. She shook her head, absently brushing her lips with her fingertips. True, she wanted him more than she should. But she did not *need* him. She would *not* have him. Not if it meant selling herself . . . cheapening herself and trading all her dreams and desires in exchange for an undefined number of nights in his bed.

She strode across her small room and lifted Lord Hunt's card from the center of the desk. Tomorrow she would call on him. Tomorrow she would accept his stipend.

Tomorrow her new life would begin.

She set the card down atop the table, smoothing her fingertips over the embossed lettering. And tonight. . .

Tonight she would say farewell to the duke.

Certainly, she could just slip away. Leave in the morning without saying good-bye, without explaining her departure. Or she could simply offer her resignation to Mr. Adams. No audience with the duke was required. She never had to clap eyes on him again.

Yet she couldn't do that. It didn't seem right. Not after . . . everything.

Wise or not, she could not leave without seeing him one last time.

Opening the door of her room, she slipped out into the silent hall.

Dominic sat in the drawing room, his booted feet stretched before the fire. Heat licked at the soles but he still did not move, preferring that the bottoms of his feet roast rather than suffer his other feelings. Feelings. *Hell.* Years of losing himself in women, drink, and painting in order to feel anything at all, and now he couldn't stop the onslaught of emotions.

Frustration swam through him, commanding he rise and set off in search of Fallon. He *should* return to his room and his own bed, but Fallon's scent still lingered there, tantalizing him. The drawing room was far safer. His eyelids drooped and he knew he risked falling asleep here for the servants to discover . . . which lent itself to the very real and unwelcome possibility of Fallon finding him in the morning. An unwelcome scenario. He could not trust himself around her. Could not trust to keep his hands to himself. Or trust himself not to lash out at the woman who preferred a life of humble servitude to him.

"Dominic."

Her soft voice sent all his nerve endings into singing awareness. It was as though he had called forth her presence.

He closed his eyes in a tight blink, forcing himself to rein in his surge of swirling-hot emotions. She was nothing to him that should bring forth such feelings. Nothing. Just as she preferred.

He opened his eyes to find her there before him, attired in the loathsome uniform all the maids on his staff wore. His gaze crawled over her, stopping at her face. "Strayed a bit far from the servants' wing, haven't you? Go away."

"I came—" she faltered, her gaze sweeping his unkempt appearance. Her nostrils flared, no doubt smelling the spirits on him. "What has happened?"

"Nothing." His hand twitched on the arm of his chair. "Merely another night of debauchery."

She stared at him some time before shaking her head, rejecting his words. "No. Something happened. I've never seen you like this."

Irrational anger burned in his chest. "Ah, proof then that you don't know me at all." *If you did, you would understand how very much in danger you are just by being here.*

She cocked her head and looked down at him as if he were a wayward child. The look ignited his temper. "Come, let's get you to your room."

"Bugger off," he snarled, despising her mothering tone and that she would dare adopt a motherly role with him. "You made it clear you were not interested in becoming my mistress. And as I have no need of a nursemaid, you are of no use to me. Leave."

Fire snapped in her amber gaze. "You're a miserable wretch." Her head nodded as though satisfied with the qualification. "Kindness is lost on you. I came in here to tell you good-bye." She started to turn.

"Good riddance," he snarled, surging to his feet even as his chest clenched at the prospect of never seeing her face again.

Scarlet stained her cheeks as she faced him again, nearly as vibrant as the hair peeking beneath her cap. "I can see the sentiment was wasted on you."

"Since when does saying good-bye require sentiment?"

"It doesn't," she raged, chest lifting on a deep, ragged breath.

"Simply turn and walk out that door." He whirled a finger in a little circle. "Easy. That is all. Done."

"Quite so." Spinning on her heels, she stalked to the door.

He swiped his hand through his hair and gave a violent tug on the ends. *Bloody hell.* With a growl, he took off after her. His hand was almost on her shoulder when she stopped and jerked herself around.

They crashed into one another.

She gave a small yelp. He grabbed her when she would have stepped back and hauled her against him, his hands hard clamps on her arms. Their eyes collided and clung, their chests heaving against each other.

With a curse of defeat, he slammed his mouth over hers in a punishing kiss. He forced her lips open, plunging his tongue inside to tangle with hers, beyond gentleness. Beyond finesse. Savage need drove him.

Her arms circled his neck and she kissed him back. Molded together, they lowered to the drawing room carpet, mouths devouring each other, the pop and hiss of the fire the only sound on the air. He slid a hand around her to the small of her back, letting her feel the evidence of his desire. She made a small sound and deepened the kiss.

He pulled up, breaking their lips apart with an abruptness that jarred. Aching and furious from the heavy wanting coursing through him, tightening every nerve in his body, he bit out, "Go. Go now, or God help me, I won't stop."

She wiggled from him, steady resolve entering her eyes. Warm amber. Red in the firelight. With a small nod, she clambered to her feet and turned, striding toward the drawing room door. Pained breath sawed from his lips as he watched her go, but he still did not move from the floor. If he moved, it would be to go after her.

Her hand closed on the latch. He watched, forcing himself to rise to his feet and watch her walk out of his life. He fought the urge to haul her back and flip up her skirts and fulfill every savage impulse pumping through him.

The grinding lock of the door clicked on the air.

He blinked.

She turned, her body falling back against the door. She had not left. She stayed. Despite his warning. Palms pressed flat against the wood, she studied him with a steadfast gaze. And yet even in that unflinching stare, a fire gleamed—a fire he had put there. And one he intended to stoke even higher.

She was staying. For now. For tonight. He intended to make every moment count. She could leave him in the morning, in the shroud of dawn, but he vowed to make her remember, vowed that she would never forget him. Of that, he was certain. Memories of him would haunt whatever bloody dwelling she called home and dared to value above him.

# Chapter 27

**F**allon had not intended for this to happen. Not again. But she could not desert him when he looked as he did. When he looked at *her* as he did. So full of savage need and hunger. Gray eyes dark with a thirst her own body felt, echoing deep in her bones.

He appeared so grim and alone when she first entered the room. Flames from the dying fire cast him in sinister shadow. It should have sent her fleeing. And yet she remained.

She knew what turning that lock signified. But as her hands moved over the tiny buttons lining the front of her gown, she decided she did not care. She would be here for him tonight.

And tomorrow she would be gone.

"Fallon," he breathed her name but said nothing more as she undressed, strangely immodest before him. Naked, she stepped out from the puddle of her clothes at her feet and strode toward him. Pressing her palm against his chest, she backed him into a chaise, a heady euphoria filling her at her boldness, making her dizzy with power and desire.

She came over him, hands curling on his muscled shoulders as she straddled him and bent to take his lips again. They kissed until both were panting and moaning, straining toward each other. The sensation of his broad palms sliding over her, sweeping her bare back, her hips, her thighs, drove her mad. She ground down against him, the hard ridge of his manhood burning into her moist heat.

His hands spanned her waist and slid up, brushing her belly and ribs until he reached her breasts. He played and toyed with them, pulling, tweaking, and rolling the nipples until she arched and cried out, ripples of sensation sizzling through her.

Quivering, she worked to free him of his shirt, her hands shaking as they roamed over his broad chest, delighting in the feel of his warm flesh, the undulation of his muscle beneath skin. She traced his tattoo, nails scoring the coiling serpent. Lowering her head, she kissed it, using her tongue to trace its form.

"Did it hurt?" she whispered, her mouth hovering over the serpent's coiling shape.

"Yes."

She winced, imagining that he must have had to sit for hours, enduring the discomfort. "Then why did you do it?"

"It's just pain."

She smiled dryly. "People usually try to avoid pain."

She felt his voice rumble from his chest. "Pain is good sometimes. It reminds you you're alive."

*He needed reminding of that?*

She peered down at him, staring into his shadowed eyes, and realized that he did. For all his outrageous ways and life of excess, he couldn't—*didn't*—feel much of anything.

She slid down his body, loosening his trousers, hot determination feeding her. *You'll feel alive. You'll feel more alive than you've ever felt.*

He watched her, his eyes a hot gleam beneath heavy lids, his hands relaxed at his sides.

Her eager hands shoved his breeches down. She took him in her hands, stroking the hard length of him, squeezing him, satin on steel in her grasp. She watched his face, studying the tight muscle flinching in his jaw, the dark want smoldering in his eyes.

Wrapping her fingers around the base of him, she took the tip of him into her mouth, sucking softly at first then harder, her tongue circling slowly, languorously, savoring him. He shuddered beneath her and wedged a hand between them, cupping her breast even as she eased more of him into her mouth.

Long fingers found her nipple and squeezed. White-hot sparks shot from her breast to the throbbing core of her. She cried out with him thick in her mouth. Determined to illicit his pleasure, to savor and taste, to know she brought him the deepest of pleasures, she slid her mouth over him, taking him deep, tongue gliding, caressing his hard length.

His hips surged and he groaned, the fingers of his other hand sifting through her hair. "God, Fallon. Now. *Now.*"

Gratified in his response, her blood burned, pushing her to the breaking point. Desperate and aching, she guided him inside her, easing down on the hard length of him with a moan, sinking until he was buried to the hilt.

Hands curling around his neck, she brought his mouth to hers again, her breasts flattening against his chest. She worked her hips as their lips fused, pumping over him. Feeling somewhat clumsy in her wild need, she tried to move slower, to control the frenzied pace. But her passion burned too hot, and she moved faster, her muscles clenching around him, tightening. Something elusive loomed ahead, just out of her reach, and she felt she would die if she did not reach it soon.

He groaned, his hands skimming her sides, clinging to her hips, encouraging her frantic pace. A desperate keening started in her throat and she couldn't stop, couldn't quiet herself, could only work harder, faster as the fever rose in her blood.

"Oh, God, slow down," he gasped, but she couldn't.

Possessed, she flew against him, with him, his desperate plea heightening her excitement, making her burst from the inside. Shuddering atop him, she arched her spine, grinding down on him with a cry.

He ran a hand over her arched spine, shouting as he released himself inside her and joined her in the sweet agony. His lips met her neck, her collarbone, dragging her skin with a kiss. She fell back over him, resting her damp forehead on his shoulder. Their bodies shuddered and heaved with exultant breaths, joined, linked. She spread her fingers in a fan against his chest, hoping they would cease to tremble that way. His fingers trailed her spine in a slow caress, tracing each and every bump.

Perfectly content to never move again, she managed to lift her head and meet his gaze, holding his gray stare for several moments and feeling a stab of embarrassment at her truly wild behavior.

"Why did you stay?"

She shrugged and broke their gaze, staring down at his shoulder, the serpent's dark watchful eye, appreciating that he had not asked why she just *ravished* him like a lust-crazed woman. "I wanted to." She moistened her lips. "And . . ." She bit her lip.

She tore her gaze from the mesmerizing serpent tattoo to his face. "You needed me tonight."

She quickly rested her head back on his shoulder, unwilling to look at him after uttering such sentimental rubbish. He didn't *need* her. At least he would never admit to it. He wanted her for one thing. And she had just satisfied him in that respect.

His fingers continued their slow dance on her spine. His chest lifted on a heavy, serrated breath beneath her, like an incoming wave. "My grandfather," he spoke beneath her, his voice a deep, vibrating rumble against her breasts. "He's dying."

She sucked in a breath, biting back the immediate comment of sympathy. He would not want that. Given his strained relationship with his grandfather, he likely did not know what to feel. But he *felt*. She was sure of it, had known something was amiss the moment she saw him tonight. Now she knew what.

She held her tongue, tracing a small circle over his chest, above his heart. A sigh rattled loose from him and his arms wrapped around her, holding her close, and she knew she had given him what he most needed. Even if he would not acknowledge it. Comfort. Companionship. Another human who knew loss, knew what it meant to want something one could never have. Her lips twisted. They had that in common.

Closing her eyes, she let the steady sound of his heart fill her head. "Will you go see him?"

"Why would I do that?"

She lifted her head to stare down at him. "I know he has hurt you, but he's dying." It made perfect sense to her. He had to go. Not for his grandfather, but for himself. So there would be no regrets later. Nothing to wonder about. He needed to close that door behind him so that he was not forever looking back.

"So."

She said nothing, could think of nothing to say. She merely stared at him, at the hard, unforgiving glint in his eyes, and realized he was everything he had ever claimed. An empty shell. Empty because he would never let anyone else in.

"He can die," he pronounced. "Alone."

She dropped her head back down on his chest and feigned sleep, unable to witness the coldness in his eyes one moment longer. Nor the cruel press of lips that had kissed her so thoroughly only a short while ago.

In that moment, she realized he was utterly and completely lacking of a heart. He felt nothing. And she needed to leave him before such a condition grew acceptable . . . before she became accustomed to loving a man incapable of loving her. Or anyone else for that matter. Who would only ever be the demon duke.

A log crumbled in the hearth, sending up a hiss of sparks. Eyes closed, Dominic heard the sound, knew it for what it was. Just as he heard the floor creak beneath a soft footstep and knew *it* for what it was. Fallon leaving him. He heard the whisper of fabric as she dressed, the quiet hush of her breath near him, the thud of his own heart in his ears, the beat quickening as she prepared to depart.

Still, he did not move, curled on his side on the chaise, muscles sated and replete. After a moment he heard the door open. A longer moment passed, and he felt her long stare on him as keenly as a ray of sun.

Then the door clicked shut and the old coldness stole over him, freezing him from the inside out. The sun was gone.

Slowly, he opened his eyes to gaze out at the silent drawing room. Empty. The murky blue of impending dawn peeked from between the damask drapes. His gaze crawled to the closed paneled doors, a live, hungry thing, searching for a glimpse of her where nothing remained.

Sighing, he rolled over and flung his arm across his forehead, considering dressing himself before one of the servants discovered him naked on the chaise.

He could have opened his eyes while she dressed. Could have spoken words that would have led to a conversation that may or may not have stopped her from leaving. He could have begged.

Or simply asked.

But to what purpose? He could not give her more than he already offered. And she wanted more. Hell, she deserved more. Deserved better than him. He'd offered all he could and it wasn't enough.

Yes, he still wanted her. She consumed him. She filled him with hunger, with need . . . with wild, desperate emotions he dared not examine too closely. But it couldn't last. It wasn't real. He would return to himself. Return to his old ways. Numbness would creep over him and he would drift from her, searching for ways, albeit temporarily, to *feel*. He closed his eyes tightly.

No, better that he permit her to find her own happiness far from him. She'd find her home. And he'd find his way back to the familiar darkness, forgetting the light he'd briefly found with her.

# Chapter 28

**F**allon waited upon the settee for Lord Hunt to enter the room, her valise at her feet. The toes of her slippered feet tapped the floor impatiently. Head cocked, she studied the striped-and-floral–patterned wallpaper of Lord Hunt's drawing room and tried not to think of the night spent in Dominic's drawing room. He would be awake by now. He would know she had left . . .

She squeezed her eyes tight against their infernal burn and opened then again, determination thick in her throat. The room's décor reminded her of the Hunt estate in Little Saums. Flowery, cluttered with all manner of knickknacks and fripperies.

Fallon had snuck into the main house a time or two to spy on Lord Hunt's sisters playing at the pianoforte. Clearly his mother's handiwork extended here as well. Fallon assumed the viscountess, a fashionable lady who had always concerned herself with making everything around her beautiful and stylish, still lived. Fallon glanced down at her worn navy wool skirts, so drab and ill-placed against the brocade settee. Likely the fine lady never imagined the likes of Fallon gracing any of her drawing rooms.

The viscount arrived, pausing in the open door of the drawing room at the sight of her, his expression all solicitousness. "Miss O'Rourke." He advanced into the room, bowing smartly before her. "I'm so pleased you called. I intended to give you more time to reconsider my offer before calling upon you again." His face adopted a look of contrition. "I'm afraid I made a muddle of it last time."

He sighed, lips curving in a lopsided fashion, rueful and apologetic, and she could suddenly understand why so many maids surrendered him their hearts. "I've given it more thought and I truly appreciate all you've gone through—all my family put you through. I apologize if I came off as a thoughtless cad. I hope I can change your mind without offending you again."

Fallon nodded as he lowered himself into a chair across from her. "That is why I've come. I would like to accept your offer now."

His face eased into a smile, relief loose about

the curved corners. "Indeed? My father would be most pleased."

She stifled the surge of bitterness and the stinging retort that burned on the tip of her tongue, eager to express how little she cared about pleasing his late father. She no longer wished to live in a perpetual state of bitterness. She wanted to change. She wanted peace. Even if that meant forgiving those who had wronged her. She wanted to stop hating the world—blue bloods in particular—for every wrong to befall her. Da would want that. Would not want her to live with hatred in her heart.

Nodding, she murmured, "As would mine."

Now ready to hear what Hunt had tried to explain to her before, she cleared her throat. "What does the provision . . . entail?"

"You will have a stipend of course." Lord Hunt leaned back in his chair, steepling his fingers together. "And there's a cottage . . ."

\*    \*    \*

*Dear Evelyn,*

*I hope this letter finds you well. I imagine you're basking in the sunshine of Barbados by now, the spray of seawater fresh on your face. Do take care of that fair complexion of yours. I've heard a tropical sun can wreak vengeance on a lily-white such as yourself. No doubt you're living the adventure you have always craved—and deserved.*

*You will find my situation much changed upon your return. Fret not, I've not landed myself in prison. I know you worried greatly over my last venture. Permit me to put your mind to rest. It will come as a surprise for you to learn that I am residing in my very own home now, a lovely cottage in Little Saums.*

*I never thought to return here, so close to where my life took such a sad turn. The late Viscount Hunt provided for me in his will. Initially, I had no wish to accept a pound from the family responsible for my father's death, but forgiveness is a grace I've learned to embrace. Astonishingly, I have a home now—just as I wished for when we were girls. I can scarcely believe it. I cannot wait until we next meet and pray it is not too long an occasion from now. Marguerite will be staying with me for Christmas. Of course, you know you always have a home with me should you ever tire of adventure. You need never beg a home from either one of your brothers again. Love and Godspeed in your travels.*

*Your dearest friend,*
*Fallon*

\* \* \*

Fallon departed the vicarage, her boots—a shiny new pair, well-crafted for the muddy-lane home—fell with cheerful alacrity on the church's tread-worn path. She pulled her thick wool scarf high at her throat to ward off the chill.

The lunch hour drew near. Depositing the arrangement of flowers had taken longer than expected. Mr. Simmons wanted her opinion regarding tomorrow's sermon. Her lips twisted. She hardly considered herself the most pious of souls, but she had done her best by the young reverend . . . even with the remembered aroma of chicken soup and fresh-baked bread teasing her nose and calling her home. She chafed her gloved palms, eager to reach her cozy cottage.

She no longer woke before dawn. And for once, when she did wake, it was to someone cooking— for *her*. A blessed change. She hastened her steps, knowing Ms. Redley's pot of chicken soup would be well ready by now. Her stomach grumbled at the prospect, and despite the chill, a warmth pervaded her at the memory of her warm cottage— *home*—and the cook and housekeeper puttering about within.

She could not complain of loneliness. Or rather, she *shouldn't*. The two Misses Redleys bustled about the house during the day, chattering like magpies. Like the rest of Little Saums, they had embraced her into their midst. The young reverend's kind reception stood out as the most discernible among all. She was certain he needed only a little encouragement to begin a formal courtship.

Life was good. Inhaling crisp air, she waited for a deep sense of gratification to sweep over her.

And waited.

She had been waiting ever since she arrived and landed herself such an ideal situation in Little Saums. With a disgusted snort, she exhaled her breath. She had achieved all she ever sought. She had no call to feel so . . . *alone*.

And yet she did.

She had fought the feeling, resisted it like a bad cold creeping into her lungs. She had plunged ahead into her new life: settling into her home, meeting and greeting the curious, well-intentioned neighbors and villagers, spending time in her garden. *Her garden.* She paused. It felt remarkable to even think those words.

On a whim, she had decided to create an arrangement for the church. A small thing to do for the community that had embraced her with such warmth. A few of the residents recalled her father. Even her. There was something in that, she supposed. Almost as though she really had returned home. Something to distract from the ache for a man incapable of emotion. Incapable of love. A man she would never see again.

She did not fear meeting Dominic here. Even with Wayfield Park a rock throw's distance, it was the last place he would visit. Her cottage on the southeast corner of Little's Saums posed even less of a threat.

She had convinced herself the ache wouldn't last. Like any sickness, it would pass and she would grow stronger from it.

She strolled along the churchyard, pausing at the gate to the cemetery. Dull light peered down through tree branches. She spied a figure bending awkwardly at a grave, clinging to a brass-headed cane as he set flowers upon it. Extravagant yellow tulips. Cheerful for the dreary afternoon.

The gentleman stood, straightening his frame and lifting his face to the muted light. There was no mistaking him. Dominic's grandfather. Mr. Collins. Not quite at death's door, it would seem. Something terrible twisted inside her at the sight of this man who caused Dominic such pain. Who made him what he was—a man who could never love. *Never love me*. Not as she loved him. And she did love him. Painful as it was to admit, painful as it was to *feel*. And she did feel it. Every day.

Jaw set, she strode ahead, her strides swift and purposeful, even if what she would *say* to him remained a void.

He looked up, startled at her approach. "Who are you?" he snapped.

"Fallon O'Rourke." She stopped.

He appraised her critically. "Am I supposed to know you?"

"I've taken residence at the cottage just beyond the old mill."

He nodded once, the motion curt, dismissive. With a grunt, he turned his attention back to the grave.

He reminded her a little of herself just then. Enough that she could only stand and stare. No doubt Wayfield Park abounded with servants. People left and right. Yet here he stood. Looking as she felt. Alone. Lonely.

Fallon had only thought to claim her home and everything would be right. Solved. Happy, even. But at night, long after the Redley sisters had departed for the day, she climbed into bed and lay alone. There she could not fool herself. Nothing felt right. She had not counted upon the stark sense of aloneness that would come with living independently. The humming silence of her house. The quiet hush of her breath in the room. In her bed. *Damn Dominic*. He had ruined everything for her.

She followed Mr. Collin's gaze, reading the marker and feeling a small flicker of surprise. "Would not the Duchess of Damon be buried with her family?"

He turned steel gray eyes on her. Eyes so familiar that she felt a second stab of surprise. "She is."

There was no family crypt at Wayfield Park? *Unusual*. Fallon shook her head, glancing at the markers near Dominic's mother, wondering why she did not then see the grave for Dominic's father.

"How do you know me?"

"I saw you in church last Sunday." She had no intention of revealing the specifics of the first time she saw him.

"Mr. Simmons needs to work more on his oration. Too many 'ahems.' " With a grunt, Mr. Collins dropped his gaze back to the grave. "The duke thought my daughter belonged *here* and not in the Damon family crypt." Resentment laced his voice. "According to him, she was scarcely his duchess before she died." Mr. Collins settled both hands on the head of his cane and shrugged as if it mattered little now.

Even knowing nothing of the situation, and little of Dominic's father, she heard herself voice with her usual candor, "That shouldn't matter."

He turned those gray eyes on her again, his expression somber as ever. "I couldn't agree with you more. She died bringing the duke's heir into this world. She earned her place in the crypt."

His words gave her a start. She was quite positive that she should not find accord of any kind with a man that reared Dominic with such cruel neglect, placing him with a governess who abused him.

And yet in that moment, standing in a graveyard with the wind whistling around them, she realized they were both two souls adrift. Cast apart from Dominic. A strange sense of kinship filled her chest and she stood a little closer to the old man who swayed at each gust of wind.

Perhaps Fallon wasn't the only one to feel the crush of Dominic's rejection. True, he would not see asking her to stay on as his mistress as a rejection, but she could see it as nothing else. Nothing more than a gouge to her heart. A heart that demanded more. Sighing, she shook her head. *Everything* it seemed.

She thought of her newly achieved home with its green ivy and sweet-smelling honeysuckle. It was more than she ever hoped for . . . and yet no longer enough.

Suddenly, impulse seized her. Lifting her chin, she heard herself asking before she could reconsider, "Do you care for chicken soup, Mr. Collins?"

# Chapter 29

This time, the secretary sent word.

The missive was brief, succinct. Dominic dropped it into the fire after reading it and rested his arm along the mantel, studying the curling fingers of fire devouring the parchment.

Still, the words floated before his eyes. *Your grandfather is dying. If you wish to see him, come with all haste.*

This was it, then. His jaw clenched.

He wasn't going, of course. His feelings on the matter had not changed since he last spoke with Meadows at his club. His feelings had not changed. But he had.

The last weeks had altered him. He hardly slept, scarcely ate. His usual brandy held no appeal. Ethan had stopped by and tried to coax him out of his melancholy. Dominic had spent the entire time quizzing him on Fallon, trying to discover the location of her long-sought *home.* All to no avail.

*If she wants you to know, she will contact you.* The response had sent him into a rage. The fact that Hunt knew her location—was perhaps maintaining contact with her—filled him with impotent fury. His hand fisted. Rather than thrash his life-long friend to an inch of his life, Dominic had ordered him from his house.

No matter how he tried, he could not stop thinking about Fallon. Wrong as it was. She had her home now. All she ever desired. And yet he had hired a Bow Street runner to locate her. He didn't quite know why. Even if he knew where to find here, he could offer her no more than he had before. He could not be the man she deserved. Fidelity, marriage, the type of husband to escort her to church on Sunday. A proper, loving husband. He could give her none of that.

If he were honorable, he would leave her in peace. Permit her to move on with her life. But then he had never been the honorable sort.

He would not stay away. He doubted he ever would . . . ever *could*. Even if he found her years from now, married with a horde of children at her skirts, he would still want her. She was a fire in his blood and he'd been a fool to ever let her go. For her sake, he hoped the Bow Street runner did not locate her. Because he was too selfish to let her slip away a second time.

The memory of Fallon as he had last seen her smoldered through him: her taste, her touch . . . her voice. In particular, the words she had last spoken to him. He jammed his eyes shut. *If you don't see your grandfather, you shall regret it.*

His hand tightened on the mantel, the flesh of his palm tight, unable to stretch. Why did he have to remember those words? Why now? He found himself shoving from the mantel with a savage curse. He strode from the room, his lips set in a grim line, one destination on his mind.

*For Fallon.* He would go for her. He shook his head as he strode into the foyer and called for Adams to ready his mount.

Because she had lost her father. Because he had never known his. Because, like it or not, Rupert Collins was the closest thing to a parent he had ever known. Dominic would see him to his Maker. Only then would he be well and truly rid of the old man and the past. With luck, all those painful memories would depart with him. Then he would be free.

With only Fallon left to haunt him.

\* \* \*

"Shall we continue with chapter sixteen?" Fallon lifted the book from the rosewood side table and flipped the crisp pages, searching for the spot where she left off last time.

A rattled breath answered her as she found her page. Her gaze caught on the brass-headed cane sitting beside the bed. As it had sat for the last fortnight. Almost as though Mr. Collins would rise and grasp it in his gnarled hand.

She wished he would. They had fallen into a pattern before he took to his bed. A pattern she missed. Luncheon or tea at her cottage followed with a walk through her garden. Granted, the walks grew gradually shorter in the days before the fall that led to his confinement. Now she called upon him at Wayfield Park, reading and chatting and pretending as though she did not sit in the home of Dominic's childhood, as though these walls had not borne witness to his unhappy youth . . . to the years that had formed him and shaped him into the hard man she happened to love.

Mr. Collins coughed. She set down the book and lifted a glass of water from the bedside table. With a hand under his nape, she helped him rise. After a sip, he lowered back down, his gray-blue eyes fixing on her. "You're still lurking about here." His voice scraped the air in low and raspy tones.

She leaned forward, as if confessing a great secret. "I have to find out how the book ends."

He gave her a shaky smile. "He was a fool to let you go."

Her own smile slipped. She had confided some of her past to him during the last fortnight. He had pressed her with questions, so she had told him . . . without revealing that the man who broke her heart happened to be his grandson.

"I'm certain he regrets it now." His rheumy gaze grew distant. "We all regret things after they're said and done."

Those few words seemed to cost him. His breath came shallower, as if he fought for each sip of air.

"Easy there," she murmured, smoothing her hand over his, knowing his words were not solely aimed at the unspecified man she told him left her heartbroken. They were aimed at himself. More than once he had spoken with remorse over the past. And on those occasions, she knew he meant Dominic. Ironic that they referred to the same person.

He worked his lips, grunting, "Read on."

Reclaiming the book, she found her page again, noticing that her fingers trembled. His words had done it. Thoughts, memories flooded her. *Not now. Don't think of him now.*

Spending time with Mr. Collins only reinforced her thoughts of Dominic. She saw him everywhere. As a boy running the halls of the great mausoleum that was Wayfield Park. In the gray eyes of his grandfather. And she felt guilty. Guilty for being in this house. With his grandfather. Guilty for finding peace with the man that Dominic could not bring himself to even visit. The peace that belonged to him, even if he was too stubborn to claim it.

And yet in some small way, she felt as though she were doing this *for* Dominic. Being with his grandfather when he could not. Would not.

*For Dominic.* For the day he realized he should have been here. Perhaps it would console him to learn that someone had been—that *she* had been.

The sound of hooves broke the quiet afternoon, growing from a faint echo to an angry din of clatter on the drive. Mr. Collins's eyes slid in the direction of the window. She pushed up from the chair and parted the damask drapes. Her heart seized in her chest at the tall figure vaulting from his horse. Even high above, she would know him anywhere. The way he moved. The brush of his too-long hair against the collar of his jacket.

It couldn't be. He wouldn't dare come here.

Her hand drifted to her throat, fingers grazing the skittery jump of her pulse. "No."

"Miss O'Rourke."

She dropped the curtains at the sound of her name. Spinning around, she tried to offer up a reassuring smile for Mr. Collins. Even so, she felt her head shaking in denial, panic and pleasure warring inside her. She took a step in one direction, and then another, unsure where to run.

Footsteps sounded outside the door, the swift tread growing, matching the thundering tempo of her heart. Unable to summon forth an answer, she shuffled back, retreating to the far shadows of the room. Her back bumped a screen and she quickly ducked behind it just as the door swung open.

From the crack in the screen she saw *him* standing there. Impossible as it seemed. His body overfilled the room, broad shoulders stretching the fine cut of his jacket. Everything else shrank away. Her palms tingled, remembering the sensation of his warm flesh beneath her hand.

*Dominic.* More than she remembered. More than she ever remembered *feeling* in his presence. Stronger. Deeper. Her chest tightened. Her breath would not come. Her stomach dipped, sank, twisted. *Grand.* She'd already come to terms with the notion of loving him. And not having him. She had not yet realized, however, that loving meant hurting. Always hurting. More so each time she saw him. Because she would never have him. Because she would forever want to.

Dominic stared at the shrunken shape of his grandfather beneath the counterpane in the massive bed. As a boy, Rupert Collins had loomed tall, an intimidating figure in his black broadcloth. This image of the past conflicted with the reality of the present.

The room felt airless, stale. A lamp burned on the bedside table but otherwise very little light pervaded the room.

"Dominic."

The feeble voice startled him. Almost as much as the use of his name and not one of his grandfather's usual designations. *Forsaken sodomite. Devil. Satan's spawn.*

He approached the bed and peered down at the waxen face, hardly recognizing him, so changed even from his last visit. Sunken cheeks moved, working for speech. "I'm glad you've come. I waited . . ." his voice twisted into a garbled mutter.

Tension knotted his shoulders. He recalled the words hurled at him during the last visit. *My last hope for your soul is to see you well and settled. I cannot embrace the comforts of Heaven until you do.*

From the looks of his grandfather, God would no longer wait on Dominic to come up to scratch.

Sinking onto the bed, he braced himself for whatever stinging reprimand his grandfather would heap upon him, knowing he would suffer it. *For Fallon.* It had mattered to her that he ventured here. When he found her, he would tell her he had. That he had found the strength to try and rid himself of the past, so that he could move on and be whole enough for her.

"I tried so hard to keep you from becoming the sinner your father was. A chronic gambler . . . to his death. A womanizer in his life. I didn't want you to grow into a man like him. He ruined my girl. Corrupted her and then broke her heart. As good as killed her, he did." He shook his head slowly on the stark white pillow. "I wasn't going to let you turn out like him." Stopping for breath, he added, "I tried. The only way I knew. Perhaps I was too hard. Perhaps I was wrong to place my trust in Mrs. Pearce . . ." His voice faded and he shook his head again. "I should have dismissed her. I know that now. I am sorry, Dominic."

Dominic stared down at his grandfather, hot emotion thickening his throat, disbelief rippling over him, puckering his skin to gooseflesh. He blinked fiercely, regarding the frail hand so close to his own on the bed. It looked pathetically small. And the man . . . the man suddenly bore no resemblance to the cold distant shadow of his youth. Dominic had come here braced and ready for familiar recriminations to be heaped upon him. He'd come prepared to feel his old hatred. But that, too, was gone. Evaporating like fast-fading smoke on the wind. He felt only loss. Regret for what could have been . . . but what he would now never know.

*But what he could perhaps still have if he would only take it. With Fallon.*

He eased his hand over the papery skin of his grandfather's hand. Incredibly, he heard himself say, "I wish we had time to start again."

A floorboard creaked and he stood in one swift motion, looking behind him. His gaze narrowed on a figure hovering in the shadows.

"Who's there?" he demanded, mortified to know someone stood witness to the intimate conversation.

"Forgive me." A woman stepped closer, her whisper a familiar caress to his starved soul. She left the shadows behind. Her face fell into the lamp's glow.

"Fallon." He breathed her name, his chest squeezing tight.

"I did not mean to eavesdrop." Her words flew in an agitated rush, her hands twisting together before her. "You entered the room, and I just panicked." She gestured to the screen. "Then you started talking—" She stopped abruptly. Even in the gloom of the room he detected the flood of color to her cheeks. She stared at him a long moment, her gaze searching. "My apologies." She fled the room, wide skirts swishing at her ankles. *Apricot-colored skirts*, he thought in stunned silence. Had he ever seen her garbed in color?

He uttered her name again, staring at the open door through which she had fled. Questions whirred through his head. What was she doing here? In this house? With his grandfather?

The rasp of his grandfather's voice penetrated his thoughts. "You're the one, then."

He turned and looked down at the bed, staring into eyes so like his own. Without even thinking, he nodded. "Yes."

"I should have guessed."

His spine stiffened. "Why is that?"

"The girl's been nursing a broken heart. She said you didn't love her. That you *couldn't* love."

"I can," he spit out fiercely, feeling challenged,

denied, and not liking it one damn bit. Especially since he had realized almost from the moment he let Fallon walk out of his life that he had to have her back. At the harshness of his voice, he swallowed, amending his tone. "I *do*."

"Go then." His grandfather's voice gained volume as he added. "You haven't run out of time with her."

The words struck him with force in the chest, winding him. Nodding again, he started from the room. First at a walk, then a run.

# Chapter 30

**F**allon halted at the bottom of the steps, cursing her poor luck to find the Reverend Simmon's smiling face beaming up at her.

"Miss O'Rourke! Splendid meeting you here. Are you visiting with our unfortunate Mr. Collins?" His pleased features fell then, adopting an appropriate look of concern as he clucked his tongue.

Fallon nodded, stepping down into the foyer, her heart racing too quickly to form coherent speech. *Dominic.* She dragged a hand down the side of her face, loathing how it trembled.

What was he doing here? This was the last place he should ever appear given his relationship with his grandfather. She had thought herself perfectly safe at Wayfield—the last place he wished to be. And yet here he was. Upstairs. With the man he most hated . . . and showing him *kindness*, saying things she never thought to hear him say.

"And how is the gentleman?"

She shook her head at the young vicar, doing her best to give him her attention. "Not well. He struggles."

"Ah, but he is blessed with a hearty constitution." His fair head bobbed. "He has been strong for so long now." He took her elbow and leaned forward as if to confide some great secret. "I suspect your arrival into his life has renewed him." His brown eyes warmed as they crawled over her face. His fingers moved a small circle over the inside of her arm. "Many an expiring soul would feel heartened in your company and find the will to live again."

"God's teeth, woman."

Fallon closed her eyes in one pained blink, recognizing the deep voice at once and wincing at his choice of words. Before the local vicar, no less.

"Every time I turn around, some man is pawing at you. Can you not try to project proper modesty?"

She turned and glared at Dominic, all remorse for overhearing his very private and long-awaited words with his grandfather fleeing in the face of his rude words.

"A lecture on propriety from *you*?"

His gray eyes glinted with what almost looked like . . . *delight*? "We're not discussing me."

"Have you no shame," she hissed, hot mortification sweeping her face.

"Whomever you are, sir, I can assure I was not pawing Miss O'Rourke." Even so, Mr. Simmon's dropped his hand from her arm as though burned. He pulled his narrow shoulders up and back, stretching to his full height, which brought his eyes level only with her chin.

"Miss O'Rourke—" he paused to glare at Dominic, "*Fallon*. Who is this person?"

"You were correct the first time. It's Miss O'Rourke to you." Dominic flicked the man the barest glance before looking back to Fallon and taking her hand. His warm fingers wrapped around hers, firm and unyielding as a vise. Facing each other, they fell utterly still. Mr. Simmons and the world disappeared for a long moment as their eyes locked, and clung. The blood rushed in her ears, a roaring buzz as she lost herself in the murky gray depths, the line of blue circling the iris especially dark. Then he blinked. The moment ended as quickly as it arrived.

Before she could tug her hand free, he hauled her from the foyer without a word. She shot a quick glance behind her. The sight of the reverend's pale, stunned face almost looked comical. Almost. She could have cracked a smile, if not for the very real feel of Dominic's hand on hers, or the small thrill of heat that sizzled through her at the contact, bringing back in a flash all they had shared. All that she had tried to put behind her.

He pulled her behind him into a drawing room she had never seen before. Not so surprising. In her limited exposure to Wayfield Park, she had yet to see all of its vast grounds or countless rooms. Mr. Collins was hardly up to giving a tour.

The room was lovely. All yellow and creams with faint accents of blue. White and ivory-striped drapes were pulled back to allow the afternoon sun inside. She would have taken more time to admire the sunny room if not for the duke backing her up until she bumped into the pianoforte, his body a very large wall of heat at her front.

"What are you doing here?" he demanded, eyes drilling relentlessly into her.

"Lord Hunt provided me his old nanny's cottage. Near the old mill east of Little Saums. It has been vacated these last—"

"You're living here?" He made a stabbing motion at the floor. "He sent you to live *here*?"

"Well, not here." She motioned to the room lamely. "Nearby."

Dominic smiled suddenly then, and she felt as though someone had thrust her from a very dark room into the warm sunshine again. "I don't know whether I should thank him or trounce him the next time I see him."

Her stomach flipped at that smile. He had smiled so few times without mockery or wicked purpose since she knew him, it was like seeing a stranger. With that smile he was a greater threat than ever before. Enticing, charming . . . dangerous. More dangerous than the wicked duke she had first thought him to be.

"Fallon," he whispered, his hand lifting, brushing back a lock of hair from her forehead. She resisted the impulse to lean into his touch. It would be so easy to fall if she let herself, to give in to all that she had resisted by running away.

*Running away.* She shook her head, her intemperate self disliking the notion. She had not run. She merely moved on with her life. A life that *still* did not include him. Nor the pitiable role of mistress he had offered her, scarcely a spot at all in his world. No matter how she loved him, she could not surrender herself to him.

*But what if he had changed?* a small voice whispered, nudging at the hope buried in her heart.

Her gaze crawled over his face, throat thickening, recalling the brief exchange she had overheard between him and his grandfather. Further evidence that a stranger stood before her. Not the duke she knew at all.

He had come. When he said he would not, he had come.

"Fallon," he repeated her name, the tender emotion in his gaze wildly at odds with all those cool looks and wicked, empty smiles he'd given her in the past. She felt something unsafe unravel inside her. *Hope.* Dangerous indeed for one who had no business feeling it.

"Don't," she murmured, afraid this time she could not walk away from him. Not again. Not when he looked at her with softness in his eyes. Not when, only moments ago, he had shown compassion she would never credit to him.

"I'm glad you came to see your grandfather. Truly I am." She tried to slip between him and the pianoforte. "I should leave you to your visit—"

His arms came up, caging her in and stopping her. "You're not running away again."

"Dominic, you need time with your grandfather right now. I will just be in the—"

"I did not just come here for me, damn it."

Fallon stopped breathing.

"I came here for you. For *us*. I need," he said thickly, "you."

She breathed again, perhaps for the first time in her life since her father died. She breathed, *lived*, drawing air deeply into her lungs.

He smiled, the grin loose, easy, even as a glimmer of anxiety flashed in his eyes. "Even my grandfather agrees with that." His chest brushed the front of her gown and her nipples peaked, hardened against the fabric. Hot mortification washed over her. "I need you, Fallon."

She wet her lips. "I can't do this. I won't be your mistress—"

He smothered the rest of her words with his lips.

She whimpered, her hands pushing and pulling at the same time on his jacket. Everything flooded back with his kiss. His taste, his heat. The magic. Her tongue tangled with his as he bowed her over the pianoforte. She clutched his shoulders, fingers curling in his jacket, yearning, desperate, ready to climb *on* him, *inside* him.

She didn't care at the hard wood digging into her spine. She cared only for him, for his mouth fused to hers. Hot tears seeped between the closed lids of her eyes, and she knew in that moment, it was over. Done. She was past fighting. She loved him. Would have him, however he wanted her.

He came up briefly, lips moving against her mouth as he said, "Be my wife."

She jerked free of his lips, her gasp a sharp rip of air in the stillness, hands flattening on his broad chest. "What?"

He smiled that smile again and this time only hot need glimmered in his eyes. Her toes curled. "I don't want to lose you. I want to spend every day for the rest of my life with you. When I thought I might never see you again . . . I felt more than I thought I ever could." His hands tightened where he held her. "I felt pain, Fallon. I hurt . . ." He stopped, blinking slowly. "It's simple. Without you, I ache. With you—" He shook his head and dove in for another kiss.

She dodged his mouth. "But *marriage*? You're a duke."

His lips twisted. "I know. I hope you're not going to hold that against me."

She snorted a rough laugh and a slow smile spread across her face. She always had before, she realized. Disliked him and every other peer, on principle alone.

"Yes, but I'm . . ." her voice faded, unsure what she was anymore. Not a servant. No longer a shadow walking the halls of Penwich waiting for a glimpse of sunlight, yearning for a place to call home.

"The woman I love," he finished. She felt her eyes widen as he continued. "Nothing else matters."

"And you're the man I love."

He cupped her cheek in his hand, the calloused pads a familiar rasp on her skin. "That matters."

She laughed, the sound strangely freeing, *lifting.*

"You've always wanted a home of your own, Fallon. I'll give you that. A house wherever you want. I bloody well don't care as long as I have you." He waved a hand about the room. "Here. In London. At your cottage. Or I'll build you the house of your dreams. Anywhere." He gave her a gentle shake. "Just say yes."

*Yes. Yes. Yes.*

She placed both hands on each side of his face, holding him as though he were the dearest thing in the world to her. And amazingly, he was. All that she *never* dared dream of. A blue blood. A rake. *A demon duke.*

"A house isn't a home." She had learned that lesson in the last few weeks. "You are. *I love you.* I can live in a stable, a shack, as long as I have you next to me."

He grinned. "A stable, eh? You don't ask for much."

She brushed her lips to his, smiling with wicked promise. "Don't fool yourself. I ask for a great deal—everything. *You.*"

"I'm yours, but I'm afraid you're going to learn that isn't much compared to what I'm getting." His hands grasped her, but it was a hold she doubted would ever feel too tight.

"No, Dominic. You're everything. And you're mine."

# Epilogue

"**T**here you are." Fallon stopped and propped her hands on her hips, looking down at her husband sprawled beneath a large oak tree, the day's fading light casting him in seductive shadow. "What are you doing here? I've been looking everywhere for you."

Dominic smiled at her—the wicked smile that *still* made her knees go weak. He reached up and tugged her down beside him. Sprawled beside him, his gaze traveled a warm trail over her. He dipped one finger inside the bodice of her dress, scraping a blunt nail across her flesh. "You look beautiful."

Her breath caught and she slapped lightly at his hand. "We're going to be late."

"Wouldn't you rather stay here?" He patted the soft grass. "It's a beautiful night."

"Here? In the garden?"

"Hmm." He inched closer, his breath a seductive rasp against her ear. Even married two years, he still stole her breath.

"I thought you wanted to attend. It's an important night for Ethan. For—"

"He won't miss us."

Fallon pouted, running her fingers over the red satin of her dress. "I did want to show off my gown . . . and it has been an age since we ventured out."

Dominic rolled her beneath him, his eyes so hot and hungry that she suddenly forgot about her dress. Or that he was crushing it. "As fetching as the gown is, I'd prefer you without it."

Bending his head, he kissed her, a deep and consuming kiss that ended abruptly at the sudden wail of a baby. His gaze shot to the window of the nursery.

"Dominic?" Suspicion settled in her chest as she watched his eyes flash with anxiety. "Is that why you're out here? To *spy* on the baby?"

Gaze still on the nursery window, he asked hurriedly, "Do you think she's all right?"

Fallon glanced up. A light soon filled the room, and the nanny's shadow passed the window. "Yes, Dominic. I'm sure she's fine. She's with Ms. Chitwood."

He scowled. "And what do we know of her?"

"She comes highly recommended."

He grunted.

"And I like her."

His shoulders slumped and he sent her a sheepish smile. "You think I'm behaving like an idiot."

She splayed a hand over his cheek, her heart overflowing with love for him, for their family. "I think you're behaving like a father. A most excellent father." Settling back against the tree, she motioned for him to join her. "We'll have plenty of evenings out."

Grinning, he settled beside her with a deep, contented sigh. A sigh that she felt reach inside her, warming her heart. Their daughter's coos and gurgles of delight floated on the air. She feathered her fingers through Dominic's hair. "I can't think of a better way to spend an evening."

"Lying here watching our daughter's window?"

"No. Lying here *with you* watching our daughter's window."